ROYAL ELITE

BLACK
KNIGHT

ROYAL ELITE
SCHOOL

RINA KENT

To you.
Yes, you.
You matter.

AUTHOR NOTE

Hello reader friend,

It's safe to say *Black Knight* is my most emotional book to date. It strikes a deep cord within me and I didn't hold back; not with the visceral details or the graphic description of the deterioration of mental health. I stayed true to Kimberly and Xander and told their story the only way possible.

If you haven't read my books before, you might not know this, but I write darker stories that can be upsetting and disturbing. My books and main characters aren't for the faint of heart. However, this time, it's different. It's deeper, rougher and can be a lot scarier on the emotional side of things.

This book deals with depression, eating disorder and cutting. I trust you know your triggers before you proceed.

To remain true to the characters, the vocabulary, grammar, and spelling of *Black Knight* is written in British English.

Black Knight can be read on its own, but for better understanding of Royal Elite world, it's recommended to read the previous books in the series first.

Royal Elite Series:
#0 *Cruel King*
#1 *Deviant King*
#2 *Steel Princess*
#3 *Twisted Kingdom*
#4 *Black Knight*
#5 *Vicious Prince*
#6 *Ruthless Empire*

Don't forget to Sign up to Rina Kent's Newsletter for news about future releases and an exclusive gift.

Love is impossible. Hate is an open game.

Kimberly

He was once my best friend, now he's my worst enemy.
Xander Knight is heartbreakingly beautiful.
Ridiculously popular.
Brutally cruel.
He's a knight but won't do any saving.

Xander

We started as a dream, now we're a nightmare.
Kimberly Reed is pathetically fake.
Terribly innocent.
Secretly black.
She can hide but never from me.

PLAYLIST

I See You—MISSIO

Ghost—Badflower

Magic—Coldplay

Drink To Drown—Stand Atlantic

Hollow—Icon for Hire

Shattered—Trading Yesterday

Under Your Spell—The Birthday Massacre

Therapy—All Time Low

Those Nights—Bastille

Zero—Imagine Dragons

Birds—Imagine Dragons

Green Eyes—Coldplay

Princess of China—Coldplay

Say Something—A Great Big World & Christina Aguilera

The Reason—Hoobastank

Past Life—Trevor Daniel

Kids—OneRepublic

Rescue Me—Thirty Seconds To Mars

Breathe Me—Sia

Someone You Loved—Lewis Capaldi

You can find the complete playlist on Spotify.

ROYAL ELITE BOOK FOUR

BLACK KNIGHT

PROLOGUE

Kimberley

Age six

Sometimes, stories end the moment they start.

Nana used to tell me that when I spent summers with her in Newcastle. At least back then, I could stay away from Mummy and how she looked at me.

As if she hated me.

Now, I have no Nana. There's no one to take me away from here or tell me stories that transport me to other worlds.

Worlds with princes and knights. Worlds filled with so much magic, I dream of them.

I trot down the house's stairs until I'm outside. The sun is so bright today, casting a bright hue all over the garden and the fence.

The sound of Mum and Dad's fighting follows me until I close the door behind me. No one can hear them now, not the staff, not the neighbours.

Not even me.

I flop down on the step and lick on the pistachio gelato stick Dad bought me earlier. Silver says all gelato tastes the same, but Silver is stupid sometimes. Pistachio gelato is the best. It's green and sweet and delicious.

If I weren't so upset, I would've gone to her house and played with her Barbie dolls, but I don't want to go anywhere.

Except for…

My gaze strays ahead to the huge mansion across from ours. It has an ancient feeling, like those castles from Nana's stories—the ones where knights and princes live. I want to go there, knock on the door, and ask him to come out.

My knight.

We agreed on that last week—that from now on, he's my knight. I even blessed him with a bamboo stick as the queen does.

Silver doesn't care when I'm upset, but he does. Because he's my knight. He always tickles me and tells me jokes until I break down in giggles.

The boy with golden hair and magical blue eyes, like the stories in Nana's books.

Still sucking on my gelato, I rise to my feet and take slow but determined steps until I'm out of our garden's gate. It's the afternoon, so maybe he's with Aiden and Cole. Maybe he doesn't want to play with me today.

I hate it when he chooses the boys over me.

Their garage door hisses open and I freeze. A red car comes out, slow at first, then it gains speed on the exit.

Aunt Samantha.

She's the one who plays the role of the queen in Nana's stories with her golden locks and big blue eyes that are so kind and caring.

Aunt Samantha, who invites me in whenever my parents are fighting and gives me snacks and food. She sits with me and does my hair because Mummy doesn't have time to. She tells me Mummy has an important job and that I shouldn't hate her for that.

She's also my knight's mother.

Her face is blank, without its usual warmth. She appears upset, but she's not crying. Or maybe she's not upset at all. She's like Mummy when she locks herself in her art studio, not wanting to see anyone.

I'm about to wave at her when I notice who's running after her car.

Xander.

The boy with golden hair and blue eyes that he stole from the ocean, the sky, and the magic in books.

Tears stream down his cheeks as he screams his mother's name. His entire body shakes, but he doesn't stop chasing her.

For a second, the whole world freezes. It's a moment, just one moment in time. It's so weird how all bad things happen in just a moment.

Nana left me in a moment, too. She was sitting with us one minute, and the next, her heart stopped. She was there, smiling at me, giving me gelato and telling me a story, and then my only grandmother was gone.

Now, it's only me, Mummy, and Daddy.

I hate it when it's only me and them. Because Daddy works a lot and I don't get to spend much time with him. And Mummy…well, I don't exist in front of her, not like when I existed with Nana.

She was my world. Now, I have nothing.

As I stand there watching Aunt Samantha's car rolling away and Xan running after her with his short legs, my chest becomes painful, the same as it did when Nana left.

My heart beats loud and hard in my ears. I'm not hearing Xan's cries and screams. I'm hearing mine when Nana dropped to the ground, closed her eyes, and never woke up.

I knew then, I just knew I'd lost something that couldn't ever be retrieved.

My life changed forever.

Just like Xan's is.

He hits the car's boot, but instead of braking, the red car makes a loud sound as it revs down the street.

"Mum, don't go!" Xan runs behind her, his flip-flops slapping against the street. "Don't leave me, please. I'll be a good boy. I p-promise."

His words bleed into each other, mixed with his tears.

My feet move of their own volition, slow at first, then I'm running as fast as Xander behind the red car.

That car resembles a monster with flaring nostrils and red horns, but neither of us stop.

He's still screaming and crying, the sound loud in the silence of the street. His shoe slips from his right foot. He kicks the other away and keeps running barefoot, uncaring about the small pebbles on the asphalt. I stop for a second to gather his flip-flops in one hand as the gelato melts in my other. It's starting to get sticky and make a mess, but I don't let go as I follow Xan.

He's in pain and I don't like it when he's in pain. I don't like it when anyone is in pain, but I hate it more when it's him.

I taste salt, and I realise my cheeks are soaked with tears, too.

"Stop, M-Mum!" Xan trips, but he catches himself and continues sprinting. The sounds he makes are winded and so guttural, it's like an animal breathing.

The car disappears around the corner. Xan doesn't stop. He keeps running and running, even when Aunt Samantha and her monster car vanish from sight.

Even when it's only the two of us on the long road adjacent to our neighbourhood.

His foot catches and he tumbles forward, falling to his knees, crying so loudly, I feel every sound in my bones.

"Muuuum!"

I rush to him but stop a small distance away, hugging his flip-flops to my chest. Then slowly, too slowly, I crouch and put them on each of his feet. The skin has turned dirty and one of them has a cut from which blood coats his small toe.

"G-Green?" He stares at me through the tears that glisten as they flood his eyes.

Xan calls me Green because it's my favourite colour. Where other girls have pink bedrooms, I have a green one.

"M-Mum is g-gone." He sniffles.

I force a smile. "She'll come back."

It's a lie. I also said Nana would come back after I slept, but when I woke up, she still wasn't there.

Adults don't come back when they leave.

"S-she won't! She said she doesn't want me and Dad anymore." His lower lip trembles, even as he tries to stop crying by turning away from me.

"Xan…" I reach a hand for him and wipe his tears with my sleeve.

For a moment, he lets me as they become fatter and never-ending.

The gelato is now dripping on the ground, and I would usually devour it all, but my entire focus is on Xan and how he can't stop sobbing.

I also thought I'd never stop crying about Nana. That I'd cry like a princess in one of her books and the tears would kill me.

I eventually stopped, though.

Daddy says nothing is permanent. Everything changes.

He's wrong. Xan and I will never change. I'll always be his Green and he'll always be my knight.

We made it official after all.

Xan places a hand on my shoulder and shoves me, then stares at the ground. "Go away, Green."

"No."

He glances up at me. "No?"

"I don't want to leave you alone. You didn't leave me when Nana died."

Slowly facing me, he watches me closely, his blond brows pinching as more tears slide down his cheeks. "Why are *you* crying?"

I sniffle, wiping my face with the back of my hand, mixing his tears with mine. "Because you're crying."

"Don't cry, Green."

"*You* don't cry." I sniffle.

He hiccoughs. "I hate it when you cry."

"I hate it when you cry, too." I inch closer and put my arms around his neck, keeping the one with the melting gelato away so I don't make a mess out of him as well.

My knight is beautiful and can't have dirt on his armour.

Xan wraps his arms around my waist, hides his face in my neck, and sobs. He sobs so hard, I feel the vibration against my skin.

I cry, too, because his pain feels like mine now. His pain is so real and close, it's as if I'm the one hurting, not him.

When Nana left, Xan hugged me while I cried. He stayed with me until I fell asleep and didn't leave my side.

Now, I'll hug him until the pain goes away. Until he can smile and show me his pretty dimples.

"Green…" He sniffles in my neck. "Promise you'll never leave me."

"Never. You're my knight, remember?"

He nods.

"From today onwards, we're one."

"We're one."

ONE

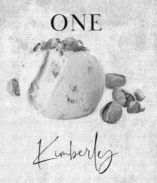

Kimberly

I'm not good enough.

I'll never be good enough.

You know that feeling when words keep hammering in your head until they form a suffocating fog? Until they're all you can think about and all you can breathe?

When you wake up in the morning, they slowly condensate around you like they're your life-long companions.

They're the first thought you wake up to and the last thought you sleep on.

That's how it's felt for years now.

That's how my battle starts, and every day, I tell it *not today.*

"Kimmy!" A small hand pulls on mine as my baby brother drags me towards the entrance of the elementary school.

Kirian reaches my waist now. His pressed uniform has a wrinkle on the shoulder that I smooth with my hand.

His sun-kissed blond hair is in a short bowl cut that he takes pride in because it's 'the thing.' His bright brown eyes are so shiny, you can almost see the world through them. A world so pure, you'd want to mass-produce it and freely distribute it.

"What is it, Kir?" I ask.

"I said, you'll do me mac and cheese later, right?"

"I can't. I have school until late."

He pouts, his hand turning lax in mine. If there's anything I hate in the world, it's killing that spark in his features.

"Marian will do it for you," I bargain.

Kir loves our housekeeper and spends time with her when I'm not around.

"I don't want Mari. I want you to do it."

"Kir…" I crouch in front of him, making him stop walking. "You know there's nothing I want more than to stay with you, right?"

He shakes his head frantically. "You disappeared the other day."

My lower lip trembles and it takes everything in me to pull it together. This is the reason I wake up every day, why I fight that fog, why I get into the shower and then put on my uniform.

People say nothing can stop those thoughts when they strike deep. You need therapy, you need meds, you need all the fucking things.

I only need this little man with his huge eyes and small pout. His face is the first thing I try to see in the morning. His voice is the one I want to hear as soon as I open my eyes.

Kirian is my own special pill. My happy pill.

But he saw something he shouldn't have last week. Or rather, he witnessed it and when I woke up, I found him bawling by the foot of my bed, hugging me and begging me not to leave him.

"That will never happen again, my little monkey."

"What if it does?" His lower lip pushes forward as he widens his eyes. "What if you disappear and I have to stay with Mum?"

"Never, Kir." I pull him to me and crush him in a hug. "I'll never *ever* leave you alone with Mum. Do you get that?"

He pushes away from me and sticks out his small finger. "Pinkie swear?"

"Pinkie swear, you baby." I curl mine around his.

As soon as he's sure of the promise, he shoves away and glares up at me, pouting. "I'm not a baby."

"You are my little baby. Deal with it."

"Whatever." He widens his eyes once more. "Are you going to come home early?"

Seriously, he has a puppy look that I'm ready to commit a crime for.

I stand up and ruffle his hair. "Fine. I'll try."

"Yay!" He hugs my legs. "I love you, Kimmy!"

Then he's running in the direction of the school, clutching the straps of his backpack.

"Love you, too!" I shout after him. "Don't run."

As soon as I make sure he's made it inside, I head back to my car. Other kids hop from their parents' vehicles, kissing them before heading to the school.

A scene neither Kir nor I have had in our entire lives. I'm probably the only sibling driving her brother today.

At times like these, the red clouds I harbour for Mum explode with passion.

I don't care about myself, but she has no right to make Kir believe he's also unwanted, a mistake, a fucking broken condom.

At least Dad tries. All my early childhood memories consist of him putting me to bed or hugging me as I slept. He's also the one who has always nursed me when I have a cold.

Never Mum.

Dad is just a busy man and rarely at home to make much of a difference. His calls are hardly enough anymore.

I arrive at Royal Elite School—or RES—in record time since it's not far from Kir's school.

At the car park, I stare at my reflection in the mirror and take a deep breath. I can do this.

For Kir.

I flip my brown hair that's intertwined with green

strands—or it's probably the other way around, more green, less brown. What? I love the colour. I'm just thankful I was born with light green eyes. Another thing to add to my green collection.

Okay, that sounded a bit off, even in my head.

I come out of my car, clutching the straps of my backpack as I stride through RES's huge entrance. Royal Elite School has ten gigantic towers and a magnificent building that goes back to medieval times.

The golden lion and shield logo is all about the majestic power of this place.

Rich, influential people send their kids to this school so they'll have an easier initiation into society. After all, most of the UK's politicians, parliament members, and diplomats have walked the halls of this school—Dad included.

He's now a renowned diplomat who works closely with the European Union in Brussels, and for that reason, we barely see him. Maybe everything will change now the country is leaving the EU.

But I'm fairly sure he'll find a way to boot himself someplace else. It's as if he doesn't want to be with us—or with Mum.

Usually, I would walk these halls with my best friend, Elsa, by my side, but since her accident and heart disease complications, she's now resting at her house. In the meantime, I'm all on my own between people who either hate me or pretend I don't exist.

The familiar jabs begin.

"She thinks she's all pretty now?"

"Once fat, always fat, Kimberly."

"Look at those thighs."

"Elsa's little bitch."

My skin prickles the more their words seep under it. I try to tune them out, but like the fog, they're impossible to ignore.

They keep multiplying by the second, heightening and filling my head with those thoughts.

The grey ones that taste like bitterness and burn like acid.

No one cares about you.

You're a nobody. Absolutely nothing.

I shake my head as I cut the distance towards the classroom. They will not get to me.

Not today, Satan. Go crawl into your little hole.

This has been my school for three years, but I've never once felt as if I belong in this place.

I turned eighteen a few days ago and I celebrated my birthday on Elsa's sickness bed with Kir by my side and Dad on Skype.

No matter how old I am, it never gets easy to walk these halls, to let the knives stab me with each word out of their malicious mouths.

I wonder if they're seeing the blood following me like a trail or if I'm the only one.

My fingers snake to my wrist, then I quickly drop my hand to my side.

For Kir, I repeat the mantra in my mind. *You're doing this for Kir.*

If I get a good college and a scholarship, I'll be able to afford a private dorm and take Kir with me, because there's no way in fuck I'm leaving him with Mum once I'm in college.

The voices around me start blurring into themselves and I lift my head high as I put one foot in front of the other.

They're nothing.

They're just a ramification of the fog and I always beat down that damn fog.

Except once.

Okay, twice, and Kir witnessed one of them.

"Scarce, fucker."

My feet come to a halt on their own accord at that voice. That strong, low voice that's been a constant in my dreams.

And my nightmares.

Okay, my nightmares more than my dreams.

That cruel voice has ended my life over and over again when he could've saved me. Instead of letting me hold on to him, he left me for dead.

That voice isn't only a part of nightmares, he's a nightmare all on his own.

The earth tilts off balance as I lift my head. I have to keep reminding myself that gravity exists and I won't actually fall over.

That he doesn't matter. He stopped mattering that day seven years ago.

But maybe I'm only fooling myself, because even though I see him every day—or rather, avoid him—his view never gets more familiar or easier or fucking normal.

But there's nothing normal about Xander Knight. He was born to become part of the elite, the ones who crush others under their boots and don't look back at the damage. He's one of the kings who leave chaos and heartbreak in their wake.

He's part of RES's four horsemen, the football team's ace striker, and nicknamed War for his ability to destroy the opponent's defence.

And war he is. Xander is the type of war you never see coming, and when you do, it's already too late.

It's already sucked you into its clutches and destroyed you from the inside out.

His golden hair is styled back but is short on the sides in a fashionable way that adds to his overall cruelty. When I was younger, I used to think he stole the blue of his eyes from the ocean and the sky.

Now, I'm sure he did, because he's a sadistic thief.

The tame blue that used to lighten up upon seeing me is now darkening to a sinister colour.

To say Xander is beautiful would be an understatement

of not only the century but of the entire common era. It's not just because of his put-together blond look—his face belongs to models, gods, and general immortals. It's sharp-cut with a slight stubble that adds to his charm.

Like everyone at school, I used to see that beauty. I used to stop at the step of my house and pinch myself, chanting that he's indeed my friend—my knight—and he's calling me over to play together.

Now, I see someone completely different. I see vindictiveness, hate, a war god out to destroy.

He used to be my best friend. Now, he's a stranger.

A bully.

An enemy.

The boy Xander just shooed away bows his head and retreats around the corner. Being part of the horsemen, Elites' ace striker, and the son of a minister gives him the right to a crown, one that's crowded with thorns and black smoke.

Still, everyone around here bows down to his authority. If he'd asked that boy to crawl, he would've dropped to the ground without asking questions.

Xander twirls a football on his forefinger, his other hand in his trousers' pocket as he stalks towards me with steady, purposeful strides. I keep my gaze on him, watching his every movement and struggling to suck air into my lungs. I don't know why I think he'll push me away, or rather, kick me down.

Not that it'd be something new. Worse has been done to me during my years of bullying—fat-shaming remarks, spilling of paint, mocking confessions, all of it.

It's stupid to think Xan would touch me. He never has.

Not even once.

The uniform's blue jacket stretches over his wide shoulders and muscular chest. Everything about him is—muscular, I mean. Including his football thighs, *especially* his football thighs.

I don't know when that happened. Okay, that's a lie. The development of his physique started exactly in the summer between Royal Elite Junior—our previous school—and Royal Elite School.

Disclaimer, I notice a lot of things around me. It's not only about him. Ever since I realised my mum wouldn't stand up for me and I'd have to do it on my own, I've learnt a lot of survival methods. The most important of all: being aware of my surroundings.

Whether I like it or not, Xander has always been a part of my immediate environment and he'll continue to be until the end of this year. Then, when I'm out of this city, everything will be over.

Breathe in. Just a few more months. *Breathe out.*

"Are you waiting for an invitation? Scarce, Berly."

His voice is light, but there's nothing light about his undertone. I know he didn't tell the boy to disappear for my sake. Xander doesn't stand up for me, and he sure as hell doesn't tell others off on my behalf.

If it were the old me, I would've bowed my head and run away crying, and his mocking laughter would've followed me as I sniffled in dark corners, not wanting others to witness my shame.

However, something's changed.

Me.

I've changed.

Ever since I woke up and found Kir hugging me and bawling, I've come to an important conclusion. If I want to survive in this world, if I want to stay with my baby brother and save him from our mum, then I have to take my life into my own hands.

I'm done playing a secondary role in my own tale.

Done letting the likes of Xander Knight walk all over me.

Done crying in corners like a damn coward.

I push my shoulders back the way Elsa always does and meet his gaze head-on. "There's room."

Okay, my voice could've been louder, but it's calm, so there's that. Baby steps.

"What did you just say?" He narrows one of his eyes as if not believing I spoke.

I don't talk back to Xander. *Ever*. I either run away or do as he tells me. I've always thought if I did, one day, he'd find it in him to forgive me. One day, he'd recall those times we used to be best friends.

But I've been a fool.

Those times only exist for me. He already wiped them clean, so I might as well do the same.

"You heard me." I motion at the rest of the hall. "There's room. Use it."

He chuckles, the sound dry and humourless, and my back stiffens. "Did you just order me, Berly?"

I *hate* that name. I fucking despise it.

It's a taunt, and a cruel one at that. The boy who used to call me his Green is long gone. It's not that I want him to call me that again, he lost the right when he said I disgusted him. He lost the right when he stood by as all the other students bullied me.

He lost the right when he was no longer my number one supporter and turned into my number one tormentor.

Still, I wish he'd just call me by my first name.

I lift a shoulder. "Call it whatever you like."

I start to move past him, but he stops twirling the ball and thrusts it in front of my face, forcing me to halt. "Not so fast."

A sigh escapes me even as a tremor shoots down my spine. Being this close to him that I almost smell the mint on his breath and his rich ocean scent rattles me in ways I don't care to admit.

Or experience.

"What do you want, Xander?"

His brows scrunch and his grip tightens on the ball. "First, lose the attitude. Second, don't say my fucking name."

"Then how about you stop getting in my fucking way?" I snap, then bite my lower lip.

Shit.

I just snapped at him. This must be the first time in…well, ever. I don't remember ever doing it, not even when we were kids. He seems taken aback, too, when his face loses the hard edge for a fraction of a second.

Before he can think about a way to retaliate—and hurt me—I brush past him and stride to class. But I don't run. No, I keep my steps controlled.

From today onwards, Xander Knight won't see me run or cry.

This confrontation is only the beginning.

A new battle has started in our war.

And this time, I'll come out as the winner.

TWO

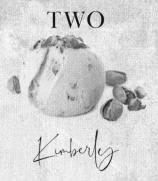

Kimberley

I heave my lunch into the toilet, the gurgling sound echoing around me like a fucked up symphony.

Do you know that distorted sound some violins make?

Yeah, me neither. Dad and Mum are into classical music—they met at a concerto. Shocker. I prefer punk and alternative rock. Thank you very much.

Anyway, I fill my mind with my favourite songs instead of the sound of heaving. You never get used to it, not the sticking your finger in your throat part and not the vomiting part; it's always disgusting. Every time I do this, I feel as if spiders are crawling over my skin with their hairy legs, leaving trails of rubbish in their wake.

Once my stomach makes the hollow sound, announcing there's nothing left, I step out of the stool. No one is here, as they shouldn't be.

I only do this right before class, after I make sure everyone is in there. That's why I sometimes arrive late, then pretend it's because of a headache.

Being invisible is easy, but being completely non-existent is a bit difficult. If I were a ghost, I wouldn't have to go through this trouble every day.

You know, the part about making sure no one is inside a public girls' toilet. If anyone is around, I just vomit in RES's back garden in the rubbish bin and only return here to brush my teeth.

As soon as I finish washing my mouth, I stare at my reflection in the mirror.

That face is also a nightmare.

In fact, it's the worst nightmare. Those cheeks that I thought would no longer be shabby, those breasts that appear too small against my blouse. My saggy arms with stretch marks galore. They're everywhere—stretch marks, I mean—at the underside of my arms, my stomach, and my thighs.

Everywhere.

I hate them and I hate this fucking body. I hate myself in it. I wish there was a way to detonate it from the inside out, aside from vomiting my lunch.

A thought assaults my subconscious.

I want to slam my fist into that mirror, break it into pieces, then take a shard of glass and—

No.

No, no!

I shake my head frantically and slap both my cheeks, resisting the urge to touch my wrist.

For Kir, you're here for Kir.

My steps are hard and determined as I exit the toilet while closing my bag.

I'm late for my next class. Or more like, I'll be late in about a minute.

That's the downside of being in the girls' room after everyone's settled in.

I'm running down the hall when an arm wraps around my shoulder. For a second, I freeze, thinking Xander has returned for revenge.

He's been ignoring me since the morning, but I know more than anyone that if Xander Knight ignores you, it's a disaster disguised as a blessing.

I release a breath when I inhale and realise it's not him. He doesn't smell this strong or feel this hard—not that I know how he feels.

And yes, I know how Xander smells. It's only because of my ability to connect to my surroundings, remember?

"You're also late, Kimmy?"

I smile up at Ronan, my first real smile since the one I gave Kir this morning.

Ronan Astor, also one of the horsemen and possibly the closest person I have to an ally in this school—aside from Elsa.

He has boyish charm, his brown hair is slightly curly, and his deep, rich brown eyes hint at a playboy in the making. Scratch that, he's already a playboy. Oh, and he happens to be a true aristocrat. His proud nose is clear proof of that.

I don't think he notices it, but his nose screams nobility from a continent away.

"Speak for yourself." I poke his side. "You didn't come in the morning."

"I had...an important meeting."

"You mean, you slept in because of yesterday's party?"

"Hey! Parties are important meetings, Kimmy. I'm going to teach you that...amongst other things." He grins. "Wait and see."

"No, thanks."

"Yes, and don't thank me yet." He waggles his brows. "I have payment suggestions for later."

"Why do I feel like I won't like it?"

"Believe me, you will." He tucks me closer to his side as we walk to class.

None of the students dares to say anything to me in front of Ronan. He might not be as brooding as Aiden and Cole or a damn popularity freak like Xander, but Ronan also has his throne in RES.

His crown is just a bit more approachable, touchable even.

He's a prince, and he's pretty much charming, too.

I still can't believe how he came to me first and decided we'd become friends just because he saw me at one of Elites' games. Oh, and he announced I'm invited to all his parties. They're legendary and with limited access, so at first, I thought maybe it was another elaborate plan from Xander to fuck with me.

However, it's been months, and Ronan remains a rock I can lean on. If it turns out to be a sick game, I might never return from it. I actually really like Ronan. He's outgoing and funny, and he always shoos all the unwanted attention away.

And sometimes, even the fog.

He's going into details about the type of weed he bought yesterday as we step into class.

"I'm telling you, Kimmy." He leans in to whisper at my ear, making me stop at the first table. "That shit was cloud nine level. Do you want to try it?"

My eyes widen. "We're at school."

"Get a room," someone says from class.

That's when I realise the position we're in. Ronan has an arm around my shoulder and I'm completely glued to his side as his lips hover near my ear. From the outside looking in, it appears too intimate.

But since I'm used to this from Ronan, I don't stop to think about it anymore.

"That's a great idea." Ronan snaps his fingers in the voice's direction. Silver. Of course, she'd say that.

I can't believe we used to be close once. Now, she's this exotic goddess, beautiful in a painful way with a model body and a venomous mouth, and she's also a top-grade student. A basic bitch.

Who was once my friend. Who hugged me when Nana died and gave me one of her favourite Barbie dolls.

That time of my life used to be so full and then, in a moment, it became empty.

"Let's go get a room, Kimmy." Ronan smiles mischievously at me.

I hit his side jokingly.

But I can't help wondering how my relationship with him would be if I'd known him as long as I've known the others.

Ronan only joined the four horsemen in our previous school. Maybe he, too, would've distanced himself if he'd known me since our childhood.

"Everyone take their seats." Mrs Stone's voice comes from behind us and I push away from Ronan to settle at the front of the class. Usually, Elsa or one of her foster siblings would be here with me, but now, it's just me. Ronan is out since he prefers to sit at the back and sleep in peace.

As I settle in, a movement catches in my peripheral vision. Xander.

He's by the window, in front of Cole, who's telling him something in his ear while clutching a book.

He doesn't seem to be listening since his entire concentration is on me. It's blank, though, as if he's not really looking at me.

But he is.

I can feel his gaze, not on my skin or on my face, but deep in my soul. It's invading me and touching parts he has no business touching.

I turn around and flop into my seat, fighting my heated cheeks. Just why the hell did I have to be in the same class with the four horsemen during my last year in RES?

I was almost surviving without having to see Xander's face in every damn class.

Mrs Stone is speaking about a test, but I can't for the life of me concentrate on what she's saying. My mind keeps flickering to the back tables, where I feel someone watching me.

My nape prickles with unwanted attention and I squirm in my seat as if that will make the discomfort go away.

Something hits my arm before a crumpled piece of paper

falls beside me. Letting my hair cover my eyes, I peek behind me to be greeted by Ronan's grin.

He's sitting right beside Xander, where the latter is clenching his pencil in a death grip. Ronan stretches both legs in front of him, twirling a black pen between his index and middle finger. He motions at the paper with his brows.

I throw a fleeting glance at Xander, but he's focused on Mrs Stone. His expression is neutral, but his shoulders are rigid. Why the hell is he so tense?

After retrieving the paper, I unfold it discreetly. It's a scribble in Ronan's messy handwriting with a smiley emoji at the top.

'Give the world a middle finger with a smile.'

I stare back at him and he winks. My lips instinctively curve in a smile.

Xander's harsh gaze slides from Ronan to me and then stays there.

On me.

It doesn't waver nor does he attempt to look away. He's trying to intimidate me so I'll be the one to cut off eye contact and cower down like I do every time he's in my vicinity.

If looks could slice me open, Xander's would be the sharpest blade right now.

But there's something he's forgetting. His war doesn't scare me anymore. It can't be worse than the fog or Kir's disappointed gaze or the fear in his little eyes when he thought I'd leave him alone.

So I continue smiling. At Ronan, not at Xander.

I flip off those who slowly broke me, who turned me into this pathetic shell of a person.

Those who took pleasure in igniting my breaking point and watched me as I fell.

Those who threw me under the bus instead of pulling me to safety.

Those who fed the fog and allowed it to rule my life.

I follow Ronan's advice and give the world the middle finger.

THREE

Xander

There's a certain company in loneliness.

Yes, that sounds crazy, and yes, I still stand by it.

This could be due to the coffee, er…vodka coffee I just had, but who cares?

The empty house sure doesn't.

The people inside it are only paid by my father to keep their mouths shut. He makes them sign NDAs that would cost them their lives and three generations of their families sold on the black market.

People keep their mouths shut when they're stuffed with the queen's bills.

At least, those my father surrounds himself with do.

Our cook didn't blink an eye when I made a coffee and poured alcohol instead of water. He just nodded and went about his business.

I stand by the huge French window, sipping my coffee and placing a hand in my pocket. You know, like a good upper-middle-class boy with decent grades, a popularity vote under his belt, and a pretty wonderful life.

Everything is laid out before me for the taking—the huge garden, the German cars in the garage, the high positions.

All of it is there.

And yet, it isn't.

Is it okay to take what you need when you don't have what you want?

The answer to that is yes, logically speaking, but I've been gradually losing that part due to my vodka.

And yes, I do answer my own hypothetical questions. Cole's philosophy shit is starting to rub off on me.

"What are you doing here? Don't you have practice?"

I slowly close my eyes, inhaling deeply, before I turn around to face the only family I have left.

The one I wish had disappeared instead of Mum twelve years ago.

My father stands in the middle of the living area, which is filled with renaissance paintings and weird fucking art that he pays hundreds of thousands for at auctions.

Lewis Knight is a man of power in this country, one of the hotshot ministers who not only regulates the economy but also controls it. He's—wait for it—Secretary of State for Business, Energy, and Industrial Strategy. Phew, I know, that's a long title, but it goes with his 'duties', as he calls them.

You know, like a typical politician.

He's in his mid-forties with a medium build and thick dark hair that he keeps styled as if he has daily dates with the queen herself. A three-piece suit flatters his frame and gives him a majesty that everyone praises in the media.

He's one of the popular ones, my father. Spoiler alert, that's why I get the popularity vote, too. That shit is genetic.

He's also friends with the 'IT' crowd, the first line of the conservative party, who are doing some internal war to crush the upcoming elections and rule the country once again. After more than ten years of consecutive wins, let's just say it got boring.

A permanent scowl lodges between his thick brows while he looks me up and down as if he objects to my jeans and T-shirt. I should always look presentable, even at home. You never know when those reporters will come to do a field visit.

For as long as I can remember, Dad has always had that look when his gaze falls on me; permanent disapproval of sorts. He's never approved of me or my existence.

Deep down, he wishes Mum would've taken me with her that day. Both of us do a fantastic job ignoring that reality.

If we could turn back time, he'd push me into her car or I would sneak and hide in her boot.

"So?" he insists. "Practice."

"We don't have one today."

"Why?"

"Because we need to rest before our next game."

He narrows his eyes the slightest bit, then schools his expression. He's pragmatic that way, my father, suspicious by nature, too. Perhaps that's why he's a successful politician. I have no doubt he'll call the school and make sure my words are accurate.

His fatherhood game is just that, a fucking game. He likes to be in control and to think he has me under his thumb where he can press anytime.

"I need you on your best behaviour, Xander. I don't have to remind you that—"

"The elections are coming." I cut him off and take a sip of my alcohol—I mean, coffee.

"Why, yes." He advances towards me but isn't too close to smell it on me. I didn't know he would be here this early or else I wouldn't have drunk in front of him. He keeps me on a leash without a reason—he'd lock me in a cage if he found out about my coffee preferences. "If you remember that, act accordingly, boy."

"I'm not a boy." I grind my molars.

"Then stop acting like one. Remember, the purpose of the football games and Royal Elite is only to establish an image. Don't lose yourself in it."

Of course, even the one thing I enjoy, playing football, is only a means to an end for dear old Dad.

"I don't have to remind you of the consequences, do I?" He raises his eyebrows in challenge.

"I know. There will be no Harvard." I'm tempted to chug the entire coffee in one go, but that will give away its contents, so I just take a sip—a long one.

It's not that I'm that keen on Harvard, but it's in the United States and that will keep me years away from this shithole of an empty house and the other house across the street.

I need to get out of here at any cost. My grades aren't that excellent for a scholarship, so I need the money only Daddy dearest can provide. As soon as I get on my feet, I'm throwing it straight back at his face.

"Correct. Remember that." He fixes his tie, staring down his nose at me, even though we're about the same height. That condescending look, the complete coldness, the absolute disregard for human emotions in those brown eyes is the reason why my mother left.

And the reason I've never made peace with this man since.

The reason why we're strangers living under the same roof.

Lewis Knight might be the nation's saviour, but he's my worst enemy.

As soon as Dad leaves, small feet pad on the wood and an automatic smile crosses my lips. I push the alcohol away—and yes, I've given up calling it coffee—and chew on some mint gum.

I always have a pack of it on me. Cole is starting to be suspicious and will soon call me on my shit and make Coach give me the 'talk', but hopefully, I'll be out of this place by then.

"Xaaaan!" A small body crushes into my legs in a tight hug. His face hides in my jeans as he nuzzles his nose against them.

"Hey, little man."

He pushes away from me, pouting and pointing a thumb at himself. "I'm no little man."

"Right." I crouch before Kirian, wiping a smudge of chocolate off his nose. "You're Superman."

"Uh-huh. That's right."

"Give me a fist." I place mine in front of his and he blows it.

It's always amazing to have this little man around, even if his presence constantly pushes me back to unwanted fucking thoughts.

"Can I have brownies, Xan?" he stares up at me with puppy eyes.

I rub my forefinger against my thumb where there's still some chocolate I wiped off his nose. "Are you telling me you didn't have some?"

"No?"

"What did I say about lying?"

"It's a white lie. Kimmy says that's okay sometimes. Adults do it all the time."

"Well, your sister is wrong. Lying is bad; don't do it."

"Fine, I had some when Mari was baking, but it was a tiny bit, promise. Can I have brownies, please? *Pleaaase?*"

I take his hand in mine. "Fine."

"Yes!"

I help him up on the stool, his short feet dangling with excitement. "Where's your cape, Superman?"

"Kimmy put it to wash."

I cut a piece of brownie and place it on a plate. Kir's eyes widen with thrill as he watches my every movement.

Neither Dad nor I eat brownies, but I always ask the cook to have pieces ready for this little guy.

The moment I slide the plate in front of him, he dives in, instantly smearing his cheeks with chocolate. No matter how old he gets, Kir will always have no willpower when it comes to his brownies.

"Where is she now?"

I regret the question as soon as I ask it. If it were anyone else but Kir, it would've been a fucking disaster.

For a long time, I've been in total control of the questions I should ask and the ones I shouldn't. I always have to keep that image I've spent years perfecting.

It could be because of the amount of alcohol I've been consuming lately.

Or the way she's been getting on my fucking nerves since yesterday; the way she talked back, the way she smiled at Ronan as if he's her fucking world.

Kimberly Reed is that rock in my shoe. It's not harmful, but it's annoying as fuck.

"At school," Kir speaks through a mouthful of brownies.

She shouldn't be at fucking school. She has no club activities to speak of and we don't have practice, so she couldn't have stayed to watch the football team.

Unless…

I retrieve my phone and check my messages.

There are several from my group chat with my three fucker friends.

Ronan: On a scale from one to ten, how many girls do you think I can fuck before my father marries me off like a whore for sale?

Aiden: Depends on whether they mean a fuck or not.

Ronan: Fuck off, King.

Ronan: Anyone else?

Cole: A hundred.

Ronan: Now we're talking.

Cole: You'll remember none of them, though.

Ronan: Fiiiine! I'll just settle with one.

He attaches a selfie with Kimberly by his side. He has an arm on her shoulder like he did yesterday, but this time, his lips are on her cheek as she laughs at the camera.

Her eyes are closed slightly, leaving only a slit of those green irises that I want to think they appear like snot but are in fact the most mesmerising green I've ever seen.

Strands of her hair fly across her face, causing the green ones to stick to her small nose and full cheeks. Her teeth show with her laughter. I wish it was forced, or for show, as she does in her mother's exhibitions.

I know Kimberly's fake smiles. I've learnt them. I have them engraved in a dark corner in my heart, the one with her name written all over it.

This isn't one of her fake laughs. She's genuinely happy, enjoying herself in what looks to be a normal grocery store. Only Ronan would snap a selfie in the grocery store like some fucking commoner.

Another text comes from him.

Ronan: I'm having a new challenge. I'll only fuck one girl and then, maybe my father will marry me off to her. Kimmy's dad is a big shot, too. Earl Edgar would approve.

I type before I realise what I'm doing.

Xander: I'm going to fucking kill you, Ron.

I delete the text before my impulsive side makes me hit send.

Fuck him and the way he's baiting me. It's not working and it never will.

Cole: And she can make your cake bunny fantasy come true.

Ronan: Fuck yes, I took her to that section and she didn't stop smiling. Next time, I'm going to have her try them on.

Aiden: When Reed visited Elsa last week, she wore those bunny ears girls put on their heads.

Give me a fucking break. Even Aiden is onto this shit? Shouldn't he not care as usual?

I make the screen go black so that I don't say something I'll most likely regret. They can see I've read the messages, but fuck them, basically.

Fuck all of them.

"Your sister doesn't have school," I tell Kir with a smile.

If she thinks she can play around without the guilt trip of leaving her brother behind, then she has another thing coming.

He pauses chewing, looking up at me through his eyelashes. "But she said she does. That's why Paul picked me up." His lower lip trembles. "I hate it when our driver picks me up. The other kids have their parents do it."

Well, fuck.

I might want her to suffer, but not at the expense of Kirian.

Besides, his case hits so close to home. I often rode with Aiden and Cole when we were kids. Neither of our parents cared enough to come pick us up personally, except for maybe Cole's mother.

"Didn't I tell you to call me when no one is there to pick you up?" I fetch another slice of brownie and slide it in front of him.

He lifts a shoulder. "Kimmy says I shouldn't bother you."

"We have bro code, remember? Next time, call me."

His eyes light up as he finally dives into the chocolate. "You'll really be there?"

"Always."

"What does always mean?"

"It means, I'll be there until the end of time whenever you need me."

Even if I move out and never return here again, Kirian will always be with me. A part I'll never try to shake off like all the rest.

He drops the piece of cake to his plate and stares at it, head bowed. "Kimmy also said that and then…"

"Then what?"

He shakes his head, his chin quivering. "I'm not supposed to tell."

I lean over until only a small space separates his hand from mine. "What happened, Kir? You can tell me. As our bro code says, you can tell me anything."

He lifts his eyes before focusing back on the brownies on his plate. "She promised that it won't repeat."

"Repeat what?"

His lower lip trembles again. It's his tell of when he's about to cry. She used to be the same when we were kids. It always happened before she started bawling.

Kirian is a lively kid and doesn't cry, so the fact he's fighting it right now should mean it's something serious. Is it about their parents, or what exactly?

"Sir." Our butler, Ahmed, stands in his elegance at the doorway. He's a short man with olive skin and light brown eyes. His forehead has that dark crease due to the five-times-a-day prayer. Even I know better than to disturb him during his prayers' time. Oh, and on Eid days—Muslim celebrations—he brings us the best kebabs from his family.

But that's not why he's the only tolerable presence in our staff. It's because he practically raised me when neither of my parents found time to.

"Miss Reed is here for her brother," he says with a slight Middle Eastern accent.

Fuck.

Perfect timing that is, as if she could sense he was going to spill the beans on her.

Kirian's eyes widen as he stuffs the rest of the brownies in his mouth until it's full, then hops off the stool.

I wipe the side of his face, and he grins as he runs outside. But first, he stops and stares back at me, placing a finger to his mouth. I make a zipping motion as I follow him.

He was on the verge of unveiling something and I'm sure, next time, with the right brownies bribe, he'll reveal everything to me. Not because he's a telltale, but because whatever happened upset him enough to make him stop eating his favourite food in the world.

"Didn't I tell you not to come here?" Her stern voice filters from the entrance as Ahmed escorts Kir to her.

"But I want to play with Xan."

"Why do you have to play with him?" She grabs his arm. "Am I not enough?"

"Of course you're not." I lean against the doorframe, crossing my arms over my chest and my legs at the ankles.

Kimberly's reddening face turns crimson under the late afternoon light. The descending sun catches in her green-ish strands making them appear rebellious. Since the beginning of this year, everything about her has been going out of that normal direction. Her uniform's skirt rides to above her knees, almost to the middle of her thighs. The jacket is too tight, I'm surprised she can breathe in it.

Fuck that and her spiritual journey and weight loss journey and all the fucked up journeys she's made.

She's starting to be as fake as the image Silver has been maintaining for years.

"Let's go, Kir." She ushers her brother in front of her, quickly cutting off eye contact with me.

That's more like it, not whatever the fuck she's been doing since yesterday.

"Go without her, Superman." I smile at him, showing him my most charming dimples. "I need to talk to your sister."

"Okay!" He doesn't pause before running in the direction of their house, probably ready to steal more chocolate cake from Marian.

"I have nothing to talk to you about." She starts to follow her brother.

"If you want to be enough for him, maybe you should stop whoring yourself around like a cheap little slut."

She comes to a screeching halt and whirls around so fast, I'm surprised she doesn't fall to her face with the force of it.

Her cheeks turn hot red as she stares at me with flaring nostrils. The old Kimberly would've turned and walked into her house, punched a pillow, and then watched one of her Korean soap operas while cursing my name.

This time, however, she storms back towards me until her chest nearly grazes my crossed arms and points a finger at me. "Who the hell do you think you are to talk to me that way?"

"Are we really going down that road, Berly?"

Her finger that was being pointed at me drops to her side. The deep green of her eyes widens until it almost swallows her face.

No, she's not beautiful. She's fucking disgusting.

D.I.S.G.U.S.T.I.N.G.

Spell it out until you learn it by heart, fucking arsehole.

Thanks for the tip, brain.

"While you were parading around, Kirian was on the verge of crying because the driver picked him up from school. Stop telling him not to call me or you won't like how I react."

Fine, so Kirian wasn't on the verge of crying because she didn't pick him up, but he was on the verge of crying because of her, so that counts.

"He's my brother." She stands her ground.

"And I'm telling you that you're not doing a good job at being his sister, considering your whorish ways and all."

"Oh, really?" She folds her arms, mimicking my position. "So I should leave him with you to learn your manwhorish ways?"

"Careful, Berly. Your jealousy is showing."

"Screw you."

"Is that what you want to see? Me screwing someone? Me

shoving my dick in another girl's mouth or cunt or arse while you bite your tongue because it's never going to be you?"

Her lower lip trembles, but she clamps it down and says in a calm voice, "You're the last person I would ever want."

Then she turns around and strides to her house, the skirt riding up her thighs with every harsh movement.

I have to spin around and stop watching her.

She better keep her word and never want me.

Lewis Knight might be my worst enemy, but Kimberly Reed is the person I hate the most on the face of this fucking planet.

FOUR

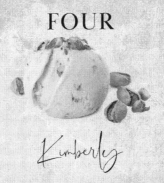

Kimberley

I fly down the stairs, carrying Kir's coat. I can't believe he almost tricked me into going out without wearing it.

That little shit and his mischievousness will be the death of me someday.

At our living area, I help him put it on and zip it.

"I can do it on my own," he whines.

"Uh-huh. Like removing it on the way out."

He grins, then pretends to be pouty. "We're late for Elsa."

"Yeah, yeah, that's not going to work. Stay still."

"I'm a grown man." He stomps his foot.

"Of course you are, Monkey."

"I'm going to be Superman one day, Kimmy, and fly you out of here. Wait and see."

"You will, huh?" His stupid obsession with the superhero would be amusing if Xander wasn't the one fuelling him with it. I really hate to admit that Xander's carefree personality is what made Kir come out of his shell and make friends at school.

If he'd followed in my footsteps, he would've become a loner like me, an outcast like me, a nobody like me.

Just me.

And being me is the last thing I'd wish on my baby brother.

Elsa was the first to approach me. Ronan, too. I'm shit at approaching people.

Whenever I think about it, that fog surrounds my head with toxic thoughts like no one would want to be friends with the hot mess that I am.

That if they get close enough and see me for who I truly am, they'll run away, or worse, they'll use it to torment me harder.

Even with Elsa, I'm always scared about when she'll figure out the truth about me and throw me behind her.

She became suspicious during my last visits, and to say I'm dreading this one would be the understatement of the century.

However, Kir will throw a fit if he doesn't see her and the rest of the 'cool guys', as he calls them, and I'm kind of weak when it comes to those puppy eyes and pouty lips.

"Come on, hurry up…" he trails off mid-sentence, his arms hanging limp, and I know who he's staring at behind me without having to turn around.

"Where are you going?" Her low voice has a biting edge like those hairy spiders—or rather, snakes, harsh and unyielding.

"To Elsa," Kirian says softly.

I swallow hard after finishing with his coat and smother his hair. "Go wait for me by the car."

He nods, appearing happy to be out of here, but then he stops, turns around, and hugs me. His small arms wrap around my neck in a tight hold, as if he doesn't want to let me go. I stroke his silky hair, biting my lower lip to not break down in sobs.

For Kir. You're doing this for this little man with a brilliant mind and delicate small hands.

"Go on, Monkey." I push him away.

He steps back and stares behind me. "Bye, Mum."

And then he's running out of the door.

I rise to my feet and slowly turn around to face the woman who gave birth to two children but has no ounce of motherly instinct.

She's taller than me, with a model body that she's maintained for decades. Her soft brown curls fall to her shoulders. She's wearing elegant trousers and a camisole that I would never be able to pull off in a lifetime.

Jeanine Reed isn't only known for her magnificent artistic talent that apparently touches souls with bare hands—the magazines' critics talk, not mine—but she's also a beautiful woman who appears in her late twenties instead of early forties.

She has high cheekbones and thick eyebrows that she passed down to Kirian. I have nothing from her. Not her talent, not her beauty, not her grace, and certainly not her model figure. The only thing we share is the eye colour, but hers are bigger and more striking, like a sparkling tropical sea.

I've always felt out of sorts whenever we've been in public together, and I stopped counting the number of times I wanted to bury myself when someone asked if I was her daughter and she hesitated as if not wanting to admit to the disgrace that I am.

"We won't be long," I say with a forced smile.

I'm surprised she came out of her studio at all. We rarely see her when she has an upcoming exhibition, and when we do, it's only so she can parade us around for the press—or parade Kirian, not me.

With this, here's to hoping she won't come out for at least another week.

And yes, my mum looks like a model when she's painting, while I resemble a wannabe beggar in my best days.

"Stop."

My feet come to a slow halt.

"Turn around." Her tone is steel-like, callous and merciless, like a general speaking to his underling, not a mother to her only daughter.

Wincing, I face her.

"How much do you weigh?"

A lump balls at the back of my throat and I fiddle with the long sleeve of my pullover. "Sixty-three."

"Sixty-three?" Her question, although lowly spoken, couldn't have been any more brutal on my mind. "Are you even still on the diet?"

"Of course, Mum."

"If you were, you would have lost three more kilos by now." She motions at me with a finger. "Come here."

"But Kir—"

"Come. Here."

I'm reduced to a small child, the one who lost her nana and cried at her grave all day, begging her to come back, to not leave her with this mother, because she hated her, because she didn't want to live with her.

As soon as I'm within reach, Mum motions at the scale she has near the dinner table. She has planted those all over the house during all these years. Dad told her to get rid of them, and he actively throws them away when he comes home, but there's nothing we can do when he isn't around.

"Get on it."

"Mum…"

"Don't make me repeat myself, Kimberly." Her voice is like a scolding teacher, biting and meant to be obeyed.

The fog surrounds me, thickening and magnifying as I step on the scale. People's hearts thunder when they're waiting for an exam result, when they have a crush. Mine nearly beats out of its place as the electronic numbers of my weight filter in front of me. The thing that defines me as a person in Mum's eyes are those numbers and nothing else.

Sixty-four kilos.

I nearly stop breathing. Shit, what did I do wrong? I ate nothing, or at least nothing I couldn't vomit back up. Was it that diet cola?

"Didn't you say it was sixty-three?"

"It was this morning." I slowly step down, as if the disappearance of those numbers will save me from the lashing of my mother's tongue.

"I expect you to be sixty by the end of the week and fifty-seven by the end of next week."

"But—"

"No buts, Kimberly." She taps her Louboutin heels on the ground. "I've been patient with you, but you're not watching your weight. You're not even tall, so you can't afford the extra kilos. I expect results or else Kir will go to that boarding school."

"N-no, Mum. You promised!" It's as if someone took my heart and pierced it open with sharp knives.

The fact she could and would send Kirian away to have more space for her art as soon as I'm in college has always given me nightmares.

I won't allow her to ruin his childhood like she destroyed mine.

"Only if you keep your promise." She flips her hair as she ascends the stairs.

"I'll do it." My voice is brittle. "I'll do it, Mum."

She doesn't even look back. I stopped expecting my mum to glance back at me, acknowledge me, *see* me.

I know I should stop asking for her attention by now, but the small child in me won't let go.

With one final glimpse at the scale, I step outside.

Moisture pools in my eyes as I search for my keys on the counter.

For Kir. All of this is for Kir.

The fog won't get to me. Not today, not tomorrow. Not until Kir is all grown up and can handle himself.

"Where are the stupid keys?" I groan in frustration, fighting the need to crawl into a dark corner and allow those morbid thoughts in.

They would devour me in no time and the next thing, I'll be in the bathroom and—

"They're in your hands, Kim." Marian's soft voice wrenches me out of my thoughts.

"Oh." I stare at her kind face with a faint smile, then back to the keys which are, indeed, dangling from my pinkie. "Thanks, Mari."

"Anytime, honey." She smiles a little. "What do you want for dinner?"

"Broccoli and a small portion of mac and cheese for Kir."

"How about you?"

"Salad—actually, forget about it. I'll grab something on the way."

I won't.

This will be another day without dinner. It's harder to vomit my food at night. It leaves me jittery with a stomachache and the inability to sleep, and if I can't sleep, that fog will eat me in a matter of seconds.

After bidding Mari goodbye, I step outside, plastering a smile on my face. No matter what happens between me and Mum, Kirian can't and will never find out about it. Not that he doesn't suspect it, but I want to protect him as much as I can.

My smile falls when I find him dragging Xander by the hand from across the street. The freaking boy next door appears. His sun-kissed hair is tousled, bedroom style. His white hoodie contrasts against his tanned skin and his black jeans hang low on his hips as if Kir found him in bed and he barely had the time to button his clothes.

Shit. I wouldn't be surprised if that were the exact case. Kirian has free access to the Knight's mansion—sort of like I did in the past. Ahmed opens the door for him, even if no one is at home. Lewis always dotes on him and the shit, Xander, treats him well.

"Hold on, Superman." Xander rubs his fingers through his hair as if submitting it, but it's only making it hotter.

Wait. No. There's nothing hot about Xander.

My blood still boils from the way he called me a slut earlier. How he said he'll make me watch as he fucks other girls.

Screw him a million times over and all the other girls he screws.

A prickling sensation has been digging at my skin since he said those words. I meant it, though—he's the last person I would ever want.

I might have been stupid enough to wait and hope for his forgiveness once upon a time, but now, he's just the boy next door.

The arsehole who lives across from me.

"You said you'll help, Xan."

"Of course."

Kir wraps both his small hands around Xan's bigger one, tugging him in my direction. "Kimmy is with Mum. You have to bring her out."

My heart warms so hot, I can feel the remnants of the fog withering away, condensing into water and falling in the distance.

My baby brother is thinking about me. I underestimated his ability to feel the tension between me and Mum.

He shouldn't have sought Xander for help, though. He's part of the problem, not the solution.

Heck, he's the worst part of the problem.

"Kimmy!" Kir shrieks upon seeing me and runs in my direction, his little feet carrying him slower than he likes.

I watch the street for any cars, even though we don't have traffic around here.

"Hey, Monkey." I ruffle his hair, completely erasing Xander from my surroundings. "Are you ready to go?"

He nods several times, then stops as if remembering something. "Can Xan come with us?"

Abso-fucking-lutely not.

I plaster a fake smile and direct it to said arsehole. "I'm sure he has things to do."

I think I imagined it, but his jaw tics before he offers me his golden boy smile that causes his cheeks to crease, and there they are. Dimples. Deep, attractive as hell dimples.

He really shouldn't have dimples. That should be exclusive to the good guys, not to bastards.

His smile and those dimples are a couple of the reasons why the girls fall all over him at school like he's some sort of Casanova.

Actually, he is one. I've lost count of the number of times he's disappeared with a girl—or two—in one of Ronan's parties, only to appear some time later with lipstick all over his shirt and neck and the girl, hair messy and lipstick smudged, grinning like an idiot as if she ascended to heaven and is now returning.

Once again, it's not me. It's my ability to notice everything. If it were up to me, I would erase him completely from my existence. Or maybe, if I had some sort of a time machine, I would go back seven years in the past and not do what I've done.

But time machines don't exist. This is what we've become and there's no changing it, no matter how much I want—or rather, *wanted* to. I no longer yearn for his forgiveness.

He'll never grant it, and I'll just be hurting myself.

"Do you have things to do, Xan?" Kir asks him as he pulls me so the three of us are standing near the middle of the street.

"Depends." He's speaking to my brother, but his entire unnerving attention is on me.

His light eyes are drawing a dark path into my soul, all paved with thorns. When we were kids, I thought magic was the reason behind the colour of his eyes. Turns out, it's black magic.

It used to be easy when I had the habit of averting that punishing gaze, when I pretended that this would be over soon.

It's never happened. And now that I've sworn to meet him head-on, it's getting exhausting.

Keeping eye contact with him is like drowning into the ocean of his irises. The harder I stare, the closer I am to the bottom.

"We're going to Elsa." Kir clutches Xander's hand with his free one. "Come with us, please?"

"Sure, Superman." He musses Kir's hair.

"Yay! Hear that, Kimmy? Xan is going."

"No, he's not." I lean over to hiss to Xander, "Since when do you go out with us?"

"Since I decided I can." His shit-eating grin never disappears. "Besides, I'm going to Aiden."

"Go to him in his damn home."

"Or I can go to him at Elsa's since he never leaves her side." He steps closer and it takes everything in me not to push back. His body heat mingles with mine and I inhale him in, mint and fresh clothes out of the dryer and... Is that a hint of alcohol?

He's still smiling, but his tone is biting as he murmurs. "And lose the fucking attitude."

"Can we go in your car, Xan?" Kir jumps, oblivious to the tension brewing between us. "Can we?"

"No."

"Of course."

Xander and I speak at the same time. I shoot him a glare. "I have a car, let's go separately."

I pull on Kir's hand, but he refuses to budge. "I want to go in Xan's car. It's *sooo* cool."

"You little ungrateful brat." I stare down at him, incredulous. "Whose car drives you to school every day?"

He pouts, blinking up at me with those puppy eyes. "But today, we can go in Xan's car. Please, Kimmy, please?"

The resident arsehole's lips tug in a smirk as he watches me fighting the Kirian pleading effect and losing miserably.

Still, there's no way in hell we'll go in Xander's stupid car. I just have to find a way to convince my baby brother of that fact.

As if sensing my intentions, Xander retrieves his keys from his pocket and throws them in Kirian's direction. The latter clutches them with both hands, staring at them with wild eyes.

"Go ahead."

"Really?"

At Xander's nod, Kirian runs towards the dark blue Porsche, trotting and grinning like an idiot. I'd hate to put an end to that joyful expression and I hate that this bastard is the reason behind it.

Maybe if I weren't such a chicken shit, I would ask Dad for a sports car instead of my safe MINI Cooper.

"You're a wanker, okay?" I sigh in both frustration and resignation.

Xander kills the space between us until his face is mere inches from mine. His mint breath intertwines with my shaky one as his eyes darken to a bottomless blue colour.

I'm so taken aback, it takes me a moment to realise the proximity.

He hasn't been this close since that time at the beginning of the year when he cornered me in the garden and told me— or rather, snapped at me—to stop wearing short skirts.

It was the first time he'd gotten close after so many years of tormenting me from afar and blatantly leaving the room whenever I came in as if I had a contagious disease.

He cornered me a few times after and they all had to do with my dress code.

Fuck him. It's not like he's my dad.

Like every time he gets close, I can't control my breathing. I know it's inhale, exhale.

In. Out.

But sometimes, even those simple steps are the toughest thing to do. For one, I keep breathing him in with every inhale and breathing my confusion out with every shaky exhale.

It's as if I'm about to vomit my heart, not my food. His lips twitch and I nearly faint, stopping the breathing struggle altogether.

Is he going to kiss me?

Shit. Shit.

"What are you doing?" I hiss, pulling my head away.

"I wasn't doing anything, but if you keep the attitude, I'll do things you won't like."

My lips part, then I quickly clamp them shut at the thought he might consider that as an invitation.

Damn him and damn me.

"Kimmy! Xan!" Kirian hops in front of the car. "Come on!!"

I raise my hand in a small wave, using the chance to pull out from Xander's orbit. It's like a magnet that keeps dragging me in despite my attempts to stay away.

When I chance a glance back at Xander, he's not intimidating me with his gaze as he was a moment earlier. He's staring at my hand, my wave, and then his focus slips for a moment.

No, no, no.

I drop my hand to my side and pull down the sleeve of my woollen pullover as I brush past him towards Kir.

He didn't see.

He *couldn't*.

FIVE

Xander

Elsa's foster sister, Teal, has taken Kirian downstairs. Judging by his sly grin, he'll probably charm her to get himself another brownie.

I was supposed to go with him or search for Aiden, but I find myself at the door of Elsa's room, staring through the small opening like a fucking creep.

Hey, don't judge. Creeps have reasons, too.

Elsa is on her bed, wearing her pyjamas. Her long blonde hair is tied in a ponytail that covers most of her back. Kimberly has a bent leg on the bed as she smiles along with something Elsa's saying about her stupid soap operas and shit.

She's been telling Elsa how much she's missed her and that the school sucks without her. Every time Elsa reaches over to her friend's hand, Kimberly tactfully pulls it away, keeping it beside her.

I tilt my head to the side as if that will give me an exclusive view of all the inside info. I'm itching to go in there and fucking rip up the sleeve of that pullover to see beneath it.

What the fuck are you hiding?

"Take these." Elsa picks up some avocado pieces with her fork and gives them to her friend. "Since Dad and Aunt learnt that avocados are good for heart disease, they've been stuffing me with them."

"I'm good."

"Come on. Try them. They're wonderful."

A smile flashes on Kimberly's lips, which is obviously forced, as she grips the fork with trembling fingers and stuffs the pieces of fruit in her mouth. The way she makes herself chew is like she's eating a dead insect.

Since the beginning of this year when she returned to school looking slim and hollow, I knew a big chunk of her was missing, aside from her curves.

She'd become this mimicking of a person who bent to others' views of what they thought she should look like.

The Kimberly I knew wouldn't have followed others' instructions about her life. She wouldn't have looked at herself in the mirror and thought, *hey, how about I become someone else?*

I might have hated her more than before, I might have watched her through the window and contemplated how to fuck her life over and ruin whatever the hell she was trying to become.

But as I watch her now, and after I saw that shit earlier and heard what Kir said when he was frantic that she was with Jeanine, I'm starting to have a different thought altogether.

Maybe the fake behaviour isn't her endgame.

When we used to play hide and seek as kids, Kimberly used to put a pillow in her bed and cover it. She said it served as her camouflage, something to hide her actual position.

Is all the fakery a camouflage, too?

She drops the fork, but Elsa urges her to eat more. Kimberly's skin is pale, so her expression is usually naked for the world to see. She couldn't hide the flustered emotions if she tried. Her cheeks redden and her ears heat under that mane of hair.

As soon as Elsa goes back to talking, Kimberly uses the chance to push the plate of fruit away as if it's a contagious disease.

"I'm feeling guilty for leaving you alone," Elsa says with a slight furrow of her brow. "I can't wait to abandon this bed and return to school."

"Me, too." Kimberly smiles. "But you don't have to worry about me. Ro and I have been having so much fun."

I shove my hand in my jeans pocket and make a fist.

"You and Ronan, huh?" Elsa hits her friend's shoulder jokingly.

"It's not like that."

"Then what is it like?"

"I don't know. Aside from you, he's the only one who's taken time to see me." Her head bows and the green-ish strands camouflage her expression.

"See you?" Elsa asks.

"The real me." Her head lifts as a grin moves her lips. How can she have so much sadness in a smile? How could she fool me all this time?

"I don't know about Ronan, but I'll always have your back, Kim." Elsa pats her hand in a motherly way. Kimberly must feel the same since she stares at Elsa's hand as if she's hit some sort of a jackpot.

"You see me," Kimberly says with a low edge to her voice.

No, she doesn't.

No one sees her. No one but me.

"Elsa, I—"

A hand wraps around my shoulder. I jerk backwards, ready to punch whoever interrupted my eavesdropping session.

Aiden.

Fucking arsehole.

He pulls me to a corner near the stairs, still not letting go of my shoulder.

I let him lead me away for no other reason than not to expose my extracurricular activities in front of his girlfriend's room. His black hair is damp as if he's been running wet fingers through it. Now that I think about it, when we first came over, Elsa was in the bathroom and—

Okay, I don't need that image.

"What the fuck were you doing there?" Aiden snaps as soon as we're out of the girls' earshot.

"Passing by."

"Funny, because I think I saw you standing there like a fucking pervert."

I push away from him. "Elsa wasn't naked this time."

"You should thank your lucky stars for that." He glowers at me. "And stop bringing up the other time before I fucking murder you."

I lift a shoulder as I lean against the wall and cross my legs at the ankles. The other day when all of us spent the night at his house, I made Aiden believe I saw him at the pool with Elsa.

I didn't, I spent most of the night outside a certain room. Still, I like using that bit against him to get a rise out of him.

Spoiler alert. I can be a dick.

"Why not?" I raise an eyebrow. "She was my girlfriend first, remember?"

Pretend girlfriend. The reason was to get back at Aiden for comforting Kimberly like a doting arsehole. Let's just say the relationship lasted for a minute, and Aiden ended it with a fist to my face.

It was the first time he got violent, and I enjoyed every second of it.

"Fuck you, Knight." He smirks. "You don't get the privilege to have me beat your arse again. Try again in ten years."

There went my plan.

"And stop fighting in those shady neighbourhoods. It won't be long before Nash knows, and if he does, Coach will, too."

"Aww, I'm touched." I place a hand on my chest. "Your words just hit me right in the feels, mate."

He continues staring at me with a blank expression, the

way cats watch their stupid owners. At least, that's how our cat used to watch us when I was a child.

Aiden has an impeccable poker face; it's impossible to see past it or through it. I'm surprised he can *see* with it himself. His dark grey eyes are unfeeling and cold. While the girls find him attractive, they usually stay away because of his closed-off attitude and 'fuck off before I kill you and your family' aura.

The only person he shows a human side in front of is Elsa. Even that part of him is dark, but she's also crazy since she kind of accepts the psycho the way he is.

"Fine." I sigh when he keeps glaring. "I'll be careful."

"You know I hate repeating myself. I said to stop it, not to be careful. If Nash focuses on your sorry arse for a fraction of a second, he'll figure you all out."

"I didn't know you loved me so much, King." I tap my chest again. "My heart is about to explode."

"You must be so lonely." He shakes his head. "I'd pity you if I knew how."

"Fuck you, King."

"Stay out of trouble. I don't and won't be the only striker in the formation."

Ah. There it is. The actual reason why he's throwing lovey-dovey shit all around. It's not that he's worried about me, it's that he doesn't want to be stuck as the only striker.

Pretty sure he'd quit Elites altogether if the situation somehow ended up going in that direction.

I waggle an eyebrow. "Then maybe I should have Nash figure it out, huh?"

"Are you ready to add your father to that mix of people?" He dusts off my hoodie as if there's something stuck in there. "How is Lewis's campaign going?"

"Wonderful, thanks for asking," I say with a grin, even though I want to punch him in the fucking face.

"If you punch, I'll punch, Knight." He shakes his head with

mock sympathy. "I'd hate to break that nose when you have so many pictures to take for the election campaign."

He steps back as I fist a hand to my side. I'm definitely going to a fight tonight. Fuck Aiden and Cole, fuck Coach and Dad. Fuck everyone, basically.

Fistfights are the only thing that allow me to blow off steam, and I need to do that so I don't blow up from pent-up frustration.

Aiden sniffles me like some dog. "Try the icy mint next time."

"What are you, my mother?"

"You must really be lonely if you want me to be your mother." He shakes his head with a mocking edge. "I'll hit you up when I consider adoption."

"Dick."

"At least I use mine. Yours is filing a lawsuit for human rights violation."

"Did I hear something about a lawsuit?" Ronan lunges at Aiden from behind in a bro-hug that the latter tries to escape. Ronan is like an octopus, though—the type that never lets go of their victim.

"Knight's dick is filing a lawsuit in search of his balls." Aiden's expression remains neutral as he says that.

I narrow my eyes on him as Ronan laughs, then stops. "But why are they searching for them? Wait a second, *mon ami*. Did one of the girls give you something? I told you to wrap it."

Aiden smirks. "Oh, I'm sure he did."

"Fuck off, King."

"What? What happened just now?" Ronan stares between me and Aiden. "You're hiding something from me again, aren't you? I swear I'm the one who'll be filing a lawsuit for neglect at the supreme court of friendship."

"That doesn't exist," I say.

"Friends?" Aiden searches around him. "Who?"

As if someone pushed Ronan's buttons, he launches into a long monologue about how he's always left out and that we're triggering his abandonment issues—the same speech he uses to lure in girls and have them suck his dick to 'loosen him up'. Girls always fall for the vulnerable act he pulls off so well.

Out of the four of us, Ronan gets the most pussy, but not the best, because he's like a fucking bus. Anyone is welcome.

Also, he's fine with sloppy seconds or thirds or even one hundredths.

Told you, he's a fucking bus.

As he talks, I'm tempted to punch him in that aristocratic nose he's so proud of, break it and watch blood ooze from it. He wouldn't be able to defend himself either, because he doesn't know how to punch, and he hasn't been in underground fights as I have. Aiden wouldn't save him either, because he simply doesn't care.

Two reasons stop me from taking action. One, we're in Elsa's father's house, and both Ro and I would be murdered by our fathers for starting shit in Ethan Steel's house; he's like a new emperor around here.

Two, and most importantly, if I hit him, the reason behind it will be as clear as day.

No matter what he does, it won't get to me.

I've already formed a thick armour around me and no one will get through it, not even Ronan's deliberate antagonising and his staged selfies.

And I know they're staged, because as much as Ronan acts like a clueless little shit, he's in fact a fucking fox. Why do you think he pretends to be supportive to girls? It's his sure way into their knickers.

Still, I hit his side harder than I should.

"Ow!" He clutches it. "What the fuck was that for?"

"To shut you the hell up. What are you doing here anyway?"

"I come to visit Ellie all the time."

"Elsa," Aiden grits out.

"Ellie is better, *la ferme*, King." He watches me up and down. "What are *you* doing here? I heard you drove my Kimmy."

Aiden's focus turns on me as if he's waiting for me to say something similar to what he's just said.

That she's Kimberly, not Kimmy.

And she's not his and never will be. Not now, not fucking ever.

But I don't say that. I have no right to fucking say that or anything remotely similar. Besides, Ronan is like a dog searching for a bone, the moment I give him a reaction, he'll latch on it and chew me out.

Not in this life, arsehole. Fuck you very much in French.

"Too bad that's none of your business." I grin.

"Both of you can leave now." Aiden snaps at the stairs. "Your presence is no longer needed—not that it was in the first place."

Ronan launches on another argument about how this isn't Aiden's place and he can't kick us out, then he goes on to remind him that he still can be Elsa's fiancé if he chooses to be-cause of two fathers' agreements and whatnot.

I'm vaguely listening to them at the beginning until I spot Kimberly's form retreating down the hall. She didn't see us, and if she heard us, she doesn't show it, appearing focused on her task.

She can't be going for Kir since she has to take these stairs to do that.

Aiden is threatening to break Ronan's nose, and his dick if need be, and while I'd love to stay and watch that show, my feet lead me away from them.

I leave my friends behind without as much as a word. They don't even pay me attention as I tiptoe down the hall to where Kimberly disappeared.

The only thing at the end of it is a guest bathroom. The sound of running water comes from inside, but there's nothing being washed since there's no interruption of the water flow.

Which means it's only used to camouflage another sound.

I know, because Kimberly always fucking used to do that when she cried in the bathroom on her own after her mum ignored parents-teacher meetings.

The fact she didn't use the bathroom in Elsa's room also means she's hiding something.

What on earth would she hide from her best friend?

I push on the bathroom's door and it opens with a slight squeak. My feet are silent as I close it behind me and stalk to inside.

What I see makes me pause. The tap is running, but as I expected, Kimberly isn't anywhere near it.

Her small frame is perched in front of the toilet as she empties her stomach into it.

But that's not what gives me a what-the-fuck-are-you-shitting-me moment.

It's when she pauses heaving, sticks her forefinger in her mouth, and then vomits again. She does it a few times more until she's dry heaving.

A red-hot rage takes hold of me at the view of her in that position.

The pieces of the puzzle all fall into place now.

It's because she ate those avocados. Now, I know why she always disappears after lunch, why I never see her eating with Kirian.

She said Ronan and Elsa see her, but she couldn't be any more wrong.

She doesn't even see herself.

Not like I do.

I see her when she's a mess, when she's fake, when she forces herself to laugh and just be there.

I see her even when she refuses to fucking see herself.

I'd hoped that the moment I was out of here and stopped fucking seeing her altogether, it would be all over, but this is a lot worse than I initially thought.

There's no way in fuck I'm going to let her be invisible to her own self. Not even if that costs me in the long run.

She had to fucking push me off the edge, and now that I'm falling, I'll drag her down with me.

I straighten and place my hand in my pocket. When I speak, my voice is low and deadly calm. The same calm before a lethal storm. "What the fuck are you doing, Kimberly?"

SIX

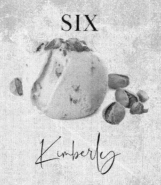

Kimberly

"**W**hat the fuck are you doing, Kimberly?"

The voice coming from behind me might as well be a bomb. Otherwise, why would I feel like I'm being detonated to pieces?

My knees shake on the tile floor as my hands fall lifeless to my sides.

No, it's *not* him.

He can't just figure me all out in one day. That's not how it works in real life.

Besides, he could've only walked in on the heaving part and nothing else.

No matter how much I reassure myself, my lower lip trembles and I bite down on the tender flesh so I don't give in to the need to run and hide.

You've got this, Kim. You've totally got this.

Taking a deep breath, I rise to unsteady feet and take my sweet time flushing the toilet. Maybe if I stay here long enough, he'll disappear and leave me in peace.

Maybe the whole thing is a play of my imagination because of being jumpy since earlier.

The prickling at the nape of my neck says otherwise, though. Razor-sharp attention is dissecting me slowly, as if cutting me open from the inside out.

It's all because of those avocados—I should've refused Elsa's offer, I should've not taken them. But if I had, she would have started to suspect me, and then maybe she'd regret being friends with me.

I can't lose Elsa. She's one of the few threads that keeps me hanging on to this existence.

Wiping my mouth with the back of my hand, I turn around, silently praying all this is a nasty nightmare.

The moment my gaze meets that ocean-deep one, I confirm it is a nightmare.

A real one.

The one I can never come back from.

"What are you doing here?" I speak lower than I intend to, but at least my voice doesn't shake like a pathetic idiot.

"The question is, what are *you* doing, Kimberly?"

Kimberly.

Kimberly?

I haven't heard him call me that in…well, ever. When we were young, he used to call me Green, or Kim when he was mad at me. After I fell from his grace, I became Berly, that stupid bullying name.

The fact that he's calling me by my full name is new and somehow…intimate.

Don't you dare like it, Kim. Don't you fucking dare.

"You never saw anyone vomiting?" I start past him towards the running tap, pretending he doesn't exist.

The keyword being *pretending*. There's no way in hell I can erase his presence, especially in the small space of the bathroom. My arm brushes against his and I falter for a fraction of a second, fighting the urge to close my eyes and soak in that contact.

I'm like a starved animal, waiting for a mere brush of clothes against clothes. What the hell is wrong with me?

I wash my hands, rubbing them harsher than needed until

they turn red, and then take a gulp of the mouthwash I always keep in my pocket.

Maybe I've overestimated what he saw. It's just someone vomiting, after all. Upset stomach, wrong food, bad weather. I have a multitude of excuses. Hell, I can even blame it on his existence and say it disgusts me.

Though, I'm not as cruel as he is—or as heartless.

"Why, yes. Of course I've seen someone vomiting." His voice is calm and steady, even though the undertone is sinister. "Nasty business, that is."

I spit out the mouthwash and clean my mouth. "Yup. Very nasty."

"Especially when you stick a finger in your throat and make yourself vomit. Nasty, indeed."

I freeze midway of pocketing my mouthwash. Shit. He saw it.

He shouldn't have seen it. Why the hell did he see it?

Or the better question is, why didn't I close the door?

Oh, I know why. I was in a hurry to lose the calories I gained from those avocados and meet Mum's requirements so she doesn't ship Kir away.

And I may have been rattled since I met this same arsehole outside my house and was forced to ride in his car earlier.

Me, in Xander's car. I might have been too stunned all the way to remember anything about the journey.

"I just had an upset stomach," I speak with a confidence I don't feel.

Last summer, I was hitting rock bottom and Dad suggested I go on a spiritual retreat; he said it helped him when he needed clarity. I didn't want to go, because of Kir, but when he said we could go as a family, I agreed. The trip consisted of Kir, Dad, and me. Mum had work—as always.

While we were there, I got to meet a lot of spiritual people from all sorts of religions, and although their beliefs didn't interest me a lot, their life philosophies did. So much, I'm actually planning to visit that mountain in Switzerland again.

Back then, a Buddhist said that even if I'm not confident, I have to think of my goals and if need be, fake that confidence.

I call it, fake it until you make it.

One day, I won't look in the mirror and practice how to talk, walk, or smile. One day, confidence will come naturally to me.

That day sure as hell isn't today, so all I can do is continue to fake it.

"Do you always have upset stomachs?" he asks with almost a sympathetic tone.

Almost, because he's faking it, too.

Xander's mirroring my fakery and using it as a weapon against me in his dickhead style.

"Yes." I don't dare stare back or in the mirror, where I'll find his eyes trying to dig a path into my soul.

No one needs to find a path to there, especially not him.

I don't want him of all people to see the mess hidden underneath all of this.

He broke me, and he doesn't get to witness the chaos left behind.

"That must be why you always carry the mouthwash, then."

"Yup."

"Funny, because I almost think you do that to hide your vomiting habits."

My fingers tremble, but I don't stop to let his words get to me. Xander might not have fat-shamed me, but he's a bully. He laughed in my face, he mocked me, and he turned my life to hell like everyone else.

When I decided to stop being a secondary character in my life, it also meant not letting him get under my skin or see me at my lowest.

"Funny, because that's none of your business," I mimic his tone.

"You think it makes you prettier? Skinnier?" He laughs, the sound hollow and harsh in the silence of the bathroom. "You can't hide behind layers of makeup, no matter how much you try to. If you think otherwise, then you need some awareness pills."

I hit the tap closed harder than needed as I try to control my breathing. His words are like tiny needles getting under my skin and puncturing the veins one by each bloody one.

"I told you," I grind out through my teeth. "It's none of your damn business."

A strong hand wraps around my wrist and I yelp as I'm yanked back so hard, the mouthwash bottle clinks against the lavatory and settles at the bottom of it.

My heart thunders so loudly, I'm surprised it doesn't follow the bottle and sink somewhere.

He's…touching me.

Xander has his hands on me. Those same long, lean fingers that are always lost in his hair or wrapped around a joint are now on my wrist.

Oh, God.

Xander's skin is on mine.

Whoa. What the hell? Is it supposed to feel this overwhelming? It's only skin against skin. Flesh to flesh. Anatomy.

But it's not just any skin. It's *his* skin.

Xander's.

Before I can get my mind to concentrate on that fact, he yanks my pullover up my wrist. The same wrist he was staring at earlier.

The wrist.

Shit.

I try to pull away from him, but he pins me against the marble edge of the lavatory, making the cold surface dig into me. He holds my other hand behind my back, disallowing me from moving as his punishing eyes study the marks on my skin.

My gaze strays away, not wanting to see how he looks at me, at that part of me no one should see. Even *I* don't like seeing it.

The cut marks are engraved in my head without having to glance at them. They're messy, but not that deep. Severe, but not deadly.

I was a failure even at that. None of it is elegant and pretty. It's all a big fucking mess.

"I suppose this is none of my business either." His voice is light, calm, as if he's not staring at the most shameful part of me.

How can he manage to make me hate myself by just looking at me? Why does he have that power?

He shouldn't.

He left me.

He didn't want to forgive me.

What right does he have to stare at me with those disapproving eyes as if we're still friends? As if my wellbeing matters?

"It isn't." My tone is biting, translating all the frustration bubbling inside me. "You said it yourself that day, we're strangers and should pretend we don't know each other, even if we cross paths, right? So be a stranger and leave me the hell alone."

More importantly, stop looking at me with those eyes.

I'm this close to melting in his touch. His soft touch, even though he's a brutal, vicious person.

"I said that, didn't I?" His gaze never leaves my wrist, like it's the first time he's seeing a cutting scar.

Or a scar altogether.

"You did," I repeat.

"Strangers can become familiar with each other again."

"Huh?"

"I changed my mind, Kimberly."

"You changed your mind?"

His pale eyes meet mine with a determination that nearly knocks me off my feet. "I'm making it my business."

My mouth falls open. I want to say something, but I can't. When I finally speak, my voice is haunted, spooked even. "You…you can't do that."

"Watch. Me."

"Are you forgiving me?" I curse the hope in my voice and all the jumbled emotions that come with it. I shouldn't feel this way after I decided I'm erasing him from my life.

"Of course not," he bites out. "That sin is unforgivable."

My chin locks, but I manage to speak without emotions. "Then let me go. My life is none of your concern."

"Told you, I'm making it mine."

"But why? Fucking why?"

"That fucking attitude." He narrows his right eye, but it quickly returns to normal. "You don't get to take the easy way out just because you can. You don't get to disappear just because you want to. I'm ruining all your plans, so you better be ready for me, Kimberly."

He gently, so gently, pulls down my pullover to hide the scar, no idea if it disgusts him like the rest of me or if it's another one of his cruel games. It's so shocking how soft and gentle he can be. He simply chooses the other route with me—the rugged edge that's meant to cut and hurt.

The one people reserve for their enemies.

"Hide while you can." He pats my hand once, and although his skin is warm, it feels so cold. "When I find you, I'll drag you out kicking and screaming."

SEVEN

Kimberley

My blood is still boiling by the next day at school. I tried to ignore it, and even spent the entire night dancing to a random list on Apple Music because that's the only thing that usually gets me out of my funk.

It helps push the fog away.

However, I was too agitated and red with anger for the fog to come. It was burned and turned into nothingness.

I barely managed to sleep after what happened in Elsa's house. It kept replaying at the back of my head on a loop, no matter how much I wanted to push it away.

Even now, as I sit next to Elsa, I can almost feel Xander's breath mingling with mine, his threats rolling off my skin like a promise meant to cut. I can smell him on me, intertwined with mint and fresh laundry and ocean scent, even though I've taken three showers since yesterday.

What the hell. Seriously?

"Kim?" Elsa waves a hand in front of my face.

"Huh?" I sound as distracted as I feel.

"Did you hear a word I said?" she asks with a tone that implies she knows I didn't.

This is Elsa's first day back at school. I'm supposed to be her wingman, but I'm totally failing at that.

"Sorry. I didn't sleep much last night." A certain face and voice kept me up, and I might have stalked his window.

When he drove me and Kir home, I sat with Kir in the back, ignoring Xander's glare, and then he went out and didn't return.

At least, not until I fell asleep re-watching *Atonement* somewhere after one in the morning.

Not that I watch him all the time. I told you, I just notice things.

Like right now, he isn't here yet, even though the class is about to start.

Xander isn't the brightest one amongst the horsemen, but he always has good grades in spite of skipping classes.

This must be one of the days he sleeps in.

Not that I care.

"Here." I push my notebooks at Elsa. "I highlighted all the sections you missed. If you need anything else, I'm your girl."

"I don't know what I would've done without you." Elsa rubs my arm with a warm smile. "You're the best."

"No, I am." Aiden's voice halts my small victory dance at Elsa's words.

He stands before her desk and taps his finger in front of her. "I told you I'd drive you."

"And I told you Kim would do it." Elsa stares up at him meeting his harsh stare with her unyielding one.

Aiden King is a ruler here, and although we were basically brought up together, he always gave me the chills, real ones, not those mixed with chaotic emotions like Xander gives me.

The moment he glares, everyone has the urge to blend with the walls or dig a grave and bury themselves in it—me included.

Elsa is possibly the only one who doesn't bow down to his authority, not even when he was her worst nightmare. Maybe that's why he looks at her as if she's his world and he'll unleash hell on everyone else just to see her smile.

He's the type of king who'll start wars for his queen.

As scary as Aiden is, I love the way he looks at Elsa, the way his brows soften under his hard face, the way he tells her without words that he's hers as much as she's his.

I've been watching them since they began, and I fell in love with them together worse than a fangirl falling for fictional heroes in romance novels.

The fangirl is me, by the way. I have more book boyfriends than I can count. Don't judge.

"Hmm." He strokes a strand of hair behind her ear. "You'll pay for that later, sweetheart."

"Show me your worst, Aiden."

God. It's so unfair to watch this and know it'll never happen to me.

Can I bury myself somewhere, please?

He grabs her arm. "Let me show you now."

"Class is about to begin," she hisses.

"Keyword being *about*." He pulls her into his side.

Elsa's face heats as she mouths 'sorry' to me while Aiden drags her behind him caveman style.

Sigh.

What's there to be sorry about, Elsa? I'm rooting for you.

I should probably start writing romance fanfiction and feed this hungry monster inside me.

I bury my head in my notebook, the one Aiden forced Elsa to leave behind, and sigh again.

That's when I notice him, or rather, hear him. His laughter echoes around me like a song, the type you can't get out of your head no matter how much you hear it. You always find yourself yearning for it, wanting more of it, like a bloody addict.

Then the beautiful song is tainted by another sound, a squeaky shrill laughter that breaks the song's melody to bloody pieces.

Veronica.

One of Silver's minions hangs on to Xander's arm as she fixes his uniform's tie. His hair is dishevelled and lipstick marks cover the collar of his shirt as if he's out of a fucking session.

He tucks a strand of Veronica's fake blonde hair behind her ear like they're just fixing each other's attire.

Or rather, fixing each other.

My grip turns deadly on the edge of the notebook as I lower my head. I want to vomit and for a different reason than the apple I had for breakfast.

Scenes like these aren't new to me. I've witnessed them time and again during the years. I've seen him cosy and playful with half the girls in school, and I've heard about his adventures more times than I wanted to.

However, to know that he went to her right after he told me those words yesterday, right after he drove me home, makes my cheeks redden with exertion.

Relax, Kim. Stay the hell down. Don't even think about showing a reaction.

That must be why he did all of this in the first place, and I won't give him the joy of seeing me crumble.

He slaps Veronica's arse, sending her to her seat as he rounds the corner to the back. Not once does he look at me or acknowledge me. If I hadn't spent the whole night thinking about that scene at the bathroom, I'd start believing it's a play of my imagination.

Veronica giggles like a strip club dancer on crack, or at least, that's how I imagine strip club dancers on crack sound.

Instead of sitting beside her eager friend Summer, her gaze meets mine.

Shit. She caught me staring.

"What are you looking at, you fat pig?" she snarls, flinging her pointy fingernails at me.

If it were any other time, I would bow my head and pray

she'd stop. If Elsa were here, she would've given her a piece of her mind, but I'm neither the old Kim nor is Elsa going to fight my battles for me for eternity.

"Oh, it was you. I'm sorry, I thought it was a street light walking into class." I grin, then this time, I do focus on my notebook.

If I speak to Veronica more, I'll be tempted to fight her, and that's probably the most stupid thought my brain can conjure.

That's because you're starving me. I need those calories to burn neurons and not be an idiot, okay?

Shut up, brain.

"What did you just say?" Veronica gasps like a drama queen in K-dramas.

"If you have a hearing problem, you might want to fix it."

She stomps in my direction and my body stiffens, but I stay my ground. "You fat pig, you must think you're all that since Ronan is protecting you as if you're his little lamb, but you're nothing without him around. You're just a wannabe fat bitch."

My entire body tightens, but I don't let those destructive thoughts out. Instead, I give her a taunting smile. "Someone is jealous."

"What the hell did you just say?"

"I told you, Veronica. Fix your hearing problem, then you might want to fix your personality while you're at it."

She lifts her hand and hits me hard across the face, making me reel in my chair. The sting burns as gasps echo around the class. I'm so shocked, my hand flies to my cheek, feeling around the heated skin.

I've always been the victim of pranks at school, the worst of all having a bucket of paint poured all over me, but no one, no bloody one, has ever put their hands on me. Violence is the last thing that can be condoned in an elite school like RES.

Xander approaches us, but before he comes closer and takes his Barbie's side, I punch her in the face. It's not a slap or pulling of hairs—I straight out drive my fist into her nose.

I don't even stop to think about it.

Instinct. This must be what it feels like. A bit impulsive, a lot liberating.

I feel the crack before I hear it. From Veronica, not me. Her face contorts and she shrieks as blood trickles down her nose and over her violet-painted lips, smudged by Xander's kiss.

The sight of her blood freezes me in place. My hand remains motionless, still in a fist, as if it can't be moved or flexed.

Blood.

Red.

Messy.

Oh, Shit. I think I'm going to faint.

The image of my own blood oozing out slow but steady assaults me. It won't stop. It won't even disappear.

It's there. It's going to end now.

Maybe Mum will find me. Maybe Mari will.

Please don't let Kir see me this way.

Don't have him remember me as a ghost of myself.

"Kimmy." The masculine voice pulls from my vision and I breathe harshly as if I'm coming out from a wave.

Ronan grabs both my shoulders, shaking me as my hand clutches my scarred wrist.

It didn't happen.

It's not happening, right? I'm not losing blood.

Oh, God. What's wrong with me?

"Are you okay?" Ronan shakes me softly again. "I'm going to get you out of here."

I don't say anything as he drags me out. I faintly hear murmurs surrounding us, lots of them. They crumble and turn into the giant fog that's gradually creeping to snatch my soul.

Veronica's shrill voice cuts in behind me like blades. I stare back at her, at the blood running down her face and soaking the hem of her shirt. She's struggling against Cole, who's effortlessly stopping her with a hand.

Xander stands beside them, not bothering with her or her hysterical state. All his attention is on me as Ronan wraps an arm around my shoulder and drags me away.

As the world focuses on Veronica and my slow retreat, he's concentrating on the hand that's gripping my scarred wrist.

An itch pushes me to let go, but I can't. If I do, blood will come out.

I'll bleed out.

Xander watches my hand and then my face as if he knows exactly what I'm thinking about.

As I round the corner, he whispers without words, "I see you."

I've never been so scared in my entire life.

EIGHT

Kimberly

The moment Mum and I are inside our house, I falter at the entrance, waiting for the inevitable.

Because of the fight with Veronica, the principal had to call our guardians. Usually, Dad takes care of anything that has to do with school, but since he's not here, Mum was forced to come out of her beloved studio for me. I could tell she was irritated by the way she snapped at the principal and Veronica's parents, telling them to rein their morbid daughter in. The video cameras showed that she slapped me first. In Mum's words, my punch was a 'knee-jerk' reaction.

I wasn't delighted she stood up for me, though. Mum is never on my side. She's on the side of the press and her image. If the great Jeanine Reed is known to have a violent daughter, it'd fuck up her upcoming exhibition.

That's why she gave it her all in the principal's office and even offered the school tickets to her exclusive pre-show that costs tens of thousands of pounds. A form of donation, she said.

Then she talked to her agent on the way home, sparing me a glare every time I breathed wrong.

Now that we're all alone, she'll tell me not to pull her name down, that she didn't spend years slaving in her studio to have a brat like me ruin her first exhibition in two years. She's been in a slump and has finally found her muse again.

Quick fact about my mum—she'd rather kill me and Kir and the whole world as long as she has her precious muse.

I steady myself at the entrance, waiting for the onslaught of her words, secretly happy Kir is spending the night with his friend Henry and won't witness this ugly scene.

Mum sighs and shakes her head, causing the perfect strands to move in an elegant kind of way. "Why do you have to be a disappointment, Kimberly?"

And with that, she retreats upstairs, oblivious to the blood trail she's left behind.

It's as if she stabbed me with a pointy knife and is taking the weapon of crime with her, letting the blood drip from it with each of her steps.

But this blood is different. It's the type that you can never wash off nor sew the flesh back together.

My chin trembles, but I inhale deeply and slowly go to my room.

"What would you like for dinner?" Mari asks me on my way up.

"Nothing." My voice is dead as I get past her. "Absolutely nothing."

The moment I'm in my room, I lock it and curl into bed, wrapping the sheet around me until my own breaths nearly suffocate me.

It's dark in here, serene almost.

The fog won't be able to get inside. It can't. If it does after what Mum said, I don't know what to do.

Kir isn't even here to stop me.

Maybe I should go get him. I can kidnap him from Henry's house or I can at least see his puppy eyes and hug him to recharge.

Without the warmth he emanates, I'm left in a cold, desolate space of my own making.

Tendrils of that fog seep under the sheet and surround me

in a tight hold. I clutch the cover harder, needing the camouflage it provides.

No, no, no…

It's not supposed to come in under the cover. It's supposed to stay the hell away.

My wrist scar tingles and my nose does, too. There's this overwhelming urge to cry, but I can't. No tears would come out, even if I let them loose. Unlike common belief, there's no relief in letting go and crying.

At least not for me.

Whenever I cry, that fog crawls faster under my skin and the next thing I know, it's invading my brain and occupying my thoughts. It turns from a need to an impulse, and without a strong presence like Kir's to stop me, I just give in to it and let go.

Completely. Thoroughly.

I'd be sitting in the bathtub and making a step I can never take back.

I blink the tears away and try to think of bright thoughts.

That's what my shrink used to say. *Bright thoughts.*

As if I can conjure them and produce them and somehow tuck them for the bad days. The days where everything disappears and everything hurts—the breaths I take, the contact of the sheet against my skin, the tingling of my veins underneath the scar, demanding release, the tears that want to come out and play with the fog.

All of it.

Every fucking thing.

"Help…" I murmur in a small, haunted voice. "Someone help me."

No one will hear me. I know they won't, because even though therapy tells me it's good to admit I need help, they also said I need to ask it from people.

And I'll never do that.

People just don't care. And if they did, they'd merely give me those pity looks that make me want to crawl to someplace no one can find me.

If my own mother, the woman who brought me into this world, doesn't care, why would anyone else?

My phone vibrates and I startle, nearly falling off the bed.

I'm about to silence it and go back to my little halo, aka a one-person party of self-pity, when I make out the name on the caller ID.

Dad.

I wince, staring at the flashing phone in the dark. Did the school call him, too? He's not like Mum. If he knows, he'll sit me down and discuss my therapy options because he recognises I wouldn't hit someone for no reason, it's an accumulation of pent-up frustration and blah freaking blah.

I can almost hear the therapist say those words, and that's why I don't like them.

Dad thinks therapy is the only solution, but there's also a simple one he could've made nineteen years ago—he shouldn't have participated in my creation.

He's a brilliant man and Mum is a successful woman. I shouldn't have been their daughter.

I don't pick up. If I do, I'll start crying, and that's a no-go right now. Besides, I'm unable to speak when the fog is wrapping its ghostly fingers around my throat like a noose.

If I break down on the phone, Dad will return on the next plane and I'll have to live with being a disappointment again.

Soon after the call ends, my screen lights with a text from him.

It's a long one. Dad is as eloquent as anyone can get, even with his texts.

Dad: Hey, Angel. If you're studying, I don't want to bother you, but I wanted to check in and see how you're doing. I'm sorry my calls were sparse yesterday and today. I've been working on an important project that will bore you to death if I talk about it. Anyway, I received a call from school, and I'm upset about what happened from the other girl. I'm sure you had your reasons, and you'll tell me about them one day. It pains me to think you've been hurt in any way. Kiss Kirian for me. Daddy loves you both and can't wait to come back and see you. We'll go on that family holiday Kir has been asking for. Stay safe, Angel.

A drop of moisture falls on my phone screen as I finish reading the text. I wipe the tear away so the others don't follow.

Damn it, Dad. Why did you have to put it that way?

Every time he calls me his angel, I'm almost tempted to believe it, to think that I'm someone's angel, that someone actually feels pain when I'm hurt.

Kimberly: I love you, too, Dad, and I miss you so much.

I erase the text before hitting send. If I do, he'll just call me, and I don't have the physical or mental energy to deal with those emotions right now.

So I check the other texts instead.

Ronan: Kimmy!

Ronan: Kim-my.

Ronan: Pay attention to me, *la merde*.

Ronan: I'm hurt, I'm going to cry in a corner.

I smile. He stayed by my side until Mum came earlier. I have a feeling it was his testimony against Veronica that saved me from suspension. I'm sure the others didn't testify in my favour.

Kim: You don't cry.

The reply is immediate.

Ronan: I do now. So, party at my place?

Usually, I would be all over that because the letting go, the drinking and dancing, takes my mind away from the fog.

Today isn't the day, though.

Kim: I have to study.

More like crawl further into my blanket and stay up all night, trying to fight these cancerous thoughts away.

Ronan: Come on, don't be a bore.

When I don't reply, he sends another text.

Ronan: Xander is here and he's so drunk, he can't stand.

I type before thinking.

Kim: Why would I care about that?

Ronan: Dunno. Thought you'd be interested in seeing me whipping his arse in a drinking competition?

No. I wouldn't be interested. That bastard is the reason behind this in the first place.

If he hadn't come in class with Veronica, blatantly parading his night with her in front of me, I wouldn't be in this damn predicament now.

Screw him.

I check the other texts from my best friend.

Elsa: Want me to come over?

Elsa: I'm worried about you, Kim.

Elsa: We can go to Ronan's party if you want?

If my parties' terrorist friend is offering to go to a party for my sake, then she really is worried.

If I don't reply, she'll burst through the front door, and I can't have Elsa see me this way.

Kim: You going to a party? Who are you and what have you done to my best friend?

Elsa: I go to parties.

Kim: Are you sure?

Elsa: Sometimes.

Elsa: So are you coming or should I come over?

Neither?

Still, I type.

Kim: Let's meet at the party!

At least that will give me time to stay with my head a bit more, bargain a little, tell it to leave me be for a while.

The whole thing.

I'm about to throw my phone away when it vibrates with another text. I expect it to be from Elsa or Ronan, but it's not.

Unknown Number: What are you doing?

Kimberly: Who are you?

Unknown Number: You better be not doing that nasty business or I swear I'm coming through your fucking window.

I pause, my heartbeat escalating. My fingers tremble as I type.

Kimberly: Xander?

Unknown Number: The one and only.

Oh, God. Oh, shit. Why is he texting me?

Kimberly: Since when do you have my number?

Elsa would never give it to him.

Xander: You think Ronan can have your number and I can't?

He stole it. I know it without a sliver of doubt. Even as kids, whenever Xander couldn't get what he wanted, he pretended not to care about it anymore, then he snuck behind everyone's backs and took it anyway. Just to prove he could.

Before I can give him a piece of my mind, another text comes from him.

Xander: What did Jeanine tell you?

I bite my lower lip so hard, I'm surprised no blood comes out. I really regret opening up to him about my relationship with Mum all those years ago. Not only does he know all my dirty secrets, but he's the only one in the know about how my mum makes me feel so small and insignificant.

I wish I could tell him things have changed since a long time ago, but that's not the case.

That doesn't mean I can't lie about it.

Kimberly: Nothing.

Xander: You expect me to believe that tyrant actually let it go as if it never happened? Try again.

Why is he being weird all of a sudden? My head has been working overtime since Elsa's bathroom. It's like being on a constant high and refusing to come down.

Kimberly: You have no right to talk about her like that. She's my mum.

I hate myself as soon as I hit Send. Why do I have to be such a hypocrite? But then again, Xander doesn't get to school me about my family as if he has every right to.

Xander: The one you wished you never had.

Damn him. Why does he remember everything I've told him? And if he does, why the hell can't he remember those times I practically begged him to never leave me alone with her?

Then he went ahead and did it.

He stepped on my heart and crushed it to pieces, so why does he think he has the right to return and tell me what to do now?

Kimberly: Leave me the hell alone.

Xander: How about no?

Kimberly: Don't you have your bimbos to keep you company?

Xander: Uh-oh. Someone is jealous.

Shit. Keep calm, Kim. Keep damn calm.

Didn't Ronan say he's drunk? This must be the alcohol, and all I have to do is ignore him.

Kimberly: In your dreams.

Xander: Good.

What the hell is that supposed to mean?

Another text comes soon after.

Xander: You didn't answer my original question. What are you doing?

Kimberly: The lack of an answer is an answer. Take a hint.

Xander: That fucking attitude will get you in trouble. Now, answer the damn question before I find out for myself.

Kimberly: And how the hell will you do that, genius?

Kirian is out, so even if Xander calls and asks him, he won't get anything.

Xander: Told you. Through the window.

Kimberly: From Ronan's house? Just how drunk are you?

Xander: Enough to run from Ronan's house to home. Or make Aiden drive me. I have plenty of options.

Kimberly: You can't be seriously serious about this?

Xander: Seriously serious, yes. That's it. I like the syntax of that.

Dammit. He pushed me back to my most basic form. Why the hell would I even repeat serious?

Kimberly: I'm doing nothing. Happy now?

Xander: Nothing, as in you're sitting around? Or nothing, as in you're hiding under your covers, trying to pretend the world doesn't exist?

My blood boils and my legs shrink further underneath me.

Kimberly: Nothing, as in nothing. Ever heard of the word? It means empty, nada. Now leave me alone.

Xander: So you can drown in that nothingness of yours?

Kimberly: Yes, which is none of your business, by the way.

Xander: Is that what you think?

I'm almost punching the keyboard with my fingers as I type.

Kimberly: Yes! You can't come here and pretend to know me. You don't, okay? You never fucking did.

Xander: Let me see, I know you dance to upbeat music on your own, and it's the only time you're not fake. I know you hide behind that makeup and new wardrobe because you see yourself as an ugly little monster on the inside. But not the hair, the green is you. It's the only real thing about you, because you've always been obsessed with that colour. You stopped eating your favourite pistachio gelato and green M&M's because they don't go well with the whole look, but you still take notice and stare when you see others eating them.

You like Elsa too much, so you do everything to appear perfect in front of her, and by doing that, you kill parts of yourself slowly, thinking if she actually saw your true self-harming, vein-cutting, pill-popping self, she'd give up on you. When you were talking to Jeanine that day, Kirian came to me frantic and told me about that night. He saw you fainted after you popped some pills, and for that reason, he's been hugging you more often lately and asking me if adults keep their fucking promises. I know you don't look long enough in the mirror, if at all, because you hate the person you see there, and if you stare long enough, you'll be out to destroy her, so you choose to hide behind the designer clothes and the layers of expensive makeup instead. But here's the thing, Kimberly, you can hide from the world and from your fucking self, but you'll never be able to hide from me.

Oh my God.

Oh. My. Freaking. God.

My hands tremble as I re-read his words and pinch my thigh to make sure this isn't some nasty dream hitting me out of nowhere.

How…how does he know all that? How can he figure out so much in such a manic, detailed kind of way?

Unless he's been watching me, too? He's been noticing me, too?

But Xander doesn't watch people. He doesn't stop to make room for me. He doesn't even look at me most of the time.

I'm the only one who does. From afar. Like a stalker.

Xander: So? How well did I do?

Xander: I can go on if you want. I can psychoanalyse your relationship with Jeanine and Calvin and Kirian, and even with Marian.

Kimberly: How about the one with you?

Xander: You have no relationship with me. Know your fucking place.

I push the covers away and jump to my feet, my muscles pumping with destructive energy.

He can't tell me all that and then decide he wants nothing to do with me. He has everything to do with me. Hell, he knows things I refuse to admit to myself. He can't pretend nothing happened and that he didn't just stab a different type of weapon in my already chipped armour.

That he isn't peeling underneath it and seeing what no one else has seen.

Me.

It terrifies the fuck out of me, to be seen by Xander out of all people.

But at the same time, it feeds a starved part that's been waiting for this since forever.

It's time I confront him about this whole thing.

NINE

Xander

A buzz starts at the back of my head. It's my cue that I drank too much and should probably cut it off.

Well, fuck that side of my brain.

I snatch a bottle of vodka from Summer's hand and chug half of what's in there in one go.

The burn picks up where the buzz left off.

The burn means I'll be able to collapse and sleep without having thoughts I shouldn't have. I'll wake up with an epic hangover, but it'll be worth it.

In other terms, I won't let my mind take me into dark mazes that have no way out.

As usual in one of Ronan's parties, it's full-blown mode. People grind against each other, and other people who won't shag tonight tell them to get a room. Post Malone is playing in the background, but he's ignored with the amount of chatter in this place.

Noise.

So much fucking noise.

It's normally my playground. Their noise means they can't hear me. Their distraction means they can't see me, and even when they do, they see what they like to see. Popularity, social status, trust funds that could boost a third world country's economy.

I'm as rotten as they are, if not worse. I just hide it better.

With the help of my friend vodka.

Summer is blabbering about the shit from today and how her best friend, Veronica, had to go to the doctor—an aesthetic one—to fix her nose and how upset she is, while she drags her fingernails up my thigh.

"If you're upset, maybe you should be with her." I smile, speaking with the slightest slur.

I'm drunk as fuck. I know because I hold my liquor well and don't typically slur. Also, I'm seeing double and Summer shouldn't have ten fingers on one hand.

Still, I don't speak as if I'm wasted. That's the power of being a drunk fool since I knew what drinking was. I would say I blame my mum and her own alcohol problem, but meh, who needs that tearjerker in their lives?

Step one into decimation: mummy issues.

Summer is protesting about some shit, but I'm not focused on the blabbering. I shake my phone as if that will make it magically light up with a text from her.

Maybe I shouldn't have said that all at once like some pubescent with a problem of holding down his wiener.

To my defence, I usually have a wingman, Ronan, to stop me when I'm drunk. He disappeared somewhere, and he's been acting like a dick all night, which probably means he's mad at me.

Fuck him, basically.

I'll have time to regret tonight tomorrow, so I might as well continue the show.

Unlocking my phone, I type.

Xander: Do you still sample Calvin's collection of tea?

No reply.

Xander: Do you still hide Jeanine's brushes to have her come out of her studio?

Nothing. Absolute fucking desert.

I don't know why I want to prove that I know her better than anyone else, that the fucker Ronan or that other metalhead arsehole Knox, Elsa's brother, would never know her the way I do.

It's not how it's supposed to go, but I continue my self-destructive path.

Xander: Are you still scared of horror films but watch them anyway?

Xander: Do you still make wishes upon the stars?

Xander: Do you still want to sleep beside me at night?

I delete the last one before I hit Send, then shake my head.

Fuck this. I'm spiralling down that rabbit hole. I stagger to my feet and Summer protests as she falls on her arse.

Huh. I forgot she was even there. Sorry, I guess.

I hit one person, or three, as I walk on unsteady feet, still gripping the bottle of vodka in my hand.

It takes me what feels like an hour before I finally find who I'm looking for. Cole sits beside the poker table, watching a game between Elites' team members. His face is calm, almost interested in what he's watching, but I know he's fucking pissed off because of a certain someone.

He and I are the same on so many levels. But I'm way worse because I'm fucked up in the head and need someone to stop my thoughts from going in that direction.

"Yo, fuckers." I raise my bottle, making a show of my drunk state.

Cole's at my face in a second, gripping me by the nape. He smiles at the others, but when his green eyes fall on mine, they turn deadly.

It's weird how he has the same eye colour as her, but his hold no beauty at all. Hers can be the reason for my free fall to hell.

"Your eye colour is fucking ugly," I say.

"What do you think you're doing, Knight?" he asks with a harsh undertone. "We have a game tomorrow and you're hammered."

"Ronan knew and he didn't stop me. If I'm going to the corner, send him with me, Captain." I laugh, even though I meant to smile. That's what happens when you're drunk—you sort of lose control over your actions.

"Jesus." He punches me across the face, but it's not mean like what I hoped for. He's only doing it to make me sober up.

It's enough to fill my thoughts with pain instead of the hell trying to break loose in there.

"Go sober up."

"Yes, Captain." I grin.

"The bottle." He extends his hand and I put it in there. "The fuck is wrong with you lately?"

"Your eyes," I slur.

"My eyes?" I swear he's smirking in one of the two versions standing in front of me.

"No, not your eyes. The colour. Fucking green." I slap my palms against his cheeks, smushing his face with the motion. "Why green, though? Just why?"

"Are you going to kiss?" Aiden's bored voice brings me out from my spiritual questioning.

My vision is slow as I turn towards him. He's wrapping an arm around Elsa's waist and tucking her to his side as if he's ready to kidnap her out of here any second—which will probably happen. Her goth sister with a tendency for sarcasm, Teal, is standing by her side, wearing a T-shirt that reads, *I don't want to be here.*

Then get out of the fucking door, sis.

Oh, wait. She won't, because she's a masochist like me.

Teal and Elsa are blushing as they watch me and Cole.

Aiden brings out his phone and directs it at us. "Let me commemorate the moment."

That's when I realise the position Cole and I are in. I'm grabbing him by the cheeks and he's staring at me with a bored expression that matches Aiden's.

"Any second now," the latter says. "If this can help with your case at the human rights court of law, you have my blessing."

"Mine, too." Cole smirks. "I'll take one for the team."

"Fuck you both." I shove Cole away.

I should bleach the colour of his eyes so this shit never happens again.

"Where's Green?" I ask Elsa, who's still watching me and Cole as if expecting the show to resume.

Seriously, as much as guys enjoy fantasising about girls together, I'm pretty sure girls fantasise about boys together, too. They're just not as vocal about it.

That was the Sherlock in me. Now, he's going to sleep.

Aiden and Cole exchange looks, smiling like two little psychos.

"Green?" Elsa repeats. "Who's Green?"

Fuck. I said that out loud? I must be drunk out of my mind. I need to get the fuck out of here before I word vomit everything.

"Yeah, Knight." Aiden feigns nonchalance. "Who's Green?"

"I think I heard that name somewhere." Cole taps his chin. "When we were young and—"

I punch him in the shoulder, cutting him off mid-sentence. The fucker is bored and out to destroy lives because of it.

There's no way in shit I'll be the next victim of his sociopathic boredom.

"I know where she is," I whisper so only he can hear.

"She?" Cole repeats with a semi-serious tone.

"Yes, *the* she." I raise an eyebrow. "She went with Ronan."

And with that, I'm out of the scene.

People hit two birds with one stone, I hit three.

One, I made Cole shut the fuck up. Two, I escaped his and Aiden's circle of sociopathic tendencies. Three, I directed his wrath towards that little bastard, Ronan.

I swear I come up with the best ideas when I'm drunk.

On my way out, I steal some boy's cup of alcohol, down it, then steal another one.

They don't even protest. No one attempts to put a brake on whatever the hell I'm spiraling into. No one dares to punch a minister's son to teach him some sense.

Fuck you, Dad.

Somewhere along the way, I find myself heading to the garden. The music fades as the chill wraps around me, but instead of waking me up, it turns me a bit more drunk.

On the night, the stars, the fucking world.

You suck, world. You really, really suck.

I throw away the last cup and head to a small covered porch at the back. Kids don't wander around the area because a) it's cold, b) Ronan will skin them alive, and c) did I mention it's fucking freezing.

So I'm surprised to find someone there. She's dancing, earbuds in her ears and hair flying behind her.

Not someone.

Her.

The one I can't have.

The only one I can't fucking have, but I still find myself roaming around and watching anyway.

Her dress falls to her knees but is tight at the waist, showing off the lines of her soft curves.

She's there, up for the taking, and for whatever scenarios my mind is conjuring at a supersonic speed.

I should go, leave, never return.

But I take a step towards her instead.

I can't have her, but that doesn't mean I can't play with her.

Love is impossible, but hate is an open game.

TEN

Kimberley

My eyes are closed as I let the music take me away from my physical shackles.

Magic by Coldplay drums in my ears and it's almost like that—magic. The lyrics speak so much to me and to the person I've been. It becomes a bit painful to listen, to be that fool who still believes in magic.

Music is the only thing that keeps my head afloat and somehow manages to keep the fog at bay.

Ever since I walked into the party and saw Summer rubbing herself all over Xander, I've been having these small bursts of nothingness.

I know I came to confront him, and I'll do that, but I need to calm the hell down first.

The shot of tequila didn't work, being with Elsa didn't, and Ronan, my own tailored distraction, is nowhere to be found, so music is my only reprieve.

I let it float me away as the melody fills my ears and my senses. My body moves of its own accord as I take refuge in the darkness and the cold, knowing no one will come out here in the middle of this wind.

As soon as this song ends, I'll walk back in there and tell Summer off. If she doesn't leave, I'll punch her like I did her friend—or not. I really don't want to witness that same expression on Mum's face again.

It's enough for one day.

Anyway, I'll just push Summer away and demand he explain whatever the hell he sent me in texts.

In and out. It'll be in a place full of people and I'll be able to disappear in no time.

I nod to myself and pluck out my earbuds as I turn around, determination bubbling in my veins.

My feet halt automatically when my eyes meet those ocean-deep ones. The ones filled with magic that I can't stop believing in.

With arms and ankles crossed, he's leaning against the tree right behind me, as if he's been watching the entire show.

Wait. He was?

The light coming from the huge mansion casts shadows over his features. I swallow, still trying to get over the fact he's been there all along.

The hell? Since when did he become such a creep?

And why are you secretly happy about it?

If he's a creep and I like it, what does that make me?

"Don't stop on my account." He twirls his finger. "How do you do that thing with your hips?"

I blush, and I'm so glad he won't be able to see it due to the lack of lighting.

"It's like a belly dancer. Is that what you practice late at night?"

My head snaps up. "How do you know that?"

He can't possibly be watching me, because his room always has its dark curtains pulled down.

"I think we've established that I know a lot of shit about you." He pushes off the tree, and my body instinctively tightens.

The way he stalks towards me is nothing short of a predator. Someone with the need to hurt and destroy. Someone who's after me, not anything else, just *me*.

Still, I speak in the most neutral tone I can afford. "Why?"

"Why?" he repeats, lifting one of his brows.

"Why do you know a lot of shit about me?"

"That's the question of the century, isn't it? Why?" He stops when his chest nearly brushes against mine.

This close, I can breathe the stench of vodka on him, strong and unyielding like everything else about him.

He's drunk. No, he's wasted. I'm surprised he was able to walk that small distance from the tree to here or even sound relatively normal.

Usually, if someone were to stare at me the way Xander is right now for more than five seconds, I would be compelled to run away. It's sinister and filled with so much anger, it's physically wounding. But I can't run away from him. I did it before and it ruined us for fucking good.

"Why green?" he asks.

"Huh?"

"You heard me. Why is it fucking green?"

"My favourite colour?"

"I hate your favourite fucking colour. I hate *you*, Kimberly."

Ouch.

I try to think that I already know that bit of information, that he's always made his feelings crystal clear, but hearing him say the words is equal to inhaling black smoke straight to my suffocating lungs.

I couldn't breathe if I wanted to.

"I hate your eyes and your fucking hair." He clutches a strand and strokes it between his thumb and forefinger as if he's memorising it—or thinking about burning it. I can never tell with him.

He's that dark well that's been abandoned for years. You never know if you'll find a treasure or vengeful ghosts in it.

"Then stop touching me," I breathe out. "Stop getting in my way, stop invading my life and knowing so much shit about me."

Most of all, I need him to stop seeing me. Because if he

keeps doing that while pushing me away and letting other beautiful girls into his bed, it'll only make the fog worse.

Why can't he leave me alone until we part ways at the end of the year?

Just why can't he do that?

"I should." He releases my hair with distaste. "But you keep being this sore thumb, making yourself noticeable all the fucking time. Don't ask for my attention or I'll suffocate you with it."

"I n-never asked for your attention."

"You want me to believe that?"

"I didn't." I push away from him. "Go away, Xander."

I'll talk to him when he's sober. Better yet, I might not talk to him at all. It's fruitless anyway. It's not like he'd answer any of my questions like a normal human being.

He'll just torment me some more, push me around some more, and then I'll retaliate and it'll turn ugly.

No, thanks.

He grabs me by my wrist—the scarred one—and forces me back against him. My breathing hitches as he dangles a pack of M&M's in front of my face. It's open and all the ones inside it are green.

"Why do you have green M&M's?" I ask in a small voice.

"I found them."

"You found them? You expect me to fall for that?"

"Yeah, and I want you to eat them."

"I won't."

"Do it or I'll turn Kirian against you. He already doesn't trust you after he witnessed your suicide attempt."

My lips part as I stare at him. "D-don't."

"Then eat them." He shoves the M&M's into my palm. "And don't vomit them or I'll shove another pack down your throat. I can do that all night."

"But Mum—" I cut off before I blabber everything. I can't tell him about my deal with her. My wanting to say something is a nasty habit from when we were children, where I ran to him and poured my heart out, then slept all wrapped around him.

Xander used to pat me to sleep, but now, he would just push me into a bottomless hole.

He's not my friend anymore; he's my enemy. I can't let my stupid memories get the better of me.

"I don't fucking care about Jeanine." His gaze hardens. "*Do it.*"

Sometimes, I swear he loathes my mother, but he has no reason to, aside from what I used to tell him. Did I paint her like an actual monster back then?

"Xander…"

"Shut the fuck up. I told you not to say my name." He releases my hand and motions at the pack. "Eat it."

Keeping much-needed distance between us, I open the pack with trembling fingers. The smell of the peanut and chocolate gets me right in the nose. Considering I only had an apple today, my stomach growls with the need for a taste.

I stare up at Xander with one final plea not to have me do this. I'll have to run or do exercises for an hour to erase the calories and I hate physical activities from the bottom of my heart.

"Hurry," he orders.

"Damn you," I curse him under my breath as I throw the first M&M in my mouth. My heart skips a beat at the taste, sweet with that rich chocolate flavour. It's been so long, a year to be exact, since I last had M&M's. Even more since I last enjoyed them.

I had them that day I lost him once and for all and since then, I haven't been able to properly taste M&M's or pistachio gelato.

The first piece is the hardest, the second tentative, but by the third, I'm popping them as if I've been dying and it's my cure to live. I want to savour it more, to commit the taste to memory, but I've been starved of this joy for way too long.

No idea if it's because a long time has passed since my last M&M or the fact that I feel Xander watching me like a hawk as I devour the entire pack.

I don't dare look up at him and meet those eyes, or else I'd offer and share. I'd stop and ask all the questions burning inside me.

The pack is empty too soon, and the moment the last bit disappears down my throat, I feel the need to throw up.

Shit.

I ate all those calories. I need to get them out and—

"Don't even think about it."

I lift my head to find Xander staring down at me with his lids half-closed, although the rest of his face is stone cold.

Only Xander wouldn't loosen up when he's drunk.

"How do you know what I'm thinking about?" I ask.

"I just do. It's a curse." He reaches his thumb to my lower lip and wipes some chocolate off. "You want to throw it back up, but don't. Rein it in. I'll stay with you until the urge goes."

My chin trembles, but I clench my mouth, not wanting to feel the softness of his touch or the dooming weight of his words.

I'll stay with you until the urge goes.

How can he say things like that so easily? How can he reach inside me and effortlessly wrench these feelings out?

He places his thumb with the bit of chocolate between my pursed lips. "Finish it."

I shake my head, but that only makes him push his thumb harsher until it connects with my teeth. "We can do it the easy way or the hard way."

Or I can just bite you.

I'm about to do that when he smirks as if he's been reading my thoughts all along. "For the record, biting me is the hard, not the easy one."

I dart out my tongue and lick the chocolate off his thumb. It's quick and I finish soon after I start.

My tongue itches for more. I'm like a newbie getting her first hit of drugs, her first high, and needing so much more of that madness.

Xander doesn't remove his finger, even after I'm done. He stares at me with a weird type of intensity.

He always has this frown whenever he looks at me, a fucked up type of interest, which I've always known is because he hates me.

But right now, it's not hate that's staring back at me. It's anger, raw and unhinged. A shudder goes through me, even though he hasn't directed it at me yet.

His thumb leaves my lips and I exhale, thinking it's finally over.

"The right green eyes," he slurs.

"W-what?"

My breathing cuts off when he cradles my cheeks with both his hands and brushes his lips against mine. Once. Twice.

It's soft, so soft, I think I'm going to die from the feeling of it. I never thought Xander's lips would be this soft. Not once have I imagined our first kiss would be this gentle, heartbreaking even.

First kiss, if we don't count the smooches we had as kids.

He groans deep in his throat as he possesses my lips and turns me around, slamming me against something hard, a tree.

Tingles erupt down my spine as I open my mouth with a moan. Xander loses all softness then. His tongue finds mine and he kisses me with a ferocity that leaves me soundless, breathless, and boneless.

I wrap my hands around his nape, letting them get lost in his thick hair as he grabs my face tighter, kissing me harder and faster, like it's the first and the last time, like he has to run right after this.

From the outside looking in, it must seem like he's sucking my soul out of my mouth, and that's probably what he's doing.

Never in my wildest dreams did I think he'd kiss me, or that he'd be this passionate about it, as if I was the only kiss that matters in his life and—

As fast as he starts, he wrenches away from me with a deep, pained growl.

My back is still against the tree, my legs shaking, and I couldn't move if I wanted to.

He glares down at me like I'm his worst enemy before he runs a hand through his hair. "Fuck!"

He kicks a pebble, facing away from me as if my mere view repulses him. "Fucking fuck."

"What the hell?" I murmur out loud, although I mean to say it internally.

He's at my face again, his eyes glimmering with deep-seated rage, and this time, he looks about ready to unleash it on me. "Don't you ever, and I mean *ever* tempt me again."

"What?"

"Get the fuck out of my sight. Your face disgusts me."

A sob catches in my throat as his same words from that day years ago cut me open all over again.

He started to mend those wounds only so he could rip them open.

I hate him.

I hate him.

I *hate* him so fucking much.

"Now!" he growls and I don't have to be told twice as I turn on my heels and run out of the garden.

My lips are swollen, heart slaughtered, and head swimming with that memory from seven years ago.

ELEVEN

Kimberley

Age eleven

"Over there?" Xan points at the path between the trees.

"Yeah," I say without smiling, even though I want to. Badly. "Go fetch her."

"Luna!" he calls for our cat as he disappears behind the trees. "Come out!"

His voice slowly fades, and I huff, throwing green M&M's into my mouth. I'll leave all the other colours for Xan.

Luna isn't there. She's at home sleeping by the fireplace—his, not mine. Mum would kill me before allowing me to have any pet.

But Uncle Lewis let Xan have Luna and after that, she became our cat.

She's not missing, but I told Xan to come look for her because he was being a meanie. Since he hates the cold, I brought him out when it's about to snow.

I sit at the rock at the entrance to the forest and grab a stick, then twirl it on the ground as I wait.

Earlier, I told Xander how much I hate being Mum's daughter and that she's stopping me from eating my favourite food.

"Ignore her; you're beautiful," he said while he was watching Kirian sleeping.

"I am?" I asked, staring at him with wide eyes.

His cheeks turned red before he nodded. "You're the most beautiful girl I know."

"Even more than Silver?"

"More than anyone." He clutched Kir's finger and my baby brother curled his fist around it.

That couldn't be true; he was lying to me. Everyone says Silver is a Barbie doll with her golden blonde hair and pale blue eyes. She's always elegant and majestic, while I'm just…me.

Fat and ungraceful. And I have some blemishes that won't go away.

"You're lying." I pouted.

"Why would I lie to you, Green?"

My face heated and I twirled a strand of my hair. "You don't think I'm fat?"

"No." His sky-ocean eyes met mine. "You just like to eat and I like it when you eat."

I hit his shoulder with mine. "Can you go with me to the grocery shop?"

"Later. I'm meeting Aiden and Cole for a football game."

"But you did that last week."

"We do that every week, Green."

"But why? Who will keep me company?"

"You have Kir."

"He's a baby and I don't think he understands when I talk."

"I have to go."

"You can't do that."

"Of course I can." He pulled his hand from Kirian's fist. "You don't get to tell me what to do, Green."

I frowned, my forehead turning painful. He'd been saying all these things lately that made me want to punch him.

Since that day Mrs Knight left and never returned, Xan

and I had become best friends. We had done everything to-gether and had shared all our lives with each other.

Then he decided Aiden and Cole were more important than me.

"You can go meet Silver," he said, watching me closely.

"Who I meet is none of your business."

He pushed me out of Kirian's room so we wouldn't wake him up. Outside, he crossed his arms. "What are you being so angry about?"

"You don't know?" I threw my arms around.

"No."

Stupid tosser.

I wanted to be with him, but he wanted to be with his stupid friends. In that case, he could go to them and leave me alone.

I stormed to my room and slammed the door shut. I flopped on my bed, fuming, and attacked a bag of crisps I hid under the covers after Mum came to check on my room.

A moment later, a knock sounded on the door. "Open up, Green."

His voice was steady, pleading even, and it almost made me want to let him inside.

I didn't, of course.

Not until he knew what he did wrong.

"You're being a baby," he said.

"So leave me alone."

"I don't want you angry."

Then don't go to your stupid friends.

Whenever I was alone, my house felt so empty, like a hor-ror film I had watched with Silver the other time. Ghosts had come out and had tried to suck the life out of any human in there.

Xan was the only one who kept those ghosts away when Dad wasn't around. I didn't want to be alone with Mum. She always looked at me as if she wished she'd never given birth to me.

Being with her was the worst, most real nightmare I'd ever had.

"I handpicked green M&M's for you."

My mouth watered, but I didn't reply.

"I'll leave the pack in front of the door. I'll come back later, Green. We'll watch a film together, okay?"

Don't go.

The words slipped to the tip of my tongue, but I bit down on a mouthful of crisps to stop them from escaping.

I jumped up and watched him from the window as he headed to Aiden's house down the street.

He really left.

Xan returned a while after and asked if I forgave him. I said yes, if he'd find Luna for me.

Which brings us to now.

Walking outside in the cold is his punishment for leaving me earlier. Once he spends some minutes out there, I'll forgive him.

Silver said she came around here with her dad and that it was so freezing, she felt the cold and even sensed ghosts.

I grin.

Ghosts are good. Xan will be scared and—

Oh, no.

Ghosts.

Ever since Xan disappeared with Aiden and Cole three years ago, he doesn't like to be left alone in unknown places.

I heard Uncle Lewis talking to Dad back then, and he said bad people kidnapped them. It took Xan two days of walking through an unknown forest until he could come home.

He snuck into our house through the servants' entrance, got into my room, and slept with me for a month after that.

Although he didn't like to talk much about that time with others, he told me how much it scared him to be alone out there.

That he called for his Mum's help, even though he knew she wouldn't come for him anymore.

I cried for him then. I just wrapped my arms around him and cried.

His pain is mine.

I feel it worse than he does because while he was simply telling the story, I felt every lash of cold against his skin and every tear he shed while he called his mother's name in that unknown dark place.

I might have also kicked and screamed in my head at the people who took him to that place.

That's how much I'm connected to him.

Why did I think it was a good idea to bring him to the cold and expose him to a situation similar to the one from that time?

Jumping to my feet, I follow the path he took. Twigs crunch under my shoes and I flinch as if someone grabbed me by the shoulder.

"Xan," I call, keeping a straight line.

The more I walk into the forest, the colder it becomes, just as Silver said. Or maybe I'm imagining it.

"Xan, come out! Luna is home." My voice breaks and I swallow.

There's no trace of him, no matter how deep I get in.

"Xan!!" Tears fill my cheeks and my chest squeezes so hard, I'm afraid it'll burst. "I'm so sorry! I won't do it again. Please!"

I'm running now, my feet moving of their own accord as I cover all the road I know and even into a road I've never been on before.

There's no trace of him.

I stop in the middle of the forest, tears streaming down my cheeks and slipping into my mouth. My unsteady legs barely carry me as I watch my surroundings, empty and desolate, and without him.

"Xaaan!"

What have I done?

After what seems like half an hour of fruitless searching, I go back home. I don't know how I do it, but I manage.

Uncle Lewis parks at his driveway the moment I reach our street. Mum went out for a meeting with her agent, so it'll take her a long time to return.

Not that she would care.

"Uncle! Uncle!" I run up to him and he meets me halfway, a frown creasing his brow.

"Xan is in there and he didn't come back. He's…he's…" I'm breathing so harshly, I'm skipping over words and unable to form a coherent sentence.

Uncle Lewis grabs both my shoulders with his comforting hands and watches me with a calm, soft expression. "Take a deep breath, Kim, and speak slowly. Let's try it, in, out. In. Out."

I follow his instructions, inhaling and exhaling as slowly as I can. When I can speak, I blurt, "Xan disappeared into the forest, Uncle. I can't find him."

"Disappeared how?"

"He was searching for Luna," I sob. "But she's already home."

"Okay, I'm sure he didn't go far. Breathe, Kim."

I nod frantically. "Please find him."

I'll do his homework for a year. I'll give him all my M&M's and even clean his room.

As long as he comes back, I'll do anything for him.

"Angel?"

My breath hitches at Dad's voice. He crosses the street as his driver closes the door.

If Dad is already home, that means it's getting late.

Uncle Lewis straightens as Dad reaches us. My daddy is tall with sandy blond hair and rich brown eyes and he looks like the models from Silver's magazines. He's wearing his perfect suit that Marian spends a lot of time perfecting.

"Daddy!" I hug his waist, ruining his suit with my tears. "Please find Xan."

"What happened to Xan?" His gaze strays from me to Uncle Lewis. They exchange a look I don't understand as I repeat the gibberish from earlier.

"It's my fault," I cry. "I'm so sorry."

"Don't say that, Angel." Dad strokes my hair behind my ear and kisses my forehead. "Let's find him and I'm sure he'll forgive you."

"I'm sure," Uncle Lewis echoes with a smile.

The three of us go back to the forest and search together. We go to where Xan and I were and try to cover the directions he could've taken.

All the way, I cry as Dad and Uncle Lewis tell me it's okay and that we'll find him.

We don't.

The late afternoon turns into dusk and soon enough, the night starts to fall.

I don't stop crying. Every time the tears begin to dry up, I think about the amount of fear Xander must be in and then a new wave hits me.

What have I done? What have I done?

"I'll take Kim home," Dad tells Uncle Lewis.

"What? No!" I shriek. "I'm not leaving until I find Xan."

"Maybe he went to his house."

"Ahmed would've called Uncle Lewis if he had," I insist.

Dad hugs me to his side as he addresses Uncle Lewis, "Call the police. This could be another case like the other time."

"I doubt it. He wasn't the target back then, Aiden was." Uncle Lewis sighs, his gaze straying towards me. "But yes, take Kim home. It's getting cold."

I struggle against Dad as he tries to drag me away. "No, Daddy. I have to find him."

"You can't, Angel." Dad's jaw tightens under the late dusk sun and I don't know why that makes me cry harder.

I wiggle free from his hold before he can trap me in again.

"Kim!" he calls and his footsteps sound behind me.

No idea where I'm running, but I don't stop.

I trip and slide down a small hill. My knee burns and stings, but I stand up and continue running.

"Xaaan!" I scream at the top of my lungs. I'm crying and running and heaving.

It's almost like that time when Nana left me and I knew I'd never see her again.

Only, now, it's worse because I'm the reason behind his disappearance.

I'm the reason he's lost somewhere unknown while he's cold and alone.

"Xan!" Something cuts into my ankle, but I keep running and calling his name.

Is this how he felt when his Mum got into that car and drove away? When she never looked behind as she left him?

A sob tears from my throat as I stand there, my chest heaving so hard, as if my heartbeat will come to halt any second now.

Just when I'm about to stop and let Dad catch me and take me home, I spot a figure by the cliff.

The denim jacket and the golden hair, the tall body and scrawny build.

It's *him*.

At first, I think he's staring down the cliff. But instead, he's facing me, a hand in his pocket and his expression blank, haunted even.

His blue eyes are the emptiest I've seen since the day he lost his mum. He's cold and so hollow, it's scary.

"Xan!" I sprint towards him, tripping twice, but I manage not to fall to my butt.

I wrap my arms around his neck and hug him so close, I think I may suffocate him. "I'm so sorry, Xan. I didn't mean to. I'm so, *so* sorry."

He places a hand on my chest and shoves me away. It's so angry and strong, I reel back with the movement.

I deserve that. I'm the one who put him into this in the first place.

I also deserve the deadly glare he's giving me. Maybe I'll have to do his homework for two years?

"Stay away from me." His voice is thick, the harshest I've heard him talk.

Okay, so I'll do the homework for three years.

"I'm so sorry, Xander."

"Don't say my name again." He glares at me. "Don't talk to me ever again."

"Xan…" My voice breaks, and I approach him slowly. My heart is on my sleeves and I sniffle as I reach out a tentative hand and clutch the hem of his jacket. "Don't make me. I'm sorry, okay? I'll do anything as long as you forgive me."

"Don't touch me. You're disgusting." He shoves me so hard, I fall on my butt on the solid ground.

It doesn't hurt.

Or it does, but it's nothing compared to the pain of his words.

Or how I feel when he turns away and leaves, without a glance, without offering me his hand.

He left me.

And never looked back.

That day was the last day I called Xander my friend.

A week later, Luna was hit by a car and died.

Seven years later, the loss of them still beats under my skin, loud, hard, and unbearable.

TWELVE

Kimberley

You know that feeling when everything and everyone seems wrong?

You wake up in the morning and instantly wish you hadn't, or worse, you want a redo of your entire life.

It's the stuff people go to therapists for, and the stuff that keeps people like me up all night, hoping against hope we won't wake up in the morning altogether.

Only to be disgusted with ourselves after.

That's how today started, morbid and awful.

I didn't have my usual happy pill from Kirian, and now, I hate myself for wanting Kir merely to feel better about myself.

Try being a human, Kim.

Not today, brain. Leave me alone.

Like any teenager with issues, *plural*, I hide from them by sneaking off to the garden. It's weird how I recognise having issues, but I don't want to name said issues.

Naming them is taboo. Naming them means I have to get into a rabbit hole of myself and I kind of don't like that. Myself, I mean.

Today is just too much. Too raw and too real, and I've had enough with everything, and everyone.

I bottle it inside the same way any good, typical teenager with issues would.

Mum is lucky to have a daughter like me. I don't take it out on people or drugs. Parties or boys. I have other purging methods, ones she approves of.

Such as starving myself.

I jab my fork at the bottom of my food container but don't take a bite of my salad. I'm not in the mood to vomit; it'll make my stomach way worse.

No, thanks.

If Elsa finds out I bailed out on her and Teal, she'll be upset, but I don't want her to see the puffiness under my eyes or the hollowness in them.

No matter how much makeup I put on, I can still feel the tears from last night.

I fell asleep crying after Xander shut me down so harshly. I can still sense the blade, hear the crunch against the bone and feel him twisting it inside.

He didn't even need a new weapon. He just used that rusty knife he left in my heart that day seven years ago.

My lips are still tingling from the way he kissed me, how he grabbed me and held me like we'll never be apart in any reincarnation.

Then he pushed me. He brought me up for air just so he could drown me all over again.

I stab my fork in a piece of tomato.

I hate him.

I hate him so fucking much.

"What did that food do to you, Kimmy?"

My war against the salad halts for a second as Ronan slides to my side, grinning wide. "There you are."

"How did you find me?"

"I have special skills, *chéri.*" He plucks a piece of lettuce, chews on it, then throws it away. "How do you eat this shit?"

It's simple. I don't.

"Where were you yesterday, Kimmy? How can you come

to my party and not wait for me? Hold on a second..." He looks me up and down as if he can read words on my clothes. "Did you get some?"

Some pushing, some kissing, some M&M's. Take your pick.

"I'm not you, Ro," I say instead.

"Of course you're not. If you were, you would've been having fun, not hiding from a certain bastard with repulsive dimples."

My eyes widen. He knows. How does he know? Am I underestimating how much Ronan is involved under the easy-going façade?

He waves a hand in front of my face. "Why do you look like a rat just died in your lap?"

"Ew, gross." I hit his shoulder with mine.

"Not more gross than that." He motions at my plate. "Go out with me and I'll take you to the best cuisine, and it's diet-friendly—my mother's style."

"Sure." I smile.

He snaps his fingers. "You just agreed."

I nod, wondering why he seems so surprised.

"It's official. We're going on a date."

"A d-date?"

"Why do you think I asked you out?"

I stare at him for a second. Ronan has always joked about a threesome of me, him, and Elsa, but that's all it's been, jokes.

Why does he seem serious all of a sudden?

"B-but why?" I ask. "You have all the girls and then some."

"You know, against common belief, I'm a fucking gentleman—unless clowns are involved, I'm not a gentleman then. Fucking creeps. Anyway, I'm doing it for you, Kimmy."

"For me?"

"Fine, for *us*." He sighs, shaking his head. "You get your payback."

"Payback?" I know I'm starting to sound like an idiot with all these questions, but I'm seriously feeling out of my element right now.

"Knight hurt you yesterday."

"You saw?"

"I felt it." He pulls up a finger. "*Premièrement*, Knight skipped today, to fight and bleed his knuckles and will probably only show up for the game." He adds another finger. "*Deuxièmement*, you've been crying and you ran away from him, which means he crossed a line. *Finalement*, I'm old-fashioned. I don't like it when ladies cry."

My lips part as I savour his every word. "So what? You think if I go out with you, it'll hurt him?"

"It will."

I laugh, and the sound is so bitter, it hurts. "I disgust him, Ro. He can't even look at me anymore."

My voice breaks at the end and I stop so the tears won't come out. I did enough crying for a lifetime last night. I won't cry again.

Doesn't mean it hurts any less, though.

The fact that Xander is the only one who sees me but is disgusted with what he sees is a different type of pain altogether.

The most crippling one.

The one therapists can't find a cure for.

I wish Dad were here so I could hug him. Since I was little, he's always made me feel safe and protected with a simple hug.

And calling me his Angel.

"He doesn't look at you like he's disgusted with you, Kimmy."

"He doesn't look at me. Full stop."

"Are you blind? You're the only one he looks at when he thinks no one is watching. He's perfected it so well, even you don't notice him."

"R-really?"

He places a hand on his chest. "I swear on my honour. Wait, I don't have that. I swear on my sacred stash of weed."

I laugh, abandoning the salad container. I'm not going to eat anyway, so I might as well stop with the pretence.

"There." He grins. "I knew you'd smile."

"You're so daft."

"Daft with a big dick, Kimmy. It makes a difference."

"Yeah, right."

"I mean it." He turns around so he's fully facing me. "For instance, I could have threesomes with you and Ellie all night long. Which brings us to my part of the deal. Both of you need to wear bunny outfits. Nash said you could definitely wear one when you're drunk, and he knows his shit. I'll get you all the tequila you like. The problem's with Ellie; we need to convince her somehow. Does she have any dark fantasies we can explore?"

I laugh at the way he's talking. I've never seen Ro so serious about such a hypothetical situation in my life. I hate to kill his fun, though, so I go with it.

"I'm afraid Elsa's dark fantasy is everything Aiden."

"*Putain.*" He rubs his jaw. "I can still spike whatever he's drinking and have him there in body, but not mind. Think about the epic expression on his face when he wakes up to find Ellie with us."

His eyes gleam with a rare type of sadistic mischievousness. Ronan might be the most playful and easygoing out of the horsemen, but I'm beginning to think he has his secret tendencies, too.

Those who hide their real selves with humour are the most cunning.

"He'd kill you, though, and I don't want you dead, Ro."

He wraps an arm around my shoulder and pats his chest. "You're the first one to ever say that to me."

"I am?"

"Marry me, Kimmy. And before you say anything, I have

an aristocratic title and a fortune that will sustain our fourth generation. I promise satisfying sex and threesomes. *Lots* of threesomes."

I laugh and the sound is relaxed compared to my earlier state of mind. "Maybe you should start looking for someone else other than Elsa. Just in case."

"You mean instead of spiking King's food?"

"And the fact that he'll murder you in cold blood."

He pouts. "But I have none other than you two on my mind."

My gaze strays ahead and I spot Teal coming from the school's direction to the garden. Upon seeing us, she turns around like a robot and marches back inside.

"How about—"

"Not her." Ronan cuts me off, his complete attention on Teal as she takes stiff, almost forceful steps towards the school.

"Why not? Teal is cool."

"She's not."

That's the first time I ever heard Ronan say something remotely bad about anyone. He doesn't even call Silver and her minions bitches, even when they act like it.

"What did Teal do to you?"

"Nothing." He grins at me. "*Yet.* But she has psychotic tendencies and I need my balls."

"Threatened, Ro?"

"*Moi?*" He feigns offence.

"Yes, *toi.*" I poke his stomach and he tickles me on my sensitive side.

We laugh as he pretends to growl, coming after my ticklish spot. I knew he'd focus on weaknesses, he just doesn't like to show his cards upfront.

My stomach hurts with the amount of laughing while I try to push him away. Even though Ronan appears harmless, he's still big, and I'm helpless in front of his sheer size.

All my swats fall unnoticed as he tickles me until I'm breathless and gasping with laughter.

I don't feel it happen until I see it.

One moment Ronan and I are struggling, him pinning me to the bench, and the next, his entire presence is wrenched off me.

I shriek as Xander throws Ronan to the ground.

His eyes are red, face bloodied, and he looks ready to finish lives.

THIRTEEN

Xander

War.

They call me that for a reason.

Wars start for a trivial cause, but they have sinister undertones. Wars are made to destroy.

Wars are the reason for death, not the other way around.

Death goes down. War remains.

My mind is bleached white as I land on Ronan, straddling his stomach. I clutch him by the collar and drive my fist straight to his face.

He had the audacity to hug her, push her against the bench, and touch her as if he has every right to.

There's that inner voice, telling me not to show my cards this clearly, but that voice is turning dimmer by the days.

I couldn't stop this need to wreak havoc if I tried.

It's been a long fucking time without a war, and wars need to happen to purge people.

Wars need to happen to Death, and now, he needs to fucking bleed.

He smirks up at me as I crush my fist into his face, but he doesn't try to fight me off, not that he can when I'm on such an adrenaline high.

A voice calls from my right, startled and soft. Somewhere at the back of my mind, I recognise it's her, but I don't focus on it. I don't stop to see her or hear the same voice she used to giggle at him.

My next punch is stronger than the previous one, and Ronan's head to lolls to the side.

"Someone is losing it." Ronan licks the corner of his bloodied mouth. "Got a problem, *mon ami?*"

I punch him again, causing his words to stop where they started.

Doesn't matter that I spent most of the night and morning fighting with thugs or that a few bruises in my body hurt like a fucker. I'm going to finish this day with an epic finale— like this bastard's death.

"Stop it!" A slender hand wraps around my bicep, forcing me back with a shove.

It's not that strong, but her touch is.

The feel of her fingers on my skin, separated only by my shirt, is like water dousing my fire.

The blurry lines from earlier and the black haze slowly dissipate when her face comes into view.

She's staring at me with those huge green eyes that have never left my head, not since yesterday, not since a century ago.

Her lips part in stupefaction—or worry, I don't know which. All I can think about is how I feasted on those lips, how they felt beneath my teeth and against my tongue.

How I tasted her, like I secretly fantasised for years, and how that single taste has opened Pandora's fucking box, unleashed the devil's minions, and even the jinn that Ahmed used to tell me stories about.

Because now, I'm hit by the need to taste her again, and this time, I don't want to stop—or finish.

I want to free fall to hell.

Fuck me.

I went to fight so I could purge these thoughts, but they

just keep magnifying. Her view isn't helping either. It's like a storm, and I'm only destined to fall, to sin, to bloody perish.

"What the hell are you doing?" she shrieks, staring at the blood oozing from Ronan's lips. "Are you crazy?"

Yup. Totally am. Otherwise, none of this would've happened.

A mistake.

It was all because of alcohol.

I can tell myself that all day, but making my brain believe it is a different story altogether.

That thing is starting to hate me for the amount of rubbish I pour in it on a daily basis.

Mutual, mate.

Kimberly pushes me away with ease—actually, no. All she has to do is use her hold on my arm and I'm out of the way as if I was never there.

Just a touch, I tell myself. One single touch.

I rise to my feet, guided by her hands around my biceps. Her hands are on me.

Hands. On. Me.

Fuck, why does that feel so good? And surreal.

And fucking wrong.

She releases me just as fast. The lack of contact is like being thirsty and given water so it can be taken away at the last second. Her attention falls on Ronan and she helps him up.

The beast inside me roars back to life as he grins down on her with an expression so pure, it stabs me a hundred times all at once.

I lunge at him again, and he smiles defiantly, not even attempting to cover his face. Kimberly moves in front of him, making me stop in my tracks.

Her stance widens and she tips her chin as she glares up at me. "I don't know what the hell is wrong with you, but stop being a morbid dog or I'll call the principal."

Morbid dog.

That's the word. A *dog*. I've been reduced to less than a dog because of her. At least a dog has principles, loyalty. I don't.

The worst part is, I have no way to stop it.

As I glare at Ronan, I pretend she doesn't exist and tell her, "This is none of your business. Get out of the way."

"Well, I'm making it my business. You don't get to hurt Ro on my watch."

Ro.

Fucking Ro.

If she's calling him that on purpose to worsen my insanity case, then it's fucking working.

Someone book the psychiatrist ward. And the ambulance because if I'm going to be locked up for being crazy, might as well kill this fucker.

"Yes, Kimmy. Protect me from this crazy twat." Ronan pouts as he holds her hand in his and strokes the back. Since he's behind her, I can see all the fakery in that expression, the taunting behind his eyes, and then he just smirks at me.

He fucking *smirks*, motioning at her hand in his.

That's it. He's dead. In his sleep, in his car, in his pool. Doesn't matter, it's going to happen.

I laugh, the sound humourless and harsh as I address her, "You think you can stop me? Know your fucking place."

"You know *your* place. You can't just push people around and punch them simply because you want to or you can. The world doesn't revolve around you."

Because it revolves around you.

Nope. No. I didn't think that.

That thought needs to be fucking eradicated.

At this rate, either she needs to disappear or I do. Otherwise, it'll be fucking chaos from now on.

"Watch. Me." I advance forward, but she doesn't move or

shrink back. There's a slight tremble in her chin, which means she is scared, but she doesn't let it take its toll on her.

Kimberly still stands in front of the fucker Ronan, unmoving, as if his safety is her purpose in life.

His safety.

His.

I come to a halt a few steps away from them, watching the scene with whatever clarity I have after all the alcohol and weed I consumed like a hippie. My head hurts, and my face burns, but the worst pain comes from the thing beating out of synch in my chest.

They were laughing and having fun earlier. She's protecting him now.

And he stopped sleeping around.

The reality hits me like a punch to the nose. I've never seen her so happy with someone other than Kir until Ronan.

I've never seen him go out of his way for a girl until Kimberly.

"Now, if you'll excuse us, Kimmy and I have to talk about our date." Ronan's voice is clear, not mocking, just stating facts.

Date.

They're going on a fucking date.

I stare at her, waiting for her denial. Kimberly doesn't go on dates. Kirian is her entire life and she doesn't like to be distracted from him. Besides, she doesn't have the confidence to. I know because I watch her more than I do myself.

She can't go on a date with Ronan of all people. It just can't happen.

I smile at them, but I'm sure it appears like some lunatic's rather than mine. "Nice try."

"Who says it's a try?" Ronan smiles back.

"Ronan," I growl.

"Xander," he coos.

I glare at him, communicating all he needs to know.

Stay the fuck away.

Don't test me or I'll crush you like a cockroach.

Apparently, that fate doesn't scare him since he speaks in a dramatic tone. "By all means, if you have any objection, say it now or forever hold your peace."

Kimberly's gaze strays my way. It's so hopeful, I want to fucking gut myself and step on the remains.

Why does she have to look at me that way?

Didn't I tell her to stop fucking tempting me? To stop hoping for things from me?

The more she does, the harder I'll destroy her.

"I do." I glare at her as I tell him, "She's a mess you don't want in your life."

Her face falls as if I've kicked her in the stomach, stepped on it, then did the same to a puppy.

This is the only way to keep her away.

Believe me, this pain is nothing compared to the other.

"Let me worry about that. I love messes." Ronan's grin is permanently irritating and wishing for my fist to erase it. He tugs on her hand. "Kimmy, anything you want to say to Xander while we're in this holy gathering?"

She's looking at Ronan as she speaks in a calm tone. "I can't talk to someone who's nothing. He doesn't even exist anymore."

Nothing.

Doesn't exist anymore

I pretend her words don't slice me open and leave a bottomless hole that's feeding on my life essence.

My smile turns threatening. "You owe me, Berly. Remember?"

She finally faces me, expression stern, determined. Closed off. "I owe you nothing. I'm done begging for a forgiveness you'll never grant. I'm done with you and your games and your cold shoulder. I. Am. Done."

And with that, she pulls on Ronan's hand and brushes past me without a glance.

Without a look behind her.

I can clutch her by the wrist and pull her back. I can bring her to my side and let the world know she'll always belong there.

But I don't have the right to.

That knowledge slices me open more than her words. It deepens the hole, making it unrecognisable. Almost as if it's from another universe.

"Say it," Ronan whispers so only I can hear him as he follows her. "One word."

Stop.

That's the word he's waiting to hear, and I know he'll let go. Or I can make him with a few more punches.

My face hardens as I watch him take her from between my fingers. I stand there like a bloody fool, unable to do the one thing I ever wanted in my life.

Sometimes, what you want is the one thing you can't get.

The one thing that will be taken away from you.

Ronan shakes his head and goes with her.

I watch their backs disappearing into the school building, and it feels as if my entire life has gone with them.

My phone vibrates with a text.

Ronan: You had your chance and you lost it.

Ronan: I'll send pictures.

I throw the phone against a tree, making it crack. The only words that keep running in my head is her voice, her words, her resignation.

I. Am. Done.

FOURTEEN

Kimberly

"Ronan?" Elsa nearly shrieks and I cover her mouth with my palm.

We're sitting around a table in her house's garden. Since it's a rare sunny day, we decided to study outside. We're sipping on juice. Or rather, Elsa is. I've only drunk water since I got here.

Water makes you full and keeps some of the hunger away.

She removes my hand and whisper-hisses, "You're going on a date with Ronan?"

"It just happened." I scribble a line with my pencil on a draft paper.

"You don't go with things just because they happen." Elsa pushes her notebook away, her eyes narrowing like a detective with a criminal. "Is it because of Xander?"

I told her about the kiss and the fight between the two of them earlier, because if I didn't, I would've gone crazy trying to figure out what the hell happened.

Even now, I have no idea what's going on.

"No. I mean maybe…" I stare at her from underneath my lashes. "Is it wrong that I want normal for once?"

"Of course not." Elsa's expression softens. "You were always a romantic at heart; it's not weird to want that. What's wrong is to push yourself to go down a road just because the circumstances forced you."

"Isn't that what happened between you and Aiden?"

"Not really. I didn't have to force myself to be with Aiden. It was the other way around. I had to force myself to ignore the connection we had, because he scared the living fuck out of me." She pats my hand once. "I don't want to see you making the same mistake."

"It's not the same. Aiden has always looked at you like you're his world and chased you relentlessly. All Xander's ever done is push me away. At first, it was painful, then it became a permanent ache, and now, I can't breathe. I want to breathe, Elsa."

My eyes fill with tears and her face scrunches as if she can feel my pain and shares it. Elsa is known as Frozen at school because she has an epic resting bitch face and that 'I don't care about the world' attitude. To see her this concerned about me warms my heart and pushes that fog back a bit.

"I'm with you, whatever you decide, Kim. If you think you'll be happy with Ronan, then I'm all for it. Just…don't force yourself into something you don't want, okay? It'll only eat you from the inside out."

I nod, wiping away the moisture with my forefinger.

"You still haven't told me what was on your mind that day at the hospital?" Her attention is still zeroed on me.

I pull my hand from hers and clutch a pen, pretending to read through my notes, even though they're blurry lines. "It's nothing."

"It didn't seem as if it was nothing, Kim."

I was going to tell Elsa about the cutting, but I chickened out again, and now, my mind is in a mush. Peeking at her, I wet my lips. Maybe I can ask her for help, maybe I can say it.

You like Elsa too much, so you do everything to appear perfect in front of her, and by doing that, you kill parts of yourself slowly, thinking if she actually saw your true self-harming, vein-cutting, pill-popping self, she'd give up on you.

Xan's words play in my mind on a loop. He hit the nail on the head with that one, the bastard.

I really do love Elsa too much to stress her out or worse, to bring something that will ultimately make her disgusted with me.

Once upon a time, Xander was my best friend and he became repulsed with me. Silver was also my friend, but she eventually pulled away from me as if we were never close.

Even though I know in my heart that Elsa is different, I can't take the risk of losing her, too.

What if she doesn't understand why I brought that blade to my veins? Or why I think about repeating it every day since?

What if, instead of understanding, there will be judgemental looks or, worse, pity?

I know I'm only buying time. When Dad returns, he'll know. He always seems to know so much about me. Maybe if I tell Dad, I'll tell her, too.

Maybe.

I'm about to deflect when Teal runs out of the house, cursing. She's wearing jeans ripped at the knees, under which there are fishnet stockings.

Elsa laughs, her attention being robbed by her foster sister. "Knox spooked you again?"

"He's a twat." Teal regulates her breathing and takes a deep one as she watches me peculiarly for a second before she joins us.

Her white T-shirt for the day reads, *No Man's Land*.

"Nice one." I smile at her, thankful she saved me from Elsa's questioning. I know my best friend will revisit the subject one day, but that day isn't today.

Besides, when that day comes, I'll just be ready for it.

Teal nods but says nothing as she sits on the other side of Elsa. Usually, she'd settle between us, and I've always thought it's because she sees me as the middle line between her and her sister. I thought we were becoming friends. Hell, she even goes to Elites' games with me.

Just not anymore.

Lately, she's been keeping her distance as if she doesn't want to be involved with me. Not that it should be a surprise. I don't have the best track record with friends.

"Are you guys going to the game?" Elsa asks us.

"Wait, you'll go?" Teal twirls the earbuds between her fingers.

"Sure."

"What happened to *I'll never go to their games?*" I poke her side.

"Aiden." She smiles like an idiot. "It's his last season and I want to be there for him."

"Ohh," I taunt her.

"Stop it. So are you going?"

"No, I have to take care of Kir." *And keep a distance from a certain arsehole with golden hair and ocean eyes.*

I don't even like football, but I've always gone to Elites' games. I pretend it's for the team, for Ronan, for the thrill, but it's for *him.*

Only him.

I stand there, watching him from the beginning to the finish. I learnt the rules because he plays the game. I bought jerseys with Xander's number nineteen for Kir because he loves him so much.

It's pathetic.

And for that reason, it needs to stop.

I meant it earlier, I'm done.

"You should go, Kim." Teal motions at Elsa's juice and when she nods, she takes a sip. "Thirteen can use moral support."

"Pretty sure Ro can use a different type of support." Elsa grins.

Teal's face remains neutral.

I laugh. "That he can. He's been talking about that three-some again."

"He mentioned it the other day, too." Elsa shakes her head. "If he keeps doing that, he'll get killed by Aiden before the end of the year."

"I told him that. I swear he has no fear for his life."

"He doesn't?" Teal's question stops us both in our tracks. "Have no fear for his life, I mean."

Elsa hums, "Actually, I think he doesn't. He said his father has his entire life planned for him, including his marriage and all, and he hates it."

I nod. "I think he's treating this as a last hurrah before he's shoved to succeed his dad's name and legacy."

Teal's lips twitch and I swear she's about to smile, but she goes back to her signature poker face.

We drop the subject and Teal returns inside, peeking first so Knox doesn't startle her again.

Then Elsa and I finish studying, and after I tell the girls goodbye, I pick up Kir.

Once we get home, we blast music and dance to it together, goofing around. He's the only human I can dance this freely in front of. I've been teaching him moves and he's been telling me I'm getting old.

The dork.

Mum comes out of her studio once to pick up supplies that are delivered. We lower the music and keep tickling each other and blocking our laughs so she doesn't hear.

However, not once does she acknowledge our presence as she directs the deliverymen to carry the canvases to her studio.

Kirian's pout appears as he watches her with puppy eyes, fidgeting, waiting for a smidge of her attention. It looks so much like me when I was a child.

You mean, even now.

I continue tickling him to divert his focus from her. As

soon as the deliverymen leave and she closes her studio—that's soundproof—we go back to dancing until we collapse.

It's his bedtime anyway, so I usher him to his room.

"Can Xan come over?" Kir asks me once he's put on his pyjamas and I'm tucking him in his bed.

"No," I snap, then smile to camouflage it.

"But why not? It would be fun to dance with him."

"I don't like dancing in front of others. Only you, my little monkey."

"And Dad!"

"And Dad."

He FaceTimed us earlier and we spoke to him for thirty minutes. Kir didn't shut up about school and his friends and how he's the most popular one.

He is. Girls are starting to give him letters.

At least one of us isn't a complete loser.

I told Dad I miss him and resisted the urge to ask him when he's coming home this time. It'll only make him feel guilty and I don't want to ever do that to him.

"Are all the tickets really gone?" He narrows his eyes.

Okay, so I might have lied about Elites' game tickets. It's the only way to keep him from bugging me, sort of.

He's a Xander fan through and through.

"Yeah, promise."

"I'll ask him for tickets next time."

Of course he will. This is just a temporary solution. Kir is smarter than I give him credit for.

"Don't bother him."

"He said I don't."

I pause. "He did?"

He nods frantically. "He always asks his cook to make me brownies and lets Ahmed play with me. Xan says I can call him when you can't pick me up."

"Don't tell me you did."

He looks away.

"Kir!"

"Don't worry, Kimmy." Kir grins. "Xan will lie and say you dance better than me."

I make my hands into claws. "Well, is he going to lie and say you're not ticklish?"

"No, stop it."

"Here comes the gorilla for the monkey."

"Nooo!" he shrieks as I attack him, tickling his side until he gasps with giggles and laughter.

It's only after he raises the white flag that I finally leave him alone and kiss him three times—two on his adorable cheeks and one on his forehead. "Sweet dreams, little monkey."

"Night, Kimmy."

I push his hair back and kiss him one more time before leaving his room.

After changing into a denim skirt and a camisole, I go outside just in time to find Ronan pulling in.

We agreed to meet once the game was over, but I never thought he'd be here straight after.

He swings the door of his Mazda open and barges outside. He still has bruises around his mouth from the fight with Xander.

It must hurt.

Just like all the bruises Xander came to school with must hurt.

No, I don't care about him.

Ronan gathers me in a hug, scooping me off the ground. "We won!"

I squeal as he spins me around before finally putting me to my feet.

"So happy for you."

"Liar." He glares at me. "You could've been happy by actually being there."

"I had to spend time with Kir."

"Or you could've brought him with you." He leans in to whisper, "Which means, you've been running away."

"Fine. Can we go?" I really don't want to run into Xan if he comes home now.

Although the football team usually celebrates the win at the Meet Up after every game, I'm not taking any chances.

"Sure." He ushers me into the car, even opening the door for me.

He's such a gentleman—protective, caring. Why can't I fall asleep thinking about him? Why can't I obsess over him? Have my chest squeeze for him?

If I'd had a choice in my heart's admission process, it would've been Ronan.

Or that's what I tell myself.

The car revs into life, leaving the neighbourhood, and I blow out a long breath.

"He didn't play," Ronan says with a smile that's different from his easy-going ones.

Xander didn't play? But why? He's always a startup, except that time the coach punished him and Aiden because of a fight.

But I won't allow myself to get sucked into that orbit. I stare out of the window at the upper-middle-class villas passing us by. "I don't care."

"Coach knows about the fighting and drinking and benched him," Ronan continues, deaf to what I said.

I face him, unable to help myself. "Fighting and drinking?"

"He has an issue." Ronan taps his fingers on the steering wheel as if he's enjoying music that doesn't exist.

He doesn't go on, and if I didn't know better, I'd say he's playing with me.

"So? What type of issue?"

His grin nearly splits his face open. "Told you, fighting and drinking. He used to control it before, but lately, he's been appearing hungover and barely holding on. His face has some cuts, and there are bruises on his body. He doesn't pay attention to practice or studies or even himself. Today, he came drunk and the captain had had enough."

"If his dad knows, he'll be in trouble," I murmur to myself, then realise I said it aloud.

"Pretty sure Coach called him by now," Ronan hums. "I think there's talk about sending him to a closed rehab and he'll only come back for his diploma. It's no secret Lewis will lose his shit on him. After all, this is an election year."

Something in my chest squeezes, tightening harder the more I ignore it.

"He brought it on himself," I say, then change the subject to the game.

Ronan launches in on his heroic accomplishments and the decisive pass he gave to Aiden so that he scored their only goal.

As we go into the restaurant, I laugh and smile at his goofy behaviour. We even commemorate the dinner with a selfie in Ronan's over the top style. He wraps an arm around me and tucks me to his side, kissing my cheek.

Although I'm laughing on the outside, there's something cutting me open and slicing me to tiny pieces on the inside.

I order a salad, even though Ronan says they have diet-friendly food, but I don't eat any of it.

My body is right here in this high-end restaurant that I shouldn't have worn a denim skirt for. The setting has an elegant brown and white combination that gives a certain type of serenity.

Not to me.

Although I'm present, smiling at what Ronan is saying, my mind is elsewhere. I'm thinking about the theories of what Lewis could do to Xander. Ronan said it. This is an election year for him and Silver's father. They completely disallow any type of mishaps in normal days, let alone when the campaign is so close to starting. I wonder if Silver's disappearance for the past two days has something to do with that.

Point is, Lewis has always been as strict with Xander as Mum has been with me. That day Aunt Samantha left, and Xander went home crying for her, Lewis fixed him with a glare and told him to not cry for her.

Since then, I've never seen tears in Xander's eyes.

"Earth to Kimmy." Ronan leans over so he's close.

"Sorry, you were saying?"

"That you should take a chance."

"Take a chance?"

"Yup."

I swallow my non-existent saliva. "On you?"

Despite my talk, I don't think I can do that. As Elsa said, it really sucks to force oneself. While Ronan adds flavour to my life, he's not my favourite flavour.

He's not pistachio.

"No, on you." He pinches my nose.

I pull away, confused. "On me?"

"Yes, Kimmy. You've been thinking about Knight all night—that wasn't supposed to rhyme—so how about you act on it?"

"I haven't been thinking about him all night." *Right?*

"Uh-huh, come on, *ma chère, c'est moi.*" He wipes his mouth, then scrolls through his phone. "I think I gave him enough evidence."

I lean sideways in an attempt to see what he's scrolling through. "Enough evidence?"

"He was home when I hugged you earlier and…" He turns the phone to show the selfie he posted on Instagram. The caption says, *New Leaf. Go Elites.*

My lips part to object, but I end up saying, "I don't think it matters."

"It does. He wants to move on, but there's something holding him back."

"Something like what?"

"I thought you would know."

"I'm not sure." If he can't forgive me because of what happened seven years ago, then he shouldn't act this way.

He shouldn't kiss me, corner me, tell me I can't hide from him.

It's too cruel.

Ronan raises a finger. "Let me try one last push."

He types for a few seconds, then shows me his texts to Xander.

Ronan: Feeling cute, I want to fuck a cute girl tonight. Like Kimmy.

Ronan: Jackpot! She just said yes.

Ronan: Wish me luck. Wait, I won't need it. Tell the school we won't be coming for a few days.

His words don't surprise me since I know he's joking. What makes my chest tighten is the fact that Xander saw all his texts, but there's no reply.

Not even currently typing.

"He'll snap." Ronan smiles

I wouldn't be so sure.

"Or we can do as planned." His grin widens. "My place? I have the best stash of weed."

My phone vibrates, and I startle.

The moment my eyes fall on the name across the screen, my heart nearly bursts out of its confinement.

Xander: Remember when you promised you'd never leave me?

My fingers tremble as I read and re-read the message. Before I can fathom a reply, another text comes.

Xander: I free you of that promise.

FIFTEEN

Xander

Get *your shit together. You're not a kid anymore.*

If Lewis had punched me, it probably wouldn't have hurt like the stab of his words.

Being a politician, he has a way with them, words. He knows which to use to make you feel as if you're the filthiest scum walking the earth. There's no differentiation between family or strangers.

Lewis has allies and enemies. Spoiler alert, I fall on the last line.

Deep down, he's always blamed me for Mum leaving, because I was an annoying little shit. I blamed him for never caring for her, for telling her to, 'Get your shit together, Samantha.'

One day, she got her shit and left.

For Lewis, people are machines. One button and they run. Another button and they stop.

Too bad he has a machine of a son who runs on a different type of liquid. I pour the last drops in the vodka bottle down my throat and groan when there's nothing.

I tap my pocket for a joint of weed I stole from Ronan's bag. Nope, nothing.

Did I smoke it earlier?

You mean when he was hugging her and you watched like a pussy?

Yes, whoever is talking to me right now. When he was squeezing her body to his and I watched through the window. Only, I did something. I crushed the glass in my hand and came out with a cut over my palm.

I bandaged it, but the cloth is red and full of dry blood.

Just beautiful.

Or fucked up—depends on how you look at it.

Kirian trotted over the moment Kim left, saying he couldn't sleep. I gave him just a small piece of brownie since it's night, and we played a video game until he dozed off, and I placed him in the room down the hall from mine.

I was about to resume my drinking session when Ronan sent me that text and I might have thrown good alcohol across the room. Then Ahmed came over. He doesn't approve of my newest habits, and it's not because of his religion.

He gave me a look. That one that says he might or might not be disappointed in how I'm wasting his efforts in bringing me up. He helped re-bandage my hand and left.

His silence sliced me more than Lewis's words and I've been kind of drowning in an ocean of my own choice. Good old vodka.

The door to my room opens and I barely stare back. I'm sitting on the chair in the dark, an empty bottle hanging from one hand and the bandaged one lying limp on the other side.

The light goes on, blinding me. I squint, but I don't move my gaze from the window.

"Turn it off," I slur. "I can't see if it's too bright."

Close to midnight, no sign of her.

Just brilliant.

Way to go, Ronan. You got me.

And we need to revisit our friendship now. Either I kill him or I kill him, there's no between.

"The fuck?" Aiden stares down at me with both his hands in his pockets. "No one mentioned a self-pity party."

"Fuck off." I motion at the door with my bottle.

"Are you okay?" Cole approaches me while Aiden flops on my bed and rummages through my CDs, making himself at home.

"Give me that." I motion at the joint in Cole's mouth. He passes it over and I take a long drag, then blow the smoke back up. "Shit, it's just a cigarette."

"You're welcome." Cole retrieves his cigarette and inhales the smoke before exhaling it through his nostrils.

If he's smoking, shit must be hitting the fan for him, too.

Cole is a mood smoker.

"What did your father say?" Cole asks.

"You mean after you snitched to Coach that I'm drunk and he called the principal and my dear old dad?"

"Everyone smelled vodka on you, Knight."

"More like breathed it." Aiden leans on an elbow and grabs a ball to twirl it on his index finger.

I lay my head back. "The usual. I'm not allowed to ruin his image and blah fucking blah."

"And the rehab," Aiden adds. "He asked Jonathan for recommendations. If my father knows, then it's happening."

"At least you'll stop getting drunk like a fool." Cole raises an eyebrow.

"And you'll stop the self-pity parties."

"And the pussy moments."

"Speaking of which, why don't you get some?"

"Great idea." Cole retrieves his phone. "I can call Summer or Veronica, or maybe both."

"Add Silver to the menu and I might be interested." I grin.

His expression doesn't change as he tucks his phone away. "None, then."

"Why not?" Aiden smirks. "I like Knight's idea."

Cole cocks his head in Aiden's direction. "You of all people get to shut the fuck up, King."

"Petty little bitch." Aiden's attention returns to me. "So, little bitch two, I don't have all night to nurse your drunk arse. Are you going to get your shit together or should we all vote for rehab?"

"He's going to take her virginity," I say the only thing I've been thinking about. There's so much pain in my voice, so much…fucking resignation.

"Who and who?" Cole asks.

"Yeah, details. Nash has a virgin kink." Aiden raises an eyebrow. Cole narrows his eyes on him, then focuses back on me.

"Ronan, that *fucker*, is going to take her virginity," I slur.

"That is, if she's still a virgin." Aiden throws the ball in the air. "This is the twenty-first century. Not everyone is waiting for a knight in shining armour. Sorry, I meant a drunk fool."

"Kimberly might look innocent, but those are the most hardcore," Cole adds.

"Take his word. He knows his shit." Aiden points at Cole.

"Not better than you. Elsa seems like the hardcore type."

Aiden's grey eyes nearly turn black as his left one twitches. "Think about Elsa in a hardcore way again, and you'll be buried in Jonathan's new construction site."

Cole smirks. "Is that a promise?"

"No, the promise is unbinding *her*," Aiden says.

"*She* is none of your fucking business."

Aiden raises a brow. "Are you sure, though?"

Cole flips him off then studies me again as if I'm one of his philosophical theories that he needs to set straight. "How are you sure Kim is a virgin?"

"She just is, okay? I know." And I heard her mention it to Elsa a week or so ago when they had their girls' sex talk, and I might have learnt shit about Aiden I can't bleach from my mind.

And yes, in case you haven't figured out yet, I'm a fucking creep.

"Not that you can do anything about it." Aiden slams me with the harsh reality. "So we might as well go back to my pussy suggestion."

"*Or* you can do something about it." Cole places a hand in his pocket, taking a long drag of his cigarette. "Fuck her. Get it out of your system."

I jerk up so fast, he doesn't even see it when I punch him in the face. People's punches turn wobbly and weak when drunk. Mine turns stronger.

Cole staggers back, placing a hand on his mouth.

"Say the word fuck and her name in the same sentence again and I'll bloody kill you," I snarl in his face.

"He technically didn't say her name." Aiden speaks from behind us and I can feel his smirk without having to look at him.

"I'm just playing the devil's advocate and saying what you're thinking about." A small, almost innocent smile curves Cole's lips. "It's not my fault your mind is already there. I only translate your thoughts, Knight. I don't form them for you."

"You can always self-destruct and let Astor do it." Aiden whistles. "I'm sure he'll take good care of her. He knows how to make love and all that shit."

I groan deep in my throat and shove Cole away, plucking a bottle of vodka from the drawer and unclasping it with jerky hands. Neither Cole nor Aiden stop me. One, they don't really care. Two, they like chaos, so they take every chance they get to watch it unfold. If my current case isn't the definition of chaos, I don't know what is.

I barely feel the burn of the first swallow before I follow with the second one.

"Does that mean Astor can do it?" Cole asks.

"It has to be done, after all," Aiden adds.

"What the fuck are you suggesting, then?" I wipe the drops of alcohol on the side of my mouth. "That *I* do it?"

"It's an option." Cole blows smoke in my face.

I glare at Aiden. "If it was Elsa, would you have done it?"

"It isn't Elsa and I don't consider hypothetical situations."

"I would have," Cole says. "No thoughts."

"You're the fucking devil. You don't count."

Cole lifts a shoulder. "Then I'll just go to hell, if there is one."

Aiden stands and stops in front of me. "Considering your human rights situation, I'll answer your question. Yes, I would have done it. There's the world and there's Elsa, and she always comes first. Now, you just have to decide if you're ready to burn."

I fall on the bed, cradling the bottle to my chest.

"Is that a no?" Aiden asks.

"At least we tried." Cole flops on the chair beside me. "This will be a long fucking night."

"Fuck this." Aiden sits on the other side of me. "I'm not supposed to be here."

"He sent me a text telling me she said yes to fucking him tonight. First date and all that." I laugh, but there's no humour. "She fucking said yes and I freed her of the promise I always held over her head."

I attempt to take a sip from the bottle, but Cole takes it away.

"You'll start vomiting and I'm in no mood to clean puke."

"Aside from babysitting your self-pity party, he means," Aiden adds.

I fall on the bed and stare at the ceiling. "I freed her of me."

"Do you think you did the right thing?" Cole stares down at me with his fucking green eyes and I'm tempted to poke out and maybe put in a jar.

"Yes." My voice breaks and I cover my eyes with the back of my hand, hiding the moisture that gathers there.

No.

Somehow, I fall asleep and somehow, I dream of her.

I always dream of her when I'm at my lowest and when I'm at my highest.

Instead of Aiden and Cole's arsehole presence, gentle hands are pulling my arm from my face. Cole's soulless green eyes are replaced by her soft, inviting ones.

There's moisture in their brightness, too, as if she also wants to cry.

The Kim in my dreams is a play of my imagination. She looks so real while she touches me, while she strokes my hair back like she used to do when we were kids.

A few of my favourite memories always begin with me laying my head on her lap, her stroking my hair, and me hand-picking the fucking green M&M's for her before I ate the other colours.

Then I fed her the pistachio gelato while she read her magical stories about wizards and princes and kingdoms aloud.

And knights.

Lots of fucking knights. Even if there wasn't one, she made them up and inserted them everywhere.

My knight, she used to call me.

Now, I'm a rusty one without armour or a sword.

I abandoned being her knight to become War.

"Why have you been drinking again?" she asks in a brittle voice. "What happened to your hand?"

"Shh, don't ruin it. Just stay like this." I lift my head and set it on her lap so that I'm staring up at her.

The Kimberly from my dreams always tells me what a fuck-up I am and that I can do better, just as before. I can be a knight instead of War.

But not today. Today is fucked up.

Today, she's with Ronan and I can't do anything about it. Today, I have Cole and Aiden as my guardians because they don't want me to do some stupid shit like getting myself killed in a gang fight.

I reach out a hand and touch her cheek with my fingers. She trembles underneath my skin as if she always wanted me to do that. My palm burns due to the cut, but I almost don't feel it.

"You're so beautiful, Green, and I fucking hate you for it."

"Xan…" My nickname catches in her mouth like she doesn't want to say it. "What the hell? You're not supposed to call me that."

"And you're not supposed to be here. I freed you."

"What if I don't want to be freed?"

"A masochist, aren't you now?"

"Maybe."

"Maybe, huh?" I smile. "I'm going to do bad things to you."

I'll hate it in the morning, and I'll hate myself for it, but if I only get this in dreams, then so be it.

Her eyes widen. "B-bad things like what?"

I lift my head and wrap a hand around her nape. "Like this."

My lips meet hers and I feast on her the way I've always wanted.

I embrace the temptation I've always run away from.

SIXTEEN

Kimberley

Kissing has always been a fantasy for me. That consuming passion, that need for more.

I blame romance books for this, by the way.

That day at Ronan's party, I thought I knew what kissing is like. A bit of passion, a bit of force, a lot of heartbreak.

Now, a different type of emotion seeps into me as Xander takes possession of my mouth.

Desperation.

That's the right word. It's the only emotion that whirls through me, and it does so with wrecking force.

I let him kiss me like it's our first and last kiss together. I don't care if we never get anything after this, as long as he kisses me with this desperation and the need to own me, be with me.

He tastes of vodka and mint, a strong mix that hits me straight in the chest. I inhale him deeply and don't dare to exhale, afraid it will end the moment and we'll go back to our separate worlds as if we were never meant to be.

When Mari told me the monkey, Kir, came here to spend the night, I might have cursed my little brother.

After the text Xander sent me, blatantly pushing me away once more, I was ready for my comfort K-dramas and my moody playlist.

The thought of confronting him made me want to cry, but I've tried so hard not to cry all this time, so I won't be doing it now.

The fog becomes stronger when I cry, and he's been feeding it non-stop for years.

Ahmed welcomed me in, saying Kir was asleep. I considered waking him up, but I couldn't disturb him. Besides, as soon as I was in the guest room Kir was in, Cole and Aiden came knocking at the door. They said Xander was in trouble.

I didn't think when I ran here, when I pushed the door and walked inside with wobbly legs. He was sleeping upside down on the bed, his head lolling over the side and his hand bandaged, covered with dry blood and dangling from the edge.

The first thing I did was check his pulse. I was going to leave once I made sure he was alive, I really was. But one touch of his hair turned into two, and before I knew it, I was sitting on his bed and then he opened his eyes and called me Green, and I kind of lost it.

I'm losing it right now.

Because I know by experience that his kisses, his slight moments of closeness, only have heartbreak tied to them. If he freed me of our twelve years' promise after the first kiss, what is he going to do now? Demand I sell my soul to the devil? Make me watch as he stomps all over my heart?

I place two hands on his strong shoulders and shove him away. His lips leave mine with a whimper—from my side, not his. Why the hell am I mourning his loss when I never had him in the first place?

"Xander, I—"

"Shh." He places an index finger on my lips, which are hot and tingly because of him. "Don't ruin it."

I push his hand away, careful not to hurt his injury, and take another deep inhale, then regret it because all I breathe is him. "You're the one who ruins everything."

"No, you did." His eyes are half-droopy, and his face is so pained, it's like being shot at and not having the ability to die.

"I did?" I repeat.

"If you didn't take me there, if you…" he trails off and shakes his head. "But it doesn't matter now. Let me kiss you."

He reaches out for me, but I struggle to push him away. He's strong, even when drunk. "No. I'm not willing to pay the price."

"No price." He grins and his cheeks crease with those dimples.

Those beautiful, beautiful dimples.

My heart might have stopped beating for a second.

He told me I'm beautiful and he hates me for it, and it's the same for him.

He's so brutally handsome, I curse him for it every day.

I curse him every time I see a good-looking man and compare him to Xander.

I curse him every time I have fantasies and he's always the main character in them.

I curse his perfect hair and ocean-deep eyes and charming fucking smile because they never belonged to me.

"I hate you," I murmur, though my fingers dig into his T-shirt. "I hate you so much."

"I hate you, too, Green." His lips hover a few inches away from mine.

"Stop calling me that."

"I'll call you whatever I fucking please. You're my Green." He grabs me by the arm and flips me so I'm lying on the bed and he's hovering above me. "Now, shut up and let me kiss you."

Even though my body is yelling for that and shouting at me to let him make my fantasies come true, because I know he will, I don't give in to that urge. I plant both hands on his chest. "Are you going to be disgusted with me afterwards?"

"I'm never disgusted with you."

"But—"

"Shut up, Green." There's no maliciousness behind his words. If anything, they're playful, amused even, with a casual appearance of his dimples.

"The other time, you—"

"Shut the fuck up, Green."

"Not until—"

My words die as he grabs me by my nape and invades my mouth. And I don't mean a simple kiss. This time, he's really devouring me.

It's like he's starving and I'm dinner. He's on a stranded island and I'm his survival.

A moan rips from me as his body moulds to mine. The friction of his hard chest against my breasts and thighs elicits a violent shiver. My nipples tighten and strain against my camisole. A tremor grips me and my hands shake as I dig my fingers into his back—his strong, sculpted back.

It's as if my hands don't believe what's happening. How do people normally react when their deepest, darkest fantasies come true?

If I had known, I would've probably done something about it. But right now, I just let myself fall into it, free fall and all.

Hard and fast.

With no landing in sight.

"Fuck," he growls near my mouth. "Why do you taste better than in other dreams?"

"W-what?"

"Shh, don't talk. If you do, I'll wake up." His fingers curl at the hem of my T-shirt and bring it over my head.

My chest heaves as his eyes trail down my body, the stretch marks and the not-so-flat stomach. It's nothing like the model figures he's used to. I despise comparing myself to them, but I can't help it.

He's my best fantasy, and it hurts to be his worst.

"You used to be more beautiful." He runs his hand down my stomach. "I hate the fake you, she's not my Green."

And then he's kissing down my stomach, over every stretch mark and every blemish, over every curve and part of me I don't even like to look at myself.

His hot lips leave scorching trails in their wake like a rapid burning fire.

"Don't change." *Kiss.* "Don't be fake." *Kiss.* "Be you." *Kiss.* "Be my beautiful Green."

A sob tears from my throat with every word out of his mouth and breathed against my skin. I cover my eyes, not wanting him to see me this way.

What the hell is he doing to me?

"Look at me." The order in his voice makes me drop my hands slowly.

He's hovering over me again, his hands disappearing underneath my back to unclasp my bra.

The deep blue of his eyes holds me hostage as he speaks in a low, gut-wrenching tone. "Always look at me, not away from me, okay?"

"Okay."

"Even if I hate you and you hate me."

"Okay."

"Even if we wake up from this."

"Okay." My voice breaks at the end.

With a single tug, he removes the bra and lets it fall to the side. My nipples harden, tightening into tiny buds, but it's not because of the air. It's due to the hungry look on his lethally attractive face.

He's not even touching them, but it's almost as if he is.

"Your tits are so perky and small." His strong fingers wrap around my breast. "So perfect in my hand. I knew it."

Still cupping my breast, his thumb and forefinger grasp my nipple and tug. I cry out, my heart squeezing in my throat.

He does it again, this time twirling, then pinching hard afterwards. The friction of his bandage against my skin adds another pleasurable sensation that shoots straight between my legs, soaking my thighs.

"Do you know how much I've wanted to do this? How much I've wanted you like this and hated myself for it? How much it fucking kills me?" As he continues to torment my nipple, his mouth latches on the other one, biting and nibbling.

My back arches off the bed with the torture. It's as if I'm being levitated. My body isn't mine anymore as it floats in the air without any landing in the foreseeable future.

His free hand travels down between us and undoes the buttons of my denim skirt. I don't think as I push it down.

"Stop," he growls against my flesh. "This is my show, my rules."

Damn him. I'm not even allowed to do anything on my first sexual experience. But then again, why am I surprised Xander is the bossy type?

If anything, I might have secretly hoped for it. I might secretly be a bit more wet by his words.

He shoves my skirt and underwear down in one merciless tug as he pushes off me and slides down my body.

The empty air makes my breasts feel abandoned, but the look in his eyes as he watches me splayed in front of him is worth it.

He reaches behind him and pulls his T-shirt over his head, revealing his sculpted abs. It's not about being fit or muscular, it's the charisma that he adds to it, the certain carelessness of being so deadly and mouth-watering.

Xander is the epitome of male beauty—tall, blond, hard, slightly tanned.

Kneeling at the foot of the bed, he stares straight at my pussy and I instinctively close my thighs.

"Nuh-uh." He shakes his head, a disapproving glare on his face. "Open them wide."

"But I can't."

"Yes, you can and you want to."

"But—"

"You don't want to?"

I bite my lower lip.

"Answer me, Green."

I can do more than answer him when he calls me that. I can fly to the moon and carve my name in the stars like he once brought me a star—that I might still be hiding.

That name means he's still my shield in the world and I'm still his.

I can do everything with that name.

I'm invincible with that name.

Slowly, I open my legs, facing away from him.

"What did I say about looking at me?"

I snap my attention to his and my breathing hitches. The approval in his gaze makes me want to purr like some kitten.

He inhales the air. "You're soaked for me. I can smell it."

God, can't he just not have commentary. It's turning the heat up a notch, and I don't think I can handle it.

"Your cunt shouldn't be soaked for me."

"What?"

"It shouldn't be, yet it is. Are you aroused because I ordered you, Green?"

Yes, I think so.

"Don't answer," he grunts. "I don't want it to be real."

Real?

Before I can formulate a response, he grips me by the ankles and places them over his broad shoulders, then dives in.

"Hello, sin." The first sweep of his tongue on my folds is like straight-up torture device, the good kind, the mind-boggling kind.

He does it again, as if tasting me, savouring me, committing me to memory.

I writhe on the mattress, my hands gripping the sheet in a deadly clutch.

"You'll kill me, Green, and I'm ready for death." The rumble of his voice against my most intimate part makes me delirious.

He thrusts his tongue inside and I'm gone for. A strange sensation whirls through me with an alarming power. My back arches off the bed with the force of stimulation and I just fall.

I do it so easily, so gracefully, and without any restraints. While I've brought myself to orgasms before, none of them were this strong or ruining.

I don't think I'll ever feel the same after this. It's like Xander reached inside me and flipped a switch, and now, there's no going back.

Now, every time I think about sex, I'll think of how he worshipped my scars, how he kissed my imperfections and called them beautiful, and how he ordered me to open my legs, just so he could worship me in a whole different way.

That brings tears to my eyes. The thought that I'll be thinking about them while he's not here turns me into an emotional fool.

I'm such a mess. This isn't the moment to be crying.

"Hey." He climbs up to crawl beside me and he does something I never thought Xander would ever do again.

He hugs me, his arm lying on the small of my back while our bodies mould together.

His thumb traces over my skin, wiping the tears. "You're not supposed to be crying."

"And you're not supposed to be better than the fantasy."

"I am, huh?" He flashes me his dimples.

"Don't be so arrogant."

"Arrogant is my middle name, Green. Did you forget?"

"How could I?" I return his smile, still unable to believe the fact he's calling me Green again. That he's holding me, wiping my tears.

If this is a dream, please end now. Don't torture me any longer.

As an answer to my prayer, Xander brushes his nose against mine, just like when we were kids. "Maybe I should burn."

"Burn?"

"Yeah." His eyes close. "Because you're worth being burned for."

And with that, his breathing evens out. I lay my head on his shoulder and resist sleep with all my might.

I'm just going to watch him all night.

Maybe then, the dream won't end.

Maybe then, we'll be trapped in this moment of eternal bliss where there's no fog and no external world.

Or that's what I plan.

But the second he absentmindedly strokes my hair, I fall into the deepest sleep I've had in years.

SEVENTEEN

Xander

There are moments where you know something is wrong, but you still do it anyway.

Moments where you stop and think, *no, I shouldn't do this*, but you forge with it anyway.

It's like that in my subconscious. My erotic, porn-fest subconscious.

My dreams should level up to this state from now on. Soft hands wrap around the bulge in my jeans and I grunt out a moan.

When my eyes open, there she is. The dream is still there, right in front of me.

She's fully naked, too, her tits begging for my mouth on those perky nipples. Kimberly kneels between my legs like a good little girl, her face flushed, her green hair dishevelled.

Still, she looks like a sex goddess.

The best to ever exist.

She fumbles with my belt, pushing my jeans and boxer briefs down. Her touch is unsure, innocent even.

Just as I would've imagined my Green.

My dick jumps to life at her inexperienced ministrations. It's been hard and painful ever since I ate her pussy, demanding to be buried inside her and get his own turn.

But I can only do so much damage, even in dreams.

You're already there. Cole's devil voice says in my head. *Might as well go all the way.*

Shut up, demon.

"What are you doing, Green?" My voice is hoarse with arousal.

Her teeth nibble on her bottom lip, that full lip I want a taste of. When her eyes meet mine, they're filled with a rare sparkle, the one she had when we used to go to new places, take risks, and then laugh out loud when we reached such place.

It's her curious nature shining, her true, non-fake one.

"I want to make you feel good, too." Her breathy voice is like a fucking aphrodisiac to my starved dick.

"Make me feel good how?" I'm still lying back, but my attention doesn't drift from her. I want to engrave her in my mind so when I wake up, these memories won't go away.

Maybe when I wake up, her taste will remain on my lips, too, and I'll recall how she writhed against my mouth and came all over my tongue.

It was different than porn. They make shallow, fake noises there. My dream's small whimpers and gasps were torture to my dick.

"I don't know." She wraps her hands around the base of my dick, and I groan deep in my throat.

"You never did it before?"

She shakes her head once.

I smirk, knowing my dream would say what I want to hear the most.

"Why not?"

She lifts a shoulder. "Promise you won't find me weird."

"You're not weird; you're a bit quirky."

"Promise," she insists.

"Fine. Promise."

She bites down on the corner of her lip. "I thought it would be icky."

"How about now?"

"It's different." Her cheeks redden. "I want it."

"Because it's me?"

She nods once, running her fingers up and down my length.

The growl that leaves my throat is that of an animal. I'm not supposed to enjoy this, but it's the most I've been turned on my entire fucking life. "Say it out loud, Green."

"Because it's you, Xan."

Her eyes remain on me as she lowers her head and takes me inside her hot, little mouth.

She's soft, way too soft, as she laps her tiny tongue around me in small strokes.

I'm tempted to let her go at that pace forever, just to see her head bob up and down, to have her this way until the end of time.

My dick has other ideas, though. It's been tortured enough.

I lean over and dig my fingers into her green strands. She moans like the best erotic fantasy.

"You're killing me, Green."

Her answer is to go faster, but it's not fast enough or hard enough.

"Look at me," I tell her.

She does, her eyes so huge, I can almost see my reflection in them.

"I'll take control and it might hurt." I don't know why I'm telling her this, but even if she's a dream, she's still my Green, and I always tell my Green everything.

She nods slowly, but her lips tremble around my dick.

Fixing her head with both hands, I ignore the pain in my bandaged palm and thrust my hips so I'm deep into the back of her throat like I've always fantasised about. Like I've always wanted to and never got the chance to.

Kimberly never takes her eyes off me, even when my pace

turns wild and brutal. She opens her mouth wide and takes me in as much as she can. If anything, that curious gleam in her eyes lights up the harder I pound into her.

The more I fuck her mouth, the more her arousal coats the air, her nipples hardening to pebbles.

She's turned on.

Well, well. Cole was right. The seemingly innocent ones are the wildest.

"Do you like it when I fuck your mouth, Green?" I grunt.

She nods frantically, her hands gripping my thighs, nails digging into my skin as if she's holding in something.

"Don't let anyone else fuck your mouth," I say like a pitiful arsehole, forgetting the part that it doesn't matter.

"Don't let them touch you or kiss you or see you naked."

Her brow furrows.

"If you were mine, no fucking one would get within two metres radius from you."

Maybe it's my words or that lustful, curious look in her eyes, but I come so hard, even I am surprised by the power of my release.

My back and balls tighten as I empty down her throat with a groan. Cum drips from the side of her mouth to her chin.

I pull from her. "Don't swallow."

She stares up at me with confusion in her eyes, but she complies. I reach over and clutch her chin, opening her mouth, and stare at my seed all over her lips and tongue.

Marked and claimed.

If only for this moment, I want to believe she's mine.

I close her mouth. "Swallow every last drop."

She does, her throat working with the motion. Then she does something that surprises the shit out of me.

Kimberly winds her arms around my neck and attacks me with a ferocious kiss, causing me to lose my balance and fall on the mattress.

I'm on my back and she's splayed all over me, kissing me sloppily, as if she's been waiting to do it for a long time.

My hand wraps around her and I return her kiss. Tasting myself on her tongue is the most arousing thing I've done in recent memories.

This is officially the best dream ever.

We kiss for what seems like forever, making out like hungry animals, like the world will end the moment I wake up.

And that's probably what will happen, isn't it?

The moment I open my eyes, I won't see the green of hers, I won't taste her on my tongue or inhale her deep inside me.

I cover her eyes with my hand, slowly erasing her from memory, making her disappear.

She doesn't resist, even as her body shivers over mine. Instead, she whispers against my lips, "What happened to us, Xan?"

"Don't talk. Don't ruin it." I flip us over so she's beneath me, small and beautiful and ready for the taking. "Fuck it. I'm going all the way."

"A-all the way?"

"Yes, Green. I'm going to fuck you hard and fast and dirty. I'll hate myself for it and wish I could take a rope to my neck when I wake up, but you know what?" I lean over to nibble on her lobe before murmuring, "It'll be worth it."

"Wait." She places her slender hands on my shoulder. "Wake up?"

"I don't want to wake up."

"You already did." Her eyes widen. "This isn't a dream, Xan."

"That's what dreams say."

"No, this isn't. We're—"

The door barges open, cutting her off.

"Xan! Ahmed says I can have brownies and—" Kirian's blubbering cuts off mid-sentence and his eyes double in size as he stares at us, then grins. "Hey, Kimmy. You didn't say you'd do a sleepover at Xan's."

"Oh, shit," she mutters, hiding underneath me and pulling the covers over us.

"What are you doing?" he asks.

"Uh…wrestling. This is like special wrestling." She struggles with the words.

"Can I join?" Kir's grin is enormous as he trots to our side.

"No, Monkey." She smiles awkwardly. "We'll be right out, okay?"

"I want to join. Why are you wrestling without me?"

He grabs my forearm, his tiny hands tightening on my muscle that's still taut from how I'm holding my body over hers.

No.

Fuck no.

I reach out and pinch her cheek and…she doesn't disappear.

Why the fuck isn't she disappearing?

Because she's real, dickhead. So very real.

I'm not drunk and sleeping while Cole and Aiden sit there as guardian demons.

Kimberly winces before whispering, "What was that for?"

Proof that I fucked up.

EIGHTEEN

Kimberly

"Where are my brownies?"

My baby brother's voice startles me from my thoughts. I've been too focused on Xander to pay him attention.

He stands behind the counter, cutting the brownies into tiny pieces over and freaking out again.

Since Kirian interrupted us this morning, Xander pushed off me as if I have a contagious disease and hasn't once looked me in the eyes.

He grabbed his clothes and washed in another room, taking Kirian with him for his morning freshening up.

I don't even recall how I took a shower. All I remember is the foreboding when I got dressed and felt his every touch like it was engraved in my skin.

His tongue, his hands. Hell, my mouth is still sore from the way he fucked it and took complete control of me.

Then he pushed me off.

Then the dream, as he called it, ended.

I try to remain calm, to not have some sort of a breakdown, but the longer he avoids me, the more I touch my wrist, the stronger the itch becomes, and I don't want that itch to come to the surface. Not now, not ever.

Xander hasn't spoken to me for thirty minutes and

whenever he makes eye contact by accident, he freezes for a second before shaking his head and looking away.

At Kirian's words, he smiles and places the plate in front of us. I reach over and throw a piece in my mouth, letting the rich chocolate taste occupy my thoughts. Kirian grins, nomming on the brownies with renewed energy.

I don't realise I've been eating with him until my mouth turns all too sweet.

Damn. Those are at least five hundred calories first thing in the morning.

Still, I don't feel as bad about them as I normally would. Probably because Mum's voice isn't at the back of my head right now. I'm not hearing her scolds or seeing the weight numbers.

The only thing that's occupying my thoughts is the person standing behind the counter, watching Kirian eat and erasing me completely, as if I don't exist.

I never thought there would be a day where I would be jealous of Kirian, but here it is.

"Xander," I murmur his name as if I'm not supposed to say it. Like before.

For years, he snapped at me for saying his name, but not last night. Last night, he loved the sound of his name on my lips. Last night, he looked at me differently when I called him what I've always loved calling him—Xan.

His jaw tightens. He's pissed off because he was erasing me and I alerted him that I exist right here in front of his eyes.

He says nothing.

I lean over to speak closer to his face. He smells fresh with that hint of mint and bottomless ocean. "I'm talking to you."

"And I'm not," he says ever so casually.

I'm about to say something else when Lewis Knight comes down the stairs. I wince, realising Xander and I might have been loud while his father is here.

Then I recall how Kir walked in on us—which was way

worse. *Wrestling?* Really? Surely I could've thought of something better. I hope we didn't scar my baby brother for life and he believes the wrestling story.

Lewis is about to head straight to the door but stops when he notices us. A rare smile lifts his face as he approaches us.

"Hey, young man." He snatches a tissue and wipes the chocolate on Kirian's cheek.

"That's right, Uncle." Kir grins, showing his growing teeth. "I'm a man. Tell everyone else."

Both Lewis and I smile.

Xander doesn't. He gives us his back as he fusses with the coffee machine. His rigid, stiff back that seems about ready to burst out of his T-shirt.

"How are you, Kim?" Lewis asks me with a warm expression, another thing that's so atypical of him to show.

He's known as a powerful politician with strict decisions. That's why he gets along so well with Silver's dad.

Despite his average appearance, he has an eloquent tongue and a charisma that makes up tenfold for the looks. Xan only took after him in the shape of the eyes, perhaps. Which is also similar to Kirian's.

I always joked to Xander when we were kids that Kirian looks like him, not me.

Wait.

No. I shake my head. That's absolutely not possible.

Go away, stupid thoughts.

I fake a smile. "I'm fine, thanks."

"How are Calvin and Jeanine?"

Why the hell are you asking about them? I know why. Because they were always some kind of friends, especially Dad and Lewis; they sort of grew up together, went to the same school—RES—the same university, and the same damn world.

However, my mind is spiralling to a completely wrong direction right now.

"T-they're good."

Xander glances back at me as soon as I stammer, his brows drawn together, then reverts his attention to Kirian, who's completely oblivious to the tension brewing in the air.

Lewis wipes Kirian's cheek again. I try to unsee the scene in front of me, of Lewis's doting gesture or his smile that's as extinct as a passing unicorn, but I can't. It's impossible.

It's all that's brewing in my mind right now.

"Let me know if you need anything," Lewis tells me.

"What do you mean?" I try not to sound spooked or on the verge of blurting these thoughts I don't completely understand myself.

His expression returns to normal as if realising how many times he slipped, smiled, appeared damn doting. "With Kirian or anything."

"Okay." *No way.*

He throws a disapproving glance at Xander, then his bandaged hand. It's uncanny how much he can communicate with only his eyes. He was welcoming with Kirian and me, but he's obviously pissed off with his son.

And it's understandable, considering the shit Xan has been getting himself into. Alcohol, fighting, and now, hurting his hand.

I swallow at that.

He cut his hand, and there was blood. Like me.

Only, is he? I'm sure he didn't do it on purpose. Doesn't mean the wound isn't hurting him, though.

Xander smiles at his father and even though his dimples make an appearance, it's a forced one that's hiding what seems like bitterness behind it. "Good morning to you, too, Dad."

"We'll talk later." And with that, Lewis is out the door.

I stare at the place he stood in, beside Kirian, my mind filled with all sorts of messed up theories.

No, nope. I'm not going to think about that.

Xander smiles down at Kir. "I'll go get ready for school. Okay, Superman?"

Kirian gives him a fist without lifting his head and then they make a blowing sound.

I would've been touched by the scene if my insides weren't melting down.

Xander leaves from the other side—Kirian's side. If he thinks he can run away from me, from this, he has another thing coming.

He doesn't get to kiss me, to murmur those words to me, and to light my body on fire just to walk away as if it never happened.

He called me Green. *His* Green.

After a whole seven years, he finally called me Green again, and I'm not going to pretend that it's a play of my imagination or some sort of dream.

I'm done being pushed around by him and letting him be the decision-maker in all this tale.

We always did things together and that shouldn't change.

I storm on his heels and plant myself in front of him, disallowing him access to the stairs. "You don't get to run away."

"Run away?" He laughs and the cruelty in it crushes me slowly. "Who are you so I'd run away from you?"

"But—"

"You're nothing, Berly."

"Fuck you," I wanted to say it with spite, but it comes out weak and with so much pain, it's pathetic.

"No, thanks."

"But you did. You can't pretend it never happened."

The malice in his eyes is nothing like I've ever seen before. This time, it's tangible and with the clear intention to break. "Watch me."

"I won't stay still this time." I fight the brittleness in my voice. "I'm not the girl who waited on your approval like a lost puppy. That girl is gone. If you erase me, I'll erase you harder."

"By all means," he snarls in my face. "Do. It."

"What the hell is wrong with you? Why do you keep doing this, Xan?"

"Stop saying my fucking name." His eyes rage until they darken into a frightening blue. "Stop talking to me. Stop being in my damn vicinity. Disappear from my fucking life."

Then he turns and takes the stairs, leaving me there, bleeding metaphorically.

I reel from the effect of his words. Each one of them is like a stab to the throat.

I was wondering what price I'd have to pay this time, and here's my answer.

It's worse than being called disgusting. This is like breaking me from the inside out with no chance of healing.

He was once my knight, my anchor, my warm shoulder. Now, he's the villain coming after my life.

Now, he's the master of that suffocating fog that's slowly wrapping its tentacles around my throat and cutting off my air supply.

His back is all I see as he ascends the stairs.

And I know, I just know that he's saying goodbye for the very last time.

NINETEEN

Kimberly

The following three days pass in a daze. It's like they're happening, but they're not.

Not really.

I told Elsa I'm down with the flu and skipped today.

Truth is, I'm down with myself.

It's one of those times where everything is too much. The air, the sounds, the people.

All of it.

I stare at the empty crisp bags surrounding me and wipe the salt from my lips.

Technically, it's called a food breakdown, where you eat everything and anything in sight. Not my M&M's and pistachio gelato, though. Those are sacred and I didn't want to ruin them in this unholy site.

So after I dropped Kir at Henry's house for a sleepover, I went to the grocery store and got all the crisps and the cola—not diet. Then I went to McDonald's and ordered the biggest menus of burgers and French fries. I finished the shopping journey by buying more pastries and cake than I could carry. Lots of damn cake. I shoved them all down my throat in no particular order. I just ate and ate and ate until my jaw hurt and my stomach protested, but I didn't stop.

Even after the puking, I brought my stash with me to the

toilet and continued eating and eating and fucking eating as if the food will somehow sew the hole inside me.

It didn't.

So I drank half a bottle of tequila and had a Xanax pill— or was it two?

I lost count after I vomited everything I ate. The alcohol was definitely after the vomiting, because it sits on an empty stomach like pure, burning acid.

This time, I didn't have to stick a finger in my throat. It's as if my body is rejecting food because it's become a foreign entity.

I lay my head on the closed toilet after I finish emptying my stomach for the second time. My gaze keeps filtering to the glinting metal amongst the mess. There isn't any energy in me to stand and freshen up anymore. I just want to stay here and…disappear.

That's it, disappear. How hard would it be?

The ironic part is, it's not even because of what happened with Xan—or didn't happen.

I can survive that, his rejection and his complete closing off. What I can't survive is the hope I had that night, the feeling of finally having a purpose.

For my entire life, I've struggled with that, with finding a place and someone I can bare myself to.

Xander gave me that. He saw me, and unlike what I've always feared, he didn't hate what he saw.

But then he pulled the carpet from under my feet.

Finding somewhere to belong just to realise you never do is like a betrayal. Perhaps, it's the worst type of betrayal.

Maybe that day I abandoned him in the forest, Xander felt betrayed, too, and that's why he's been taking revenge ever since.

I understand that—I think I can anyway. I just can't pretend it's not affecting me or that I can be strong.

What's being strong even like?

Is it waking up in the morning and not looking at the sharp

blade I stole from Mari's kitchen? Is it smiling while FaceTiming Dad, even though I want to scream at him to return? Is it forcing myself to look in the mirror so I can have my makeup done?

Or maybe it's staring at my knight in the eyes and having a stranger staring back at me and not flipping there and then.

Once upon a time, he used to be mine. Now, he's anything but.

The fog turns thicker with every breath I take, wrapping itself like a noose around me.

For the first time in my life, I have no energy or will to fight it.

I have absolutely nothing to lose, and everything to suffer.

"What the hell, Kimberly?" Mum's voice rings like an alarm before her shadow falls over me in the bathroom.

Like a small kid with broken wings, I crawl up so I'm sitting and face her. No idea how I look. I'm wearing my pyjamas and my hair is in a messy bun. I put mascara on this morning, so it could be smeared all over my face. I didn't check, because the thought of seeing that face made me want to ruin it.

Mum, however, has on her designer trousers with a khaki shirt and Louboutin heels. Her rich brown hair is elegant and with a beautiful wave to it.

"Hi, Mum," I slur, then slap a hand over my mouth.

I'm drunker than I predicted. Oops.

"Have you been drinking?" She shakes her head and points at the food containers, the half-empty crisp bags "And what is that junk food? What did I say about losing that weight, Kimberly?"

"I'm sorry." My chin trembles. "I'm sorry I'm a disappointment, Mum. I'm sorry you have to be stuck with someone like me."

With every word out of my mouth, tears stream down my cheeks. They're not only tears, though. They're everything I've felt since I was a child.

Every time Mum is in sight, I feel so small; I dress wrong, breathe wrong, act wrong.

I exist wrong.

"If you're sorry, fix it." She stares down her nose at me. "Be worthy of being my daughter for once in your useless life."

I nod frantically. "I'll fix it."

She does another glance over and her lips thin in a line, in disgust, in disappointment, in distaste.

Mum isn't seeing me or the scar that's visible since my pyjamas are short-sleeved. She doesn't see the tears pooling in my eyes or the screams behind those tears.

She's seeing a mess that she's stuck with. She's seeing someone who can ruin her image.

That's all that I've been to her since I was born, a liability, a damn mistake.

I heard her tell Dad that last year, around the time my mental health took a sharp dive and the fog became my constant companion.

We shouldn't have let her come into the world. Look at her. She's a mess, Calvin.

Dad fought with her and stood up for me, but I don't remember his words. It's strange how the human mind only focuses on certain things, but not others, how I can only remember her saying I'm a mess, but not Dad calling me an angel.

Perhaps it's because I've always craved attention she's never given, love she'll never grant, and care she's not capable of.

Still, I find myself begging her with my eyes.

Look at me, Mum.

Help me.

Be my mum.

She turns around and leaves without as much as a glance. On her way out, she mutters to herself, "What have I done to deserve this?"

A strong wave of nausea hits me and I open the lid, clutching the sides with both hands, and heave until nothing comes out. I'm dizzy, and I feel as if I've been vomiting my soul aside from my gut.

The fog invades the bathroom like a being. It has a large body, all filled with black smoke while its invisible hands wrap around my throat.

Fix it, Kimberly.

Be worthy of being my daughter for once in your useless life

Look at her. She's a mess.

Mum's words tighten the imaginary noose around my neck, or is it imaginary? Maybe those are the words I've always needed to hear. Those are everything I am.

A loser, rubbish. No one wants you.

You're nothing. How about you become nothing?

Those voices heighten and tighten around my chest like thorns, prickling away at my heart.

Disappear from my fucking life.

Xander's words are like that last stab. It's not even the strongest one, but it's the most fatal.

Since we were children, he's been my sanctuary against Mum. Not only did he take that away, but he also took his position as my support, my safe haven.

Then he pretended I didn't exist.

He's even worse than her. At least she never pretended to care about me.

He showed me the world, then pushed me off the edge.

He painted the stars into the dark sky, then pulled them down in one go.

When we were young and I told him I loved stars, he got me one, a special star. *It's from an actual star*, he said. He stole it from his dad and I should keep it a secret.

I dig into my pocket and bring out the bracelet with the ugly black motif in the middle.

He said it's ugly on the outside, but only because it travelled planets to be with me, just like he always will.

Liar.

I retrieve my phone and type the text I always wanted to send him but never had the courage to.

Could be the alcohol or the pills or both.

Kimberly: I wish you were never my friend. I wish you had never told me you'd be there for me. I wish you didn't know so much about me and still chose not to be with me. I wish there was never me or you or us.

I let the phone fall to my side.

The fog's hold on my neck turns into rope, tight and hard.

It's a place where everything and anything are possible. The world is at the tip of my finger, so I take it.

Reaching under the empty bags of crisps, I bring out the blade. It's been there the entire time with the food and the alcohol and the pills—the ones Mum didn't see, because she never sees me.

When did it start getting so bad so fast? When did I start losing myself this hard and with no way to come out?

Is this how it feels when nothing is left and it's all just… fog?

Fog doesn't tell lies. The fog has been here many times before when I've lost myself to that impulse and I couldn't get out.

Or is it an impulse?

Maybe it's what I was always supposed to do.

This time, my hand doesn't tremble; it's steady and precise. This time, I don't cry and look at the door expecting, *hoping* Mum will come here and tell me she's here for me.

This time, it's all over.

I slice through the veins vertically in two long, swift moves. At first, it's just a sting. I feel it, but I don't at the same time.

Blood oozes out in a steady rhythm, red and vibrant. With it, all the pain filters out and it's…relief. Complete utter relief.

But it's not enough.

So I cut harder, not horizontally like a newbie, but vertically and deep until blood splashes in a small fountain all around me.

It's a mess, just like Mum said.

Maybe she'll call it a mess, too, when she finds me.

Dizziness assaults me almost immediately. My gaze is focused on the blood as my head lolls back against the wall. I try to concentrate on the wound and how it purges the fog out of me, how it frees me, but all I see is that bracelet and that stupid star.

The star I didn't have the chance to wear, because I was always scared he'd take it away.

Now, nothing will.

Now, I'm the one taking everything and leaving it empty. The fog slowly dissipates, but no one comes through, no one barges through the door and tells me not to go.

Maybe it's because I was always meant to go.

The sound of everything ending is just that…the end.

A tear slides down my cheek as I close my eyes and surrender to the darkness.

TWENTY

Xander

Today has been a clusterfuck since the morning.

Or maybe my life has been a clusterfuck since the beginning and I'm only starting to see it.

Dad and I had the talk about rehab—secret, of course, because he can't risk his political enemies or the press finding out that his loser son is detained.

Obviously, I said no. Then he reminded me of Mum's drinking problems and that I'm becoming like her.

So I told him, I wish I'd stayed with my mum and her drinking and mental problems and not with him.

He gave me a strange look, something that made me kind of regret what I said, then he left.

I shouldn't feel sorry about Dad; he should be feeling sorry towards me. He ruined my life in more ways than one, and I don't even mean with Mum.

He did something way worse that's been slowly but surely destroying my life.

After all, he's Lewis Knight. If he can survive the parliament's questioning, he can survive his son.

Then I kind of tried to beat Cole and Aiden up for allowing Kimberly to come to my room that night and instigating it. I have no doubt in my mind that they're the reason behind it.

Cole just laughed and said, 'so something did happen'.

Aiden smirked like a fucking psycho and patted me on the back.

I was too drunk to hit them anyway, so it ended up being half-arsed punches.

They might have prepared the ground, but I was the one who kissed her, claimed her tongue, ate her like a starved animal, then fucked her mouth as if it's always belonged to me.

My insides shrink at the thought, at the memory, at what the fuck I've done.

I lied to her.

There's no way I can pretend it didn't happen. For three days, that night is all I've been thinking about.

I can lie to myself and say that it'll wither away with time, but like all my memories with her, they'll just strengthen and magnify, and all I'll want to do is to bust into her room and repeat it for eternity.

Fuck you, twisted up mind. You should burn with Cole.

As if my week hasn't already been complete shit, I'm also sitting with none other than the main bastard whose murder I've been plotting for a while now.

Ronan and I are at the Meet Up because the captain called a meeting for the football players. I'm ready for anything that'll stop me from acting on my impulses.

I might have had a drink on the way here, but it's only one. I'm not losing my mind enough to not recognise that the fucker, Cole, set us up.

Ronan is grinning like a fucking idiot as he sits opposite me. My fist clenches to pound him to the ground.

"Long time no see, Knight. You know, remotely sober."

"Fuck you, Astor." I stare anywhere but at him.

The Meet Up is a small cottage owned by Aiden with direct access to the forest and a lake at the back. It's cosy with warm wooden colours. The four of us always come here to escape our families. There's something liberating about shedding our confinements and our names and the shit expected of us.

We were taught what we should become before we learnt what it was like to be kids. That's probably why we were never actually children.

Young in bodies. Elderly in minds.

I recall when Elsa brought Kimberly here for the first time. She watched the space with wonder in her green eyes. It's the same look she has when reading her books and watching her dramas.

For years, I made it a point to separate her from the group because if she was close to my friends, she'd be close to me, and I couldn't do that.

Until I fucked it up.

I might have ignored her for the past few days, but she's been the only one I see. The only one I watch. The only one who exists in a sea of blurry existences.

There are people and there's her. And she always shines bright amongst them.

"Why has she been absent today, Knight?"

"I'm not her fucking guardian." I made it a point not to watch her today, if I don't count the time she picked up Kirian. I was watching him, *not* her.

"You're right, I should visit and ask myself." He grins. "After all, we're dating."

"Or I can beat you up." I smile back.

"Fine. Get all that energy out. The faster you're finished, the sooner I'll go to her."

"What the fuck is wrong with you, Astor? Since when do you care about her this much?"

"Since you don't care, *mon ami*. I'm all for tortured heroines."

A sigh rips from me. "It's not what you think."

"Then tell me what I don't think."

I considered doing that since he started being a little fucker about this whole situation. After all, Aiden and Cole know. I only told Aiden on a drunk night, and Cole figured it out on his own.

Astor, however, has a big mouth. If he knows, she will, and I don't have any state of mind to deal with that.

"You'll tell her." I lift a shoulder.

"If it's something about her, then damn straight I'll tell her." He pauses. "*Attend une seconde.* The others know?"

"Define know."

"What the fuck, Knight? I tell you all my shit."

"And I don't publish it on the *Daily Mail*, unlike you, fucker."

"Well, since we're at it." He smiles his innocent but secretly evil smile as he stands up. "I told her about the rehab, leaving the country, and oh, that you always watch her."

"What. The. Fuck."

He glances back at me. "You know what? I'm taking her away, Knight. It's done."

One moment, I'm sitting there, the next, I jerk up, crash with him to the ground, and start beating him up. This time, he doesn't stay still and he fights me as well. We roll around, wrestling and hitting each other. A table falls and something breaks, but we don't stop.

"You're supposed to be my friend, *my* fucking friend." I punch him.

"And you're supposed to be better than this." He punches me.

I don't know how long we go at it, but it's long enough that I lose the feeling of my fists and Ronan's mouth and nose become bloodied. Mine is probably the same, considering the burn in my bottom lip.

We fall back on the carpet, lying side by side, breathing harshly in the silence of the room.

"I'm just disappointed in you," Ronan says in the most

serious tone I've heard on him. "I hate seeing you hurt her and being hurt in return. What the fuck are you? A masochist?"

I laugh, but it's humourless. "Probably, yes."

"Your mum left because your dad hurt her. How can you repeat the cycle, *connard?*"

"Believe me, it's not the same."

"How so?"

I release a sigh, and I'm about to cave in and just let it all out. I might have grown up with Aiden and Cole, but Ronan is the closest to me. We always gravitated towards each other like Aiden and Cole did. It's nature. And ever since Ronan told me his deadly secret a few years back, I connected to him more than ever before.

The only reason why I haven't told him my secret is because, unlike me, he really doesn't keep his mouth shut.

Before I can carry on with the crazy idea, the door opens.

Aiden and Elsa come inside, arms around each other while Teal walks alongside them. We're watching them upside down, considering our position.

My chest tightens when I search behind them and there's no trace of her.

Not that I want to see her.

Lie.

You're a fucking liar.

I need a drink—or two—right about now.

"Fuck, I missed the fight." Aiden appears genuinely offended. Arsehole.

Ronan stands up first and offers me his hand. I take it as I rise to my feet and wipe my bottom lip with my thumb.

"Where's that fucker Nash?" I ask.

"Busy." Aiden motions at us. "By all means, don't stop on our account. Can we have a redo?"

"Sex and drugs and now violence." Teal stares down at Ronan like he's a stray, dirty dog. "What a charmer."

Since he's close to me, I notice the change in his demeanour, the way his body leans forward as if for a fight, but he grins, showing his teeth.

"Glad to be of entertainment, *ma belle*."

"Entertainment?" She rolls her eyes. "More like a war zone."

"Then you should take shelter, huh?"

"Are you okay?" Elsa leaves Aiden's side and retrieves tissues from her bag to wipe the blood off Ronan's mouth and nose.

Teal puts earbuds in and saunters to the midst of all the mess as if it doesn't exist. Then she sits on the sofa, saying in no uncertain terms that she's lost interest in the scene.

No idea why she's here anyway.

While Elsa wipes Ronan's face, Aiden's left eye twitches, which means his inner demon is about to come out.

Just to be a dick, I say, "What about me, Elsa? He ruined my face."

"Not you." She doesn't break her attention from Ronan.

"Not him either." Aiden pulls her by the arm and throws the tissues at Ronan's chest.

The latter smirks. "But I like Ellie's soft hands."

Aiden offers him a mock smile. "I'm sure you'll also like the grave I've been digging for you. I'm making it nice and cosy."

"Why not me?" I ask Elsa.

"You're acting as if you don't know?" She folds her arms over her chest, pinning me with a scowl like a stern teacher.

"I don't know."

"I can't believe this. You're such an arrogant bastard."

I give her a smug grin. "I'd probably take the compliment better if we put it into context."

"Kim pretended to have a fever so she could escape you today. She's not even answering my calls or texts."

Ronan glares at me as if to say, 'I told you so.'

I resist the urge to flip him off. "As I was saying, I'm not her guardian."

"Then stop confusing her, damn it," Elsa snaps. "Leave her alone so she can pick up her life without you polluting it."

"Too bad you don't get to tell me what to do." I wave at them. "I'm out of here."

"You're just a coward!" Elsa shouts at my back. "You'll never deserve her."

I glance at her over my shoulder as Aiden holds her in place with both arms around her stomach while she struggles to be set free to no avail.

"We agree on that," I say, and then I'm out in the night.

The cold air causes goosebumps to erupt over my skin. My face turns numb and the freezing air seeps to my bones.

I stop in front of my car, retrieve a joint, and light it. The smoke is like an instant tranquiliser. I close my eyes for a bit, savouring the pungent taste.

My options are either to drink or to fight.

Or I can do both at the same time.

After all, I'm on a limited time until I'm shipped off to where Dad sees fit. I'm eighteen and could leave on my own, but where would I go?

Maybe it's the thought of being alone that grates on my skin more than the lack of the luxurious life.

I can see myself ten years from now, partying and fighting and drinking. Or maybe I won't be alive ten years from now, because I'll get myself killed in one of those fights.

Or because of drowning my liver in alcohol.

My phone vibrates.

I leave the joint in my mouth as I retrieve it.

The thing in my chest picks up speed immediately. It's as if I'm in a bleak world and then she barges in like a spark.

A spark I've been slowly killing—while also killing myself.

It's a text message.

Kimberly: I wish you were never my friend. I wish you had never told me you'd be there for me. I wish you didn't know so much about me and still chose not to be with me. I wish there was never me or you or us.

My lips part and the joint nearly falls to the ground as I read and re-read the text.

No.

No, she didn't.

I hit her name and call her. She doesn't pick up. I kick the car and don't stop to think about the pain as I type.

Xander: Pick up the fucking phone, Kimberly.

No answer.

Xander: I don't wish I didn't meet you. I never did.

Still nothing.

Fuck!

I throw the joint away and jump into my car, driving back home in a speed I've never done before.

I arrive in five minutes sharp. All the time, I keep calling her over and over again.

Then I call Kir and he says he's spending the night with his friend.

That makes me hit the steering wheel as soon as I hang up on him. He's been her balance, and the one she's looked at when she's had those destructive thoughts.

Now that he isn't there, there's nothing that stops her.

Don't you dare, Green. Don't you fucking dare.

I swerve the car to the Reed's driveway and barge outside, not bothering to close the Porsche's door.

I don't pretend to be clueless as I hit in the code to their house. I've seen her put it a thousand times. Besides, Kir often forgets it and I have to help him.

No one greets me when I step inside. That bitch Jeanine must be in her studio, and Mari is probably fast asleep.

I hit in the code again to shut off the alarm, then I ascend the stairs two steps at a time.

There's been this something in my chest since I read her text. Something morbid and dark and so fucking wrong.

Don't.

Don't.

Don't.

I pause outside her room, my fingers hesitant as I push the door open.

There hasn't been a day where I forgot where her room is or how we used to sit and watch shows together, or how she used to tell me jokes that weren't funny, but I laughed anyway because her expression was adorable.

The fact I'm coming back here under these circumstances is like a jab straight to the groin.

"Kimberly." Her name catches in my throat as my feet slowly drag on the floor.

No answer.

"I'm coming in."

Still no reply.

I step into her room, and there's no one there. Just her made-up bed and the open wardrobe that's filled with green clothes.

Instead of releasing a breath of relief, I'm unable to breathe at all. My lungs burn as I head to the bathroom, a strange premonition telling me she's there.

"Kimberly?" I call in a helpless try to get an answer. Or a sound.

Anything from her would do.

I drag my feet to the entrance and the worst-case scenario materialises in front of me.

Blood.

So much fucking blood.

Kimberly sits on the floor beside the toilet, her back

leaning against the wall, and she's surrounded by bags of crisps, pills, and a bottle of alcohol.

Her head lolls at an awkward angle and her green strands half-camouflage her expression.

My eyes go straight to the trail of blood soaking her cat pyjamas and the tiles beneath her.

So much fucking blood.

One of her hands holds a blade and her previously scarred wrist is now cut open, oozing blood all over the white tiles.

I run towards her, cursing out loud like a lunatic and grab towels on the way.

The first towel soaks immediately after I wrap it, so I add another one. Then something glints in her cut hand.

A bloodied bracelet dangles from her fingers.

I almost break at the view. It's the bracelet I gave her for her eleventh birthday. The last gift I ever gave her, which I thought she threw away.

I push that thought out of the present and place two fingers on the pulse point in her neck while keeping pressure on her wrist.

The waiting time is probably seconds, but it feels like centuries. The more she doesn't show any sign of life, the more I stop breathing altogether.

"Come on, Green." My voice is hoarse with the pent-up emotions swirling inside me.

My grip tightens around her wrist as I lean my forehead against hers. "Don't go, please. I'll be the one to go, I promise."

The moment her pulse thumps under my thumb, I release a long breath. It's as if I'm coming from the dark, suffocating underground.

Her pulse is weak and barely there, but it exists.

I bandage one more towel around her wrist, keeping the pressure as I dial 999.

From here on, there are only two options. Either she lives or I don't.

TWENTY-ONE

Kimberley

N umb.

That's the only feeling that remains in my head as I slowly open my eyes.

It's something strange. Being numb, I mean.

There's nothing in there. No emotions. No thoughts. And most of all, no pain.

It's like a blank canvas.

I always loathed blank canvases when Mum brought them over. At least she paid them attention and made them pieces of art.

People think the 'nothing' state of mind is the best to have.

It's not.

Slowly, that nothingness morphs into irrevocable darkness that you can never escape.

A fog. A numbness.

While I never had Mum's artistic streak, I always wanted someone to touch my blank canvas, paint on it, somehow revive it.

Make it a piece of art.

Slowly, too slowly, my surroundings register. The white walls and the bleach. The unfamiliarity and then…the familiarity itself.

The hospital.

I'm at the hospital because I cut myself. This time, I went in too deep that I had to be admitted. This time, I don't have to google ways to stop the bleeding or hide the scars.

That's when the most dooming realisation hits me.

I'm not dead.

A tear slides down my cheek as I soak in that reality, in the fact that I went all the way but still couldn't die.

How could I be a failure even in death?

I'm still breathing, and the fog will soon cover my senses and envelop me in its tight embrace, and this time, it'll never let me go.

The pain will be tenfold worse.

The harshness will be a hundred times crueller.

The reality will be so much more brutal.

Then that 'something' will attack me and I'll find no reprieve from it.

Who found me? Why did they do it? Should I be thankful? Mad?

"Angel?"

My muscles lock at Dad's voice.

No, not him.

Please, not Dad.

I don't want him to see me this way. Why did he come back?

Facing away, I screw my eyes shut so tight, hoping against hope that he'll think I went back to sleep and leave.

Just leave, Daddy. Don't look at what I've become.

Big hands wrap around mine and I nearly lose the fight against the overwhelming emotions whirling inside me.

"Angel, please look at me. It's Daddy."

"It's because you're Daddy that I don't want you to hate me."

"I'll never hate you, Kimberly." His voice turns non-negotiable. "Never, do you hear me?"

My lids slowly open and I take him in, sitting by my bed-side, holding my bandaged hand so softly, as if it'll break any second.

Dad, Calvin Reed, is a clean-cut man in his mid-forties. A slight stubble covers his sharp jaw. He has a strong, tall build that gives him so much charisma and power. His blond-chest-nut hair is always styled and perfected, his suits are tailored for him and him alone.

Dad and Mum are dubbed as one of most beautiful cou-ples in the media, and while Kir fits in that picture-perfect family, I never have.

Right now, Dad isn't in his usual impeccable attire. His hair sticks out as if he's been running his fingers through it. His tie is gone and the first buttons of his shirt are undone. Black circles surround his eyes as a reminder that I disturbed his life.

"Did you have to take a night flight because of me?" I whis-per, my voice spooked.

"I'd take a million flights because of you." He reaches a hand to loosen his tie, then realises it's not there and lets his arm drop to his side. "You're not a burden, Angel. You're my only daughter. I know I've been a failure, but I'll work harder for you—for us and our family. I just need you to talk to me."

My chin trembles and it takes everything in me not to take refuge in him. I can't bother Dad. He's a busy man and doesn't need this whole mess in his life.

"Please, Angel. *Please* let me help you…" His voice breaks and the first tears flow down my cheeks simultaneously.

"D-Daddy, I don't want to see Mum, please? I don't want to see how much she hates me and is disappointed in me."

His jaw tics and he says in an eloquent voice, "You won't. I promise."

"What if… What if Mum hates me, what if she—"

"Fuck her," he snaps, then forces a smile. "If she hates you, it's only because she thinks you're a reflection of her ugliness.

It's not you, Kim. It's her and her self-image and her damn artistic philosophy. I'm so sorry I didn't take the time to tell you this earlier. I'm so sorry, Angel."

Those words are my undoing.

I lunge at him, wrapping my arms around his waist and burying my head in his shoulder.

The sobs that rise from my chest are ugly and unhinged, but I don't stop.

I *can't* stop.

It's as if I've been waiting my entire life for a moment like this. It's even better than the purge I felt whenever I cut or popped those pills.

Those were imaginary and temporary releases; this one is real.

All too real.

Dad smells of sandalwood and cosy nights. His embrace brings back my childhood days when he used to carry me on his shoulders and just take me out.

When he used to let me sleep in his embrace whenever I was spooked by a nightmare.

When he used to play with me and read me stories after Nana couldn't.

That Daddy was a part of my armour against Mum.

I lost him to his job and was never able to get him back.

"K-Kir," I manage between sobs. "I-is he here? Don't let him see me this way, Dad."

"Don't worry, he's with Henry."

Oh, thank God. I can't scar him again.

What is wrong with me?

How could I do this without thinking of the other people my life? How could I not think of Kirian and how alone he'd be in the world? How could I not think of Dad, who, even though he's holding me and whispering soothing words to me, his chest rises and falls with harsh breaths as if he's about to combust?

I was going to leave Dad and Kir behind. I was going to stab them in the chest and go without thinking about the depth of the wound I caused.

"I'm so sorry, Daddy." I hiccough, my voice muffled with his shirt.

"I'm sorry, too, Angel. I'm sorry I didn't see this sooner or protect you sooner."

"D-don't say that, Daddy. You always protected me."

"Not enough."

"Dad…"

He reaches between us and wipes my tears away. "From today on, promise you'll talk to me."

I nod, sniffling. For a long time, I've dreamt about a moment like this. I practised it every night, too.

Yes. I practised the time I'd open up to someone about the fog that's been residing in my brain.

I couldn't be any happier that it's Dad, not some therapist.

"Promise you won't hate me?" I ask anyway.

He strokes my hair back. "Never, Angel. You're my only daughter."

I inhale a deep intake of air, my heart slamming against its cavities so hard, I can almost hear it.

No idea how or where to start, so I let my gut lead me as I pour it all out.

"You know when you sometimes wake up and you're disoriented and don't know where or who you are? I'm that way every day. It's not a phase and it doesn't go away. Every day, I remember I'll meet Mum, talk to Mum, and see the disappointment in her eyes. Every day, I remember I'll go to school and see the boy who used to be my best friend, then realise I don't exist for him anymore. Every day, I wonder if I'm invisible and if maybe I stopped existing altogether at a moment in time. Every day, I struggle with the need to stay afloat, to eat, to keep fighting because Kirian needs me. But other times, I think maybe he's better off without me. Other times, I get too weak and can't fight anymore. Sometimes, Mum snaps at me and I just have to relieve that pain someplace else, so I cut and watch the pain disappear with the blood. I know it's wrong and I feel so bad afterwards, to the point I can't look at myself in the mirror, but I can't stop, because the physical pain is better than the emotional pain. The blood is better than being suffocated by the fog."

I'm sobbing by now. A tear slides down Dad's cheek, but he continues holding me close as if he's afraid to let go.

I grip him by the shirt, digging my nails in. "Help me stop, Daddy. I need help."

TWENTY-TWO

Xander

People can become ghosts.

They can exist, even if at the same time they don't.

They can go unnoticed so that even though everyone looks at them, they don't really see them.

That's how I spent the last two days at the hospital, sleeping on benches, using the bathroom's soap to freshen up, surviving on coffee—actual coffee, not the one cocktailed with vodka.

Being sober for two days straight sucks. It's like seeing the world from non-grainy eyes, and the view isn't pretty.

Alcohol makes it less harsh, more tolerable. Being drunk makes me accept myself, or maybe it makes me think less about myself and as a result, I kind of accept it.

I considered going to the grocery store and fetching a bottle of vodka, but I stopped.

This isn't the time to lose myself. I have plenty for that later.

So I nursed a two-month hangover.

And yes, it hurts like a bitch with an STD.

But it doesn't hurt as much as that night.

Witnessing Kim bleed out will haunt my nightmares for life. I still can see her blood marring the tiles, bright and red. It was life leaving her with no intention of returning. I had my suspicions, but when I heard the confirmation that I'm one of the reasons behind that decision, something inside me broke to bloody pieces.

That night she told her father everything and asked for his help, I stood in front of the door with my fists clenched by either side of me.

Every sob she released was like a stab, and every confession she made twisted the knife deeper.

She just needed someone, and I did everything not to be that someone, and as a result, I almost lost her.

I thought I could never hate myself more than when I woke up and realised touching her wasn't a dream. Seems the self-hate has huge degrees and mine reached its max that night, listening to her confessions and sobs, seeing her hold on to Calvin like she'd break to pieces if he let go.

She's been doing that a lot these past days, holding on to people, hugging them. First Calvin, then Elsa, Teal, and the fucker, Ronan.

Those are the only four people she's allowed to visit her. The only people she's allowed to see her in her true form, not the fake Kim who hid behind the façade, but the real one who held back tears as she talked about her scars.

Elsa cried and Ronan comforted her. Teal, the goth girl, who doesn't touch anyone, let Kim hug her.

And yes, I watched all that through the opening of the door or the glass like a creep.

I've been contemplating the best way to go in there and tell her, to relieve her from the pain, even if it'll add a different type of pain.

However, I haven't managed to.

I'm not only a creep but also a coward and a selfish bastard, because even now, I want to protect her in my own fucked up way.

Calvin is the only one who spends the nights with her and she sleeps almost immediately whenever he sits beside her.

I've never seen a father so devoted as him, even if he is a bit late at it. He brought the psychiatric doctors and they had some sort of a family therapy—without Jeanine.

That bitch is now sitting on the bench, glaring at a boy who's playing with his parents, probably because he's making some noise. As usual, she's holding a phone to her ear and speaking in her typical snobbish tone. She's acting as if the girl inside isn't her only daughter.

As if she didn't attempt to kill herself.

Kill herself.

Thinking about those words drives the knife in deeper still. I can try to put roses and unicorns on it, but that's what Kim did. She wanted to leave this world and never return.

Fuck.

I'm in the corner, watching the entrance to Kim's room, but staying away from Jeanine's field of vision.

"Yes, of course," she snaps. "I will not delay the exhibition for any reason at all. She'll be fine, she's not a kid."

I'm about to go in there and punch her in the face. Maybe she'll delay the exhibition if her damn image is disfigured.

I hate that woman. And not only because of the past, but it's mainly because she never deserved a daughter like Kim.

Selfish people like Jeanine are not fit for motherhood. Just like my mum.

Kim's room door hisses open and Calvin comes outside, his face worn, but he doesn't appear sad, just tired.

"Go home, Jeanine," he tells his wife, stopping in front of her.

"This is the second time I've come and haven't seen her." She rises to her feet and places a hand on her hip. "I have things to do."

"And I'm telling you to go back and do those things. You won't see her until she's ready."

"You're spoiling that brat and I won't stand for it. I'm her mother."

He laughs with a biting edge. "Mother? When was that, Jeanine? When I caught you hitting your stomach, saying this demon needs to disappear? Or when you didn't want to hold her when the nurse brought her over? Or was it when you threw her at me and refused to even look at her, let alone feed her? Newsflash, she was never your daughter and from today onwards, you have no right to speak to her or try to exercise your motherly rights on her."

For the first time in her life, Jeanine appears speechless. It only takes her a few seconds to recuperate, though. "Is that what she said?"

"Go home and take care of Kirian."

She taps her shoes on the ground. "He keeps asking about her."

"Then you tell him she's at camp and will call in the morning. Be useful for once in your entire useless life."

"Fuck you, Calvin." She yanks her bag from the bench. "I won't be coming again."

"Even better," he calls behind her back as she stomps out of the hospital as if her heels are on fire.

Bitch.

Calvin is about to head inside when he notices me lurking there, both hands in my pockets.

I haven't released the star bracelet, scared it'll disappear the moment I do. Just like she almost disappeared.

He sighs. "Go home, Xander."

Calvin has seen me over the past few days and always tells me to leave. I'm like a dog who keeps coming back even after being told off.

I remain silent, but I don't make a move to go.

Another sigh rips from him. "Lewis must be searching for you."

I scoff. "He's not. He has long conferences, he probably doesn't know what time it is right now."

"Still, go home and freshen up. You look like you've been in a fight."

That's because I have.

When I still don't move, Calvin motions behind him. "Or go in."

"I'll probably make it worse," I confess, my voice thickening with emotion.

"As long as it's real, I don't think you would. Besides, sometimes, things have to get worse before they get better."

I stare at him for a beat as I weigh his words.

You know what, a human can be a ghost only for so long.

I make a move towards the door, but Calvin clutches my shoulder forcing me to halt in my tracks. "If you blame her for what happened, I'll beat you up worse than in those newbie fights you get yourself into."

How the hell does he know about those?

"Yes, sir," I say, and there's surprisingly no sarcasm like when I speak to Dad.

Maybe it's because I respect Calvin and the role he's playing in his daughter's life.

"I'll go grab a coffee." He releases me and vanishes around the corner.

I continue watching him, making sure he's gone before I step inside the room. It smells of antiseptic, but there's also that slight lime smell from her.

Kim leans sideways, rummaging through her drawers. Her skin isn't as pale as that night. Her hair falls on either side of her shoulders like a green halo.

She's so beautiful, it's physically painful.

And she's alive, breathing, moving.

She's alive and right there.

If I don't do something, she might try it again, and maybe next time, Calvin or I won't be there and it'll be too late.

"Dad, did you see my Kindle? I think I put it here, but maybe—" Her words cut off as her eyes meet mine.

They widen to a huge green colour and sparkle a little, shine a little, but die a little, too.

Ouch.

I deserve that.

"What are you doing here?" she whispers. "Get out."

I deserve that, too.

But I'm not leaving until she knows everything.

It's the moment of truth.

TWENTY-THREE

Kimberley

Today, the therapist told me to say what I hate, that I should let it out.

I said I hated how Mum treated me and how the bullies at school talked about me. I said I hated fat shaming and diets.

But I kept what I hated the most to myself.

I hate how much my heart flutters when Xander is in sight or how I forget what I was trying to do the moment he comes into my vicinity.

Both his hands are shoved into his jeans. His lower lip is busted and cut and his ocean-deep eyes appear even more bottomless, exhausted, as if he hasn't slept for days.

He appears a little bit broken, a little bit haunted, a little bit wounded.

Just like me.

And I hate that even more.

I hate that he was the one who found me and that he saw me in that state.

I hate that I'm grateful to him in ways words can't express.

I hate that I keep looking at the door, expecting him to come in any second, and how I feel gutted every time he doesn't.

I hate that I wanted to see him, even though I have no interest in seeing my mum.

But most of all, I hate *him*.

The boy, the person, who cut me off from his life and left me to fend for myself.

The knight I took refuge in, but he offered no shelter.

The person I shared my life with, but he erased me as if I were never there.

I trusted him and he betrayed me. I can forgive anything but that.

"Get out," I repeat in a firm voice.

Now that I had my fill of him—as dishevelled as he is—I can live without wondering about him one more day.

I told Elsa and Dad about everything, although I had to struggle with the tears in Elsa's eyes and how they both blamed themselves for not seeing the signs sooner.

They couldn't have, because I was pro-level at hiding them. Besides, they both had a lot to deal with. Dad had his demanding work and Elsa had her complicated family situation and volatile relationship with Aiden.

Now that they offered their full support, I don't need Xander to see me anymore.

I might be broken, but I'll pull myself together. I might have fallen, but I'll get up. There'll be a day where I look behind and say I survived.

And I don't need him to be there for that.

Xander sits on the chair Dad usually occupies, his attention never leaving my bandaged wrist. A small voice inside me tells me to hide it, but I squash that voice.

There'll be no more hiding. This is me, the *only* me.

"Didn't you hear what I said?" I continue in my confident tone. "I told you to go. I don't want to see you, just like you don't want to see me."

"I lied about that." His voice is calm, too calm. It raises goosebumps on my skin.

"You lied?"

"I lie about a lot of things. I'm a liar." He's still speaking in that neutral tone as if any other range will ruin his composure.

"Things like what?"

"Like how much I hate you. I don't. Or how much you're nothing. You aren't. Or how I can live without you. I can't."

My breathing hitches and I dig my nails into the hospital's sheet. "If you're saying that because of what happened to me or out of pity, I swear—"

"I don't pity you." He cuts me off.

"Then why are you saying those things now? Why do you think you can come in here and say shit like that after you told me to disappear from your life?"

"I told you—"

"You lied, you don't mean them." I cut him off, repeating his earlier words. "Doesn't mean I didn't believe them. Doesn't mean you didn't make me cry every time you pretended I was nothing. Why would you ever do that to me? That child prank doesn't warrant this much torment. It doesn't warrant that you treat me as if I'm invisible. I'm visible, I'm here, and I'm always looking at you, so why don't you look at me?"

"I can't."

"Why not?"

"You'll hate me if you know."

"Tell me and I'll decide myself. I lived through this torment for years; I have the right to know."

He lifts his eyes and the wretchedness in them nearly breaks me all over again. "The truth isn't always good, Green."

"I want to know why. Tell me why!"

"Because you're my sister."

TWENTY-FOUR

Xander

Age eleven

"Luna!" I call the cat's name as I walk into the forest. "Come here, kitty."

She's such a pain, like Green sometimes.

I called her for more than five minutes and she still didn't show up. Here's to hoping she didn't get caught in one of the trees.

Actually, if she did get caught, she would've brought the entire world down with her mewling.

I slide down a small cliff to the riverbank. Maybe she came here to drink.

Kim must be worried. She's always weird whenever Luna disappears, saying things like maybe she was hit by a car and died.

Luna doesn't even go to the road. She's too lazy for that.

There are many weird things about Kim, like the way she smiles and the way she eats and the way she laughs.

I say weird, but Cole says that's because I want to kiss her. He's wrong, I don't want to kiss her.

Okay, maybe I do, but I also don't want her to hate me, so I only did it once.

She smiled, though, her eyes sparkling, so maybe she doesn't hate me?

Cole says I have to do it a few more times to find out and that's what I plan.

I search beneath the bushes for a silver tabby, but there's no trace of Luna. It's getting dark and it reminds me of that time when Cole, Aiden, and I were taken away.

It was dark and cold, and I kept hearing voices, speaking in hushed tones, but no one gave me any food.

I remember thinking about Dad and Aiden and Cole and if they were okay.

After I was thrown out of the van into a similar forest like this one, I didn't cry or call for help. I couldn't, even if I'd wanted to. It could have been because Dad said to never cry and to think of solutions instead of thinking of problems.

But I remembered having one purpose: I had to go home to Kim.

She hates spending time with her mum and I promised to never leave her alone. I'd planned to keep that promise, just like she kept her promise about never leaving my side.

And that's exactly how I got home.

I fought the cold and the hunger and continued walking until I found a police station.

Since then, Kim and I have grown even closer. She's the only one I told about the kidnapping and how cold it was. She's the first person who comes to mind when I wake up in the morning and the last thought in my head when I go to bed at night.

Aiden and Cole have been making fun of me, saying I'm being controlled by a girl and that I should wear her skirt. I punched Aiden and kicked that tosser Cole in the chin.

He said that she'll grow up and not care about me anymore, because that's what girls do. They change their minds.

That's why I've been keeping a distance from her, not because I don't care about her anymore like she said, but because I don't want her to hate me with time.

I don't know what I would do if she hates me. It'd be worse than losing Mum. At least I had her back then. If I lose her, I'll have no one.

"Absolutely not!"

I come to halt at the very familiar voice. Jeanine, Kim's mother. What is she doing here?

Tiptoeing behind a tree, I peek through the branches to find her standing in front of her white car, folding her arms. She's wearing huge sunglasses that cover half her face and a scarf around her head, but I know it's her from the voice and the car and the shiny brown hair.

Kim is always jealous of that, wishing she had hair like her mum, a body like her mum, and everything like her mum.

If only she knew she's more beautiful than her mum.

"I want my daughter, Jeanine. You're obviously not doing a good job with her."

My nails dig into the trunk as the person she's speaking to comes into view.

Dad.

He stands in front of his Mercedes, wearing his hunting hat.

His words slowly trickle in my brain. Daughter. He said, *daughter*.

"Fucking someone doesn't make you a father, Lewis." She flips her hair back. "I'm the one who carried Kimberly in my womb for nine fucking months."

"Doing that doesn't make you a mother either." He glares down at her.

"You should've fought for her as soon as she was born. But no, you had that other bitch to worry about. Your home and your pretty little family. Remember what you told me back then?" Her voice turns mocking as she mimics his, "I already have a son, Jeanine. Don't get on my nerves, Jeanine."

"Well, I didn't think you'd be this useless as a mother. She was crying the other day because you yelled at her."

"I get to raise her any way I like. Mind your own business and take care of your precious son."

"Jeanine," he mutters her name through clenched teeth.

"I have a reputation, okay? I can't just announce I have a daughter outside of marriage, an affair, and with my neighbour and my husband's friend. Do you even realise how that would smash my and Calvin's careers? Yours, too, in fact."

"I'm not asking you to announce it, but to at least tell her about it, so I can openly treat her as my daughter. She already spends so much time with Xander anyway."

"No way. That brat will start calling you Dad in public and I can't have that." She points a finger at him. "Keep our deal or I'm telling Xander the truth. How do you think your precious son would feel, huh?"

"Don't you dare come near him."

"Then stop this nonsense."

"I'm warning you. Treat her well."

"Oh, I'm sorry. Did you miss the part that says you don't get to tell me what to do? Even Calvin doesn't, so why should you?"

"I'm her father, damn it. I can't let you mistreat her like that."

"Or what? You'll demand custody? I guess you can't, huh?"

"I'm keeping my eyes on you." He heads towards his car.

"You know I love the attention."

"Rot in hell, Jeanine."

"I'll see you there, Lewis." She waves at him with a venomous smile before she yanks her car door open and slides inside.

Both of them head in opposite directions, leaving dust in their wake.

And me.

I stand there, not believing what I just heard. A blade slashes through my chest, and although I can't see it, I feel it. It's deep, burning and painful. So, so painful.

My legs shake and I fall to a sitting position, unable to remain standing anymore.

I stare at the road they just took as if I can bring them back and ask them about what they revealed.

A daughter.

Kim's father isn't Uncle Calvin, it's my dad. That means she's my sister.

My. Sister.

I always told Kimberly that I wanted a sibling like she had Kirian and she said he could be both of ours.

I felt so happy back then, to have a sibling, but now, after I found out she's my real sibling, I want to cry.

She can't be my sister. If she is, that means I can't kiss her anymore.

It means I have to be with her like I am with Kirian.

I *hate* that.

I hate Dad and Jeanine.

And now, I have to hate Kim.

TWENTY-FIVE

Kimberley

Present

My mouth hangs open. I couldn't close it if I tried.

The whole time Xander has been telling me his version of that day seven years ago, he hasn't looked at me.

Not even once.

He's the only one I can look at, though. I feel like if I don't use him as a visual anchor, I'll have some sort of a breakdown.

The wound at my wrist itches, tingling and scratching for a touch. I clutch it with my other hand, not wanting to feel that need for pain.

If I let it loose, it'll just devour me alive.

"After that," he says in the calm voice he's been using since he came here. "I had to stay away because I didn't trust myself around you."

My nose tingles, but I ask anyway. "Trust yourself around me, how?"

His ocean eyes meet mine. They're dark, desolate, as if he's hanging at the bottom. "You're my sister, Kim."

He says it with harshness, like he's trying to jam that information in my head.

He's trying to hit that fact home.

And he should.

Because even as I hear those words out loud, I can't believe them.

No—I don't want to believe them.

Xander can't be my brother. He just *can't*.

"Maybe you heard wrong," I say. "Maybe they weren't—"

"I heard them again a few years later. Dad always gave Jeanine shit for the way she treated you. He made it his job to threaten her for not taking care of his daughter, of *you*." He runs a hand through his hair. "You never noticed how he looks at you?"

"I-I thought it was Kir and that maybe he was Kir's dad." God. I didn't even want to think about that option, but now, it turns out to be way worse.

Xander is my brother, half-brother, but it still counts as a blood sibling.

I kissed my brother.

I had oral sex with my brother.

I've fantasised about my brother my entire life.

Oh, God.

Oh. My. Freaking. God.

I think I'm going to throw up.

"Hey." He leans over, reaching a hand for my face.

I slap it away, my heart beating so loudly, I'm scared it's going to come to an imminent halt. "Don't *touch* me."

"I won't; you're right." He sits back down, his shoulders hunched.

Defeated.

He looks like a knight out of a lost battle, his armour broken, and his face bruised.

I've never hated someone as much as I hate him right now.

"Why did you tell me?" My voice raises. "Why didn't you take it with you to the grave?"

He could've just rejected me like always, and I would've

moved on. Eventually. Now, I'll always think of him as my brother.

And that is torture.

The worst fucking torment he could inflict on me.

"Because you did that." He motions at my bandaged wrist. "I can't watch you self-destruct because of me, Kim. I can't watch you being hurt."

"You did that just fine all these years. Why now? Why did you decide you care now?"

"I've always cared. Every time I pushed you away, I sliced myself deeper. The more I pretended you don't exist, the harder I noticed you. There hasn't been a day where I haven't thought about you or watched you. And that's not right, Kim. That's not right at fucking all."

"Because we're siblings?"

He shakes his head. If pain could be tasted, I'd be burning in acid from the way his expression falls. "Because I never thought of you as a sibling. Because I want you as a woman and because I'm considering hell as a permanent resident as long as I get to be with you. Because I feel jealous and fucking crazy whenever anyone gets close to you. Because I want to be your first and last and fucking everything."

He's breathing harshly by the time he finishes, as if it took all his energy to say those words. Then he sighs. "But as I said, that's not right, not to you."

My chin shakes so hard until my jaw hurts. Hearing those confessions out of his lips is like being shoved into a dark murky tunnel with no way out.

There's a strange ache in my heart, something a lot different than the fog and depression. It's deeper and scarier, and all I want to do is let go.

But to go where?

To who?

"Dad mentioned rehab and some school in the north," he says.

I couldn't speak if I wanted to, so I stare up at him with widened eyes.

"I'm leaving, Kim." He smiles, and although his dimples appear, it's the saddest, most wrenched smile I've seen on his face. "It's better for all of us."

My gulp is loud in the silence, but I don't say anything. I can't.

"You're strong, so don't believe otherwise. You're loved, so don't let that bitch Jeanine tell you any different, and don't be shy to lean on Calvin, Elsa, and Kirian. Don't hesitate to ask for help when you need it. They care about you more than you know."

No.

"Instead of dancing alone, dance with others. Instead of living alone, lean on others. Instead of purging the pain, talk about it."

No.

"Live well."

No!

I want to scream, but no words come out.

He heads to the door with steady steps. My heart weeps as his back remains the only sight. His tight, broad back that I probably will never see again.

Without turning around, he says, "You'll always be my Green."

And with that, he's out of the door, leaving trails of blood in his wake.

TWENTY-SIX

Kimberley

Two days later, the psychiatric ward decides I'm good to go home.

The trip back is like a one-way journey to hell. As I come out of Dad's car, I stand there for long seconds, staring at the Knights' mansion.

A part of me is yearning for one more look. I don't even have to talk to him, all I need is to see him.

We can just watch each other from afar like we have all these years.

Until we crossed lines. Or he did. I didn't know we were blood siblings.

If I had, I would've…what? What exactly would I have done?

God, this is messing me up.

Dad escorts me inside with a hand around my shoulder. I'm like a zombie, following him, but not exactly participating.

"Welcome home!"

Some confetti flies in the air as I focus on the smiling faces waiting for me—Elsa, Ronan, Teal, Knox, Cole, Aiden, and even Silver.

What the hell is Silver doing here?

I don't focus on her, though, since a small man attacks me in a hug. I crouch and wrap my arms around Kirian in a strong embrace, my heart thudding loudly in my chest.

"Kimmy, I missed you so much!"

"I missed you, too, Monkey. Have you been a good boy without me?"

"Always." He grins, then motions at Marian. "I helped Mari with everything."

I mouth thank you at her and she nods with moisture pooling in her eyes.

Crouching, I kiss his cheeks harder than needed. "That's my monkey."

Elsa hugs me next, her eyes welling with tears. She's been with me the whole time and she didn't blame me for not telling her. She said she understands and that's all I need.

Dad smiles at me, motioning upstairs. I nod back, knowing he needs to freshen up and change. He never once left my side during all those tests and doctor meetings. We already agreed on a therapy plan and he said he'll be there with me every step on the way.

Still, even with Dad's support, nothing can get rid of the lump that's been lodged in my throat since that night.

It's asphyxiating and slowly robbing me of life.

Mum isn't around and I'm not surprised. Dad said he told her not to come out of her studio—not that she would.

"Look at you, all rosy and shit." Knox grabs me by the shoulder in a side hug. "May I have this dance?"

Ronan slides to my other side, glaring at him. "Hey, hands off, fucker. Kimmy is my girlfriend."

"As if you'd ever have a girlfriend." Knox shoots back.

"I would. It's Kimmy."

Teal scoffs.

"Do you have a problem, *ma belle?*" Ronan grins at her.

She pushes them both away with surprising strength, considering her size compared to theirs. "You're suffocating her. Leave her alone."

"That's right." Elsa glares at all of them. "Leave Kim alone or I won't sit still."

I squeeze her hand and Aiden smiles at her, pride shining in his eyes.

Everyone goes on about what's happened in school and how it's been boring as hell, but no one mentions Xander or if he's already gone.

I want to ask, but I feel like it's taboo to even talk about him.

Did he leave without saying goodbye?

The hospital was your goodbye. What else do you need? A hug? A fucking kiss?

I close my eyes against the onslaught of emotions, trying to keep up with the semi-party everyone is throwing for me.

A part of me wants to sneak upstairs and hide underneath the covers, but that will only invite the fog and I don't have the energy or confidence to push it off right now.

"You know what?" Elsa's voice brings me out of my head. "I'm just going to address the elephant in the room. What are you doing here, Silver?"

I stare at the bitch queen of the school, the one who used to be my friend but now participates in my bullying.

She's wearing one of her elegant dresses and her 'fuck-me' heels. Silver isn't only beautiful, but she's also hot, even from a girl's point of view. She has provocative features and waist and breasts and everything. She's basically the whole package wrapped with 'bitch' ribbon.

It's crazy how someone can change from childhood. She has never been mean—secretive, yes—but not a bitch who lives to make other people's lives hell.

She now stands an inch in front of Cole and stares back at him at Elsa's question. He doesn't even acknowledge her as he slowly drinks from his cup.

"True." Ronan snaps his fingers in her direction. "We don't need the presence of someone who bothered Kim."

She remains silent, her face blank. But I know Silver to an extent. Her silence is hiding her flustered feelings or frustration.

"If you came here out of pity, I don't need it," I say aloud for everyone to hear. "You can go."

She doesn't move. Not even an inch. Instead, she stares at Cole again. This time, he does make eye contact, even though his bored expression doesn't change. Silver must be able to read whatever's in there, since she releases a deep sigh.

Her attention falls on me as she speaks low. "I'm not here because I pity you. I'm here because I know how it feels to want to end the pain. I tried it before, but it only made it worse."

"You…did?" I ask, not believing what I'm hearing. Silver isn't the type who talks about herself this openly. She's too arrogant to enumerate her weaknesses in front of so many people who can use it against her.

"What I'm trying to say is, I'm sorry if I participated in that pain. It's not you, Kim. It's how I deal with…" she trails off and her shoulders lock like someone is throttling her from behind. Cole is still drinking with nonchalance as if she's not speaking at all.

"Things," she breathes out and places her untouched cup on the table. "It's clear I'm not welcome here, so I'll just go."

She doesn't spare any of us a glance as she walks out, carrying herself with her usual high and mighty posture. Cole stares after her for a second before a slight smile—or smirk—lifts his lips. It's gone as soon as it appears, making me wonder if it happened in the first place.

"Wow, can you believe that?" Elsa leans in to ask me. "Silver apologising. I swear something is wrong in her head lately."

"Or she's scared," I whisper, more to myself than aloud.

"What?" Elsa asks.

"Nothing." It's none of my business, even though I'm pretty sure something is completely wrong with her.

Silver has been acting out of character more often than not lately. That means she's either being threatened, or she has a life-altering situation.

Maybe I should tell Dad about it. He's friends with her father, the mighty future prime minister, Sebastian Queens.

The party goes on. The boys put on a football game, and it's a nostalgic reminder of the times where we used to meet in Aiden's house for game nights when he started going out with Elsa.

How I used to sit in a position that gave me a discreet view of Xander's side profile. I've lost count of how many times I watched him while pretending to focus on the game. Or how much I smiled when he and Ronan jumped up to celebrate a goal.

Now, he's gone.

I shake my head once, not wanting to think about that particular subject.

"So, hear this." Elsa brings my attention to her and Teal. The three of us are sitting with Kir around the dining table as he devours the cake. "Teal says love is only a chemical reaction."

"It is." Teal crosses her arms over her T-shirt that reads, *Don't Know. Don't Care.* "It's just a dopamine rush like drugs and other things."

"You can't get drugs to fuck you." Elsa raises an eyebrow.

"You can have them get you high, and that's better than fucking." Teal keeps her ground.

"Drugs can make you feel high, but it's temporary." I wipe the corner of Kir's mouth. "Love can be temporary, too, but it has an everlasting effect. Sometimes, it becomes hard to breathe or think or even be without it."

"That." Elsa's eyes brighten up.

She's saying that because she's living it with Aiden—who's

been watching her instead of the game, by the way, but why the hell am I saying it?

"You guys need help." Teal shoves an earbud in her ear. Elsa laughs, hitting her shoulder with hers.

"Can I get juice, Kimmy?" Kir asks me.

"Sure thing, Monkey. And slow down."

"Mmmm," he speaks through his bite of cake, grinning up at me.

Teal and Elsa are still in their friendly banter. Knox and Ronan are shouting at the game while Aiden watches Elsa. Cole flips through a sociology book from Dad's library.

The scene and the sounds disappear as I go into the kitchen. I open the refrigerator, but I don't find Kir's favourite apple juice.

I try the cupboard, but the top one won't open. I stand on tiptoe and pull it hard, but still nothing.

Frustration bubbles into my blood, and it's not because of the stupid cupboard.

My gaze strays to the house opposite us. It's quiet, lifeless, and appears deserted.

Is this how I will act from now on? I'll look at that house and fight the need to cry or something?

He could've not told me. He could've left and kept the entire thing to himself.

But is that what I want, really?

"Here."

I push back as a taller body opens the cupboard for me. Cole smiles down at me as I retrieve the bottle of juice.

"Thanks." I take it, then steal one last glance at the Knights' house.

Will we meet on holidays now? Or will he cut off any relationship he has with Lewis—and, therefore, this place?

Lewis is my father. Uncle Lewis is my…father.

I shut down that idea before I can focus on it.

"He's probably watching," Cole says.

"W-what? Who?"

He leans against the counter and crosses his legs at the ankles. After Xander, Cole is probably the most attractive of the horsemen. His beauty is that calm, refined type. The kind that can belong to a handsome professor or a hotshot CEO.

His green eyes are dark and he gives off a composed façade—façade, because from what Elsa says and what I've noticed, Cole runs a lot deeper than what meets the eyes. While he's kind and doesn't talk much, he seems to know everything, and he has moments where he completely changes—like when he smirked as Silver ran away to hide her fear.

No good person would enjoy that. I'm not even close to Silver anymore and even I didn't like seeing her that way.

He's her stepbrother. He's supposed to care more, not take pleasure in it.

"He can't stop watching. It's an impulse. He used to control it better in the past, but the alcohol is screwing up his judgement," he continues in his neutral tone. "Xander, I mean."

"Is his drinking issue bad?"

"Bad? He's becoming an alcoholic."

I swallow, my fingers shaking around the bottle. "Maybe it's better he leaves then."

"Better?" Cole's eyes light up as if he's a dog who found a bone. "So that means you've thought of another option to the situation."

"Y-you know?"

He nods. "So does Aiden."

Oh. That must be why Aiden said he might have information that explains Xander's hatred. It was around the time he started getting involved with Elsa, but he never told me anything.

"Since when?" I ask Cole. "Why the hell did he tell you but not me?"

"He didn't tell me. I connected the dots myself. He did tell Aiden, though, when he was drunk and vomiting his gut. He was complaining about how close you got to Knox after he beat him up."

"Xander did that?" I release the bottle and it falls on the counter with a thud.

Knox, Teal's twin, had come to school with his face beaten up and Elsa was dead sure Aiden had done it because he was jealous of him. I never imagined it was Xander. Although I should've suspected it since he snarled in my face to stay the fuck away from 'the new boy'.

I would've laughed if it were under different circumstances.

But all of that doesn't matter now.

It's done, finished, over.

"About that second option," Cole repeats. "What did you have in mind?"

"N-nothing." I swallow. "How can there be a second option in our situation?"

"I see." He appears thoughtful for a bit. "But before you close all doors, remember, the impossible is nothing if you decide it isn't."

He reaches the threshold, then glances over his shoulder. "Oh, and he leaves tomorrow."

TWENTY-SEVEN

Kimberley

S ometime later, everyone goes home.

Elsa wanted to stay the night, but she's spent a lot of time with me lately and I can tell Aiden isn't amused, so I sent her home, saying I need time with Kir.

And I do.

We talk for what seems like hours and he tells me all about the new letters he received and that he might consider replying to one of them.

My baby brother will grow to become a heartbreaker.

He falls asleep as soon as I lie beside him, after making me promise him I'll never leave him for long again.

I make that promise, and unlike the other time, I have a strong belief that I'll keep it.

After I tuck him in and kiss his cheeks and forehead, I untangle his small arm from around my waist and leave his room.

As if on autopilot, I find myself down the stairs and standing in front of the huge window that overlooks the Knights' mansion.

Cole was right, it's an impulsion and can't be stopped.

My fingers trail to my scar, feeling over the bandage. Why do I feel like ripped tendons aren't as bad as the pain creeping under my skin?

It's slow and almost invisible, but it'll surely break my heart.

I'm holding my breath for the moment, hoping against hope it won't ruin me again once and for all.

"Here you are, Angel."

I smile at Dad as he passes me a mug of Lady Grey tea, then takes a sip of his, its bergamot scent filling the air in no time. Dad is a sucker for tea, British through and through.

For a minute, we just stand there sipping our tea and watching the house opposite us.

"Xander said something that night, didn't he?" Dad asks.

I pause mid-sip, gulping the liquid as if it's poison. "How do you know?"

"You were showing signs of improvement before he came in. Besides, you haven't stopped watching his house since we got here."

I glance at Dad, unable to understand how he knows so much about me, even though he's not my real dad.

No—he's not my *biological* dad.

Calvin Reed is my real father and the only father I'll ever have.

That's why I don't want to hurt him by revealing Jeanine's affair, or worse, disclosing I'm not his biological daughter. He's probably keeping up with my mess because he's my father. Once he figures out he's not and we share no familial ties, he'll throw me away.

My chest squeezes at the thought and I take a large gulp of the tea in a helpless try to hide it.

I'd rather suffer in silence than lose my dad.

"You're hiding again, Angel. Didn't we agree you'd tell me everything?"

I keep my mouth on the cup, not wanting to meet his eyes. *I'm hiding so I don't lose you.*

Lewis is okay, I guess, but he's not my dad. He's not the one who has been taking care of me since I was a baby.

I'm not his Angel.

"Hold on." He pauses, watching me intently. "Did Xander mention any familial ties by any chance?"

I cough on the tea, some droplets splattering on my hands. Dad pats my back, telling me to take it easy.

"How…" I breathe, then clear my throat. "How do you know?"

"I always have." His brow furrows. "I'm only surprised Xander does. Did he say how or when he figured it out?"

There's no way I can keep it inside anymore. I tell him everything about that incident seven years ago and what Xander overheard from Mum and Lewis's conversation.

"Why did she do that, Dad?" My voice is brittle. "Why did she do that to you and me? How can she make Xan my brother? I don't want him to be my brother. Please tell me he somehow heard it wrong."

"Unfortunately, it's all true." Dad leads me to the sofa and takes the cup from my hand to place it on the table. "You are indeed Lewis's biological daughter."

The tears I've been holding in since the hospital flow down my cheeks and my chin and soak the hem of my T-shirt.

"Don't cry, Angel. It breaks my heart when you do." He plucks tissues and wipes under my eyes.

"How can you care for me this much when you know I'm not your daughter?"

"The moment I saw your beautiful eyes, I decided you were my daughter. I didn't care what the world says. DNA doesn't make a family, Angel. Jeanine is a prime example of that."

It takes everything in me not to throw myself at him in a hug and ruin his cardigan sweater. "You're the only dad for me, too."

He clears his throat. "Lewis isn't bad either."

"How can you defend him? Mum had an affair with him."

"Jeanine lied to him, giving proof that Samantha and I had an affair first."

My lips part. "S-Samantha Knight?"

He nods. "We had a fling before our marriages, but that's all it was, a fling. It ended before our respective marriages and each of us went on different roads. We became neighbours, but Samantha and I remained platonic. Jeanine made Lewis believe it was a long affair and demanded revenge. They had their own affair, but it only lasted until she discovered she was pregnant with Lewis's child. After he found out the facts from me, their affair came to an end."

I squirm in my seat, but I manage to ask, "So everyone knows I'm Lewis's biological daughter? Aunt Samantha included?"

"Yes."

How could she be so kind to me, knowing I'm her husband's daughter out of an affair?

"Everyone also knows Lewis isn't Xander's biological father."

If my jaw could hit the ground, it would. "T-then who is?"

"I am." He smiles a little. "He's the result of that fling with Samantha. Lewis knew about it from the beginning and we made the decision that he and Samantha would raise him as their son. Just like we made the decision that Jeanine and I would raise you as ours."

My head spins with the amount of information shot in my direction at one go.

Xan is Dad's son.

I'm Lewis's daughter.

But we've switched fathers. It makes my head hurt.

"Then whose son is Kir?"

He smiles. "Mine and Jeanine's. There's nothing in there."

Oh, okay.

"I know this is too much to take, Angel, and I'm sorry you had to find out this way, but I don't want you to kill your happiness because of adults' mistakes." He pats my hand. "You live in the present, okay?"

I'm an adult, too, and I've already made a lot of mistakes.

Most of all, hiding and allowing the fog to swallow me whole.

"So..." I gulp, the question burning at the back of my throat. "So this means Xander isn't my brother?"

"Not at all."

I smile as I give Dad the hug I've been meaning to. "I love you so much, Dad."

Xander isn't my brother.

Not at all.

TWENTY-EIGHT

Xander

"I'm here if you want to talk."

I stare at my room's door after Dad leaves. I might need some sort of alcohol for my ears because I think the almighty Lewis Knight just offered to listen.

It's already weird as fuck he didn't tell me to get my shit together, but to go as far as being an actual parent?

Who knew that concept existed in his vocabulary?

Dad is the last one on my mind, though. After our decision—or rather, his—the only thing I keep craving is a look at her, or even a peek would do.

I can be fucking selfish and ask for a touch, but that would be torture in the long run and I've been tortured enough through the years.

Apparently not enough, fucker, because you're still thinking about it.

Shut up, brain.

I stand in front of my balcony, in the middle of my last spying session. However, the Reeds' house is dark and silent, which means they're probably asleep.

My fucker friends left earlier and Ronan made sure to wave at me from down there, ensuring I saw him.

Wanker.

The bright side, she was smiling and appeared happy,

considering the way her eyes brightened and her shoulders didn't droop.

I meant what I said in the hospital, she's strong and will get through this. She'll stand tall and embrace her scars and blemishes and everything in between. Kim has an unyielding spirit and while it broke, it can be mended now that Calvin and Elsa know.

It might take time, but she'll be fine.

I'm the one who won't.

I'm the one who'll stay up every night thinking about her, then curse myself for thinking about her.

It'll be an endless, vicious cycle I'll have neither the power nor the will to stop.

Maybe I should go confess or something. Or is my sin too big for that? I don't want the priest to drown me in holy water or chase me with a bat.

There's another simple solution that's hiding in my drawer in the form of a bottle. Dad banished all the liquor from the house and told Ahmed to donate them. The joke's on them. I always have a hidden bottle somewhere.

If I'm going to quit, I might as well go out with a hurrah. Being sober for days sucks. The itch is like an urge that consumes me from the inside out. It won't leave me until that burn tickles my throat.

The door opens and I sigh. Of course, Dad would return to ruin my fun. I understand the sudden hit with parenthood, but come on, we need a break from each other.

I need a break from hating my father because he's her father.

I need a break from thinking he ruined my life.

I need a break from him. Full stop.

"I'm not interested in talks, Dad. Leave me the fuck alone."

I expect him to reprimand me for 'language' in his stern politician voice, but there's no answer.

Maybe he got the memo this time.

Small arms wrap around my waist from behind. "I'm not leaving you alone anymore."

What the…? Am I getting drunk without alcohol now?

Either that or I'm going crazy, because nothing explains the soft hands resting on my stomach or the voice that should only visit in my dreams.

And my hell once I'm dead.

Because I have no doubt I'm going straight there. Do I regret it? For her, yes. For me, not at all.

I kind of made peace with my demons after long years of struggle, and they're against the holy water idea.

My demons spill out to invade my space and whisper those thoughts that, while sinful, feel so fucking right.

One last time.

One last touch.

One last push into madness.

What do you have to lose?

It could be the demons or my demented mind, but I remain still, soaking in her warmth that's creeping into me and filling me with a weird sense of comfort.

It's when she tightens her arms around my waist that I realise it's neither because of the alcohol or a dream, like the other time.

Kim is here and she's hugging me.

I grab her hand and attempt to yank it. While a part of me wants her to stay there forever, this will only fill her with regrets later.

A moment of weakness will rule her life and before she knows it, all her actions will be eating away at her soul like cancer.

That's how I felt after the kiss and the oral sex. I felt so much guilt towards her, it drew a hole in my chest and I had to fill it with bottles and bottles of alcohol.

Spoiler alert, it never worked.

She doesn't release me, her clutch turning hard and unyielding while her chest presses against my back.

Fuck me.

"Let me go, Kim." My voice is thick, wrong.

She shakes her head against my T-shirt.

"Let me the fuck go," I snap for her sake, not mine.

She has to stay the fuck away from me because I'm this close from ruining us both for life.

When she doesn't comply, I grab her arms and shove her away. She releases me with a gasp, but she doesn't leave.

We're both breathing harshly as we stand across from one another. She, because she probably took the stairs running—like when she was excited as a kid. Me, because of all the black thoughts swirling in my mind. Thoughts about hugging her again, kissing her, and being a sinful fucker fit for hell and all its friends.

"Why are you here?" I speak in my cruel tone, the one I've always used to push her away.

This is how I pretend her presence doesn't tilt my world and refuses to let it snap back to normal balance.

"Because of you." She smiles, her eyes sparkling as if she's reading one of her books.

"Didn't you hear a word I said at the hospital? You're my sister, Kim."

The more I say that word, the harder I dig in that blade from seven years ago. It's becoming rusty and it hurts like a fucking bitch whenever twisted.

She lifts her chin. "I'm not."

"Just because you want it to be that way doesn't mean it's true. You're not a kid anymore. Grow the fuck up."

"Screw you, okay?"

That'll be impossible. Or possible if she doesn't get the fuck out of here, *now*.

"Didn't know you had incest as a kink, Kim." I grin.

"Apparently, you do. You always thought about it, didn't you, Xan?"

My jaw tightens, but I remain silent.

"I'm not judging you." She sighs. "I probably would've been the same."

"Well, I'm judging you, so get the fuck out of here."

"So you can leave and never return?" She stares up at me with those huge, gut-stabbing eyes.

Those eyes will be the reason for my free fall to hell. I see it, feel it, can almost fucking taste it.

"Yes," I mutter.

"You know, even if we were siblings, I would rather have you close than not here at all."

"What the fuck is wrong with you? Do you think I can stay here after all that's happened?"

"I hope so."

"*What?*"

"Listen to me first, okay? Dad told me everything."

I pause. "What do you mean?"

"We're not siblings, not biologically, at least."

Then she goes on to tell me what Calvin said about his relationship with my mum and how Dad and Janine retaliated.

The entire time, I listen to her, but I'm not even sure if the words are reaching me right.

The fact that Calvin is my biological father.

The fact that Dad willingly chose to be my father.

The fact that Mum wasn't a saint as I tried to convince myself.

But most of all, one fact remains with me through the whole retelling.

One fact revives my heart and allows it to beat.

After Kim finishes talking, she stares up at me with that spark in her eyes, the hope and excitement I thought I killed once upon a time, but they still find their way back to her life.

This time, I have no intention of murdering it. If anything, I'll protect it, thrive on it.

"So?" she asks.

"So what?"

She grabs my arm. "You have nothing to say?"

I smile at her impatience. Some things never change. "Like what?"

"Xan!" she snaps.

My palm finds her cheek, and my thumb strokes the puffiness under her eye. This means she was crying before coming here.

Once again, I made her cry.

She leans into my touch like a kitten and sighs.

Kim and I are the same in so many ways. We're both broken, flawed, and have unsatiated hunger.

A hunger so furious, it chips at our souls.

A hunger so strong, nothing but the other one can satiate.

"Does that mean you're not my sister?" I ask the question she's wanted to hear since she ran all the way here.

"Not at all. Not even close."

"Thank fuck." I tilt her head up and capture her lips with mine.

TWENTY-NINE

Kimberly

Xander devours me.

I don't even have to open my mouth or participate or do anything.

Both his hands are on my face as he sucks my soul into his, or that's what I think happens with the way he nibbles on my lip, how he dances with my tongue, how he robs me of air.

He pushes me against the wall and I moan in pure bliss as my back hits the solid surface. My legs wrap around him as he lifts me up and my arms wind around his neck.

God. He's so strong and agile, his waist taut and narrow and perfect for my legs.

Or is it?

Should we be doing this now?

He lifts my skirt up and I tighten my legs around him, wrenching my lips away. "Wait."

A groan spills from him. "I've waited long enough, Green."

My breath hitches at the sound of my nickname out of his mouth. That's the only name I want him to call me until the end of times.

"Maybe we should talk first?" I don't know why it comes out as a question or why I'm so breathy as I say it.

"I can talk during." He yanks my skirt up my thighs

and it bunches around my waist. "What do you want to talk about? You? Me? How about me fucking you?"

I bite my lower lip as if that will make the reddening cheeks go away. "How about the fact we were siblings not five minutes ago?"

As soon as the words are out, I regret them. It's like I'm putting a damper on the entire mood. While I never considered him my brother, he did—for seven years.

All these years, he thought we were blood-related, and it must've destroyed him from the inside. It bruised his heart and ate away at his knight armour like acid.

"That didn't stop me from wanting you, it just stopped me from acting on it." He leans over and traps my lower lip into his mouth. "Partially, at least."

He fiddles with something between us and my core tightens every time there's the hint of friction.

While his words should have some sort of a negative effect on me, they don't. If anything, I'm wetter, hotter.

Xander is the fire and I'm the gasoline waiting to burn.

He's the ocean in his eyes and all I want to do is drown. Maybe never return.

It'll be worth it.

"Do you hate me for wanting you?" He wraps a strong arm around my back and aligns his hard cock with my entrance.

This is happening.

Oh, God. This is actually happening.

Don't faint. Don't you dare faint and ruin the whole thing.

I force my gaze on him, using him as an anchor, and say the truest words I've ever said. "No."

"How about if I don't use protection because I want to feel you strangling my dick?"

Why does he have to word it like that and why are my thighs coated with arousal.

"No. I-I'm on the shot." I've been on it for years, secretly hoping he'd one day take me, own me, make me his.

Little did I know, he'd never do that. Until now.

"Fuck, Green." He breathes harshly against my face. "I waited so long for this, I don't even know how to start and finish with you."

"Then don't finish," I murmur.

"You bet I won't. I'll fuck all this wasted time out of you."

I lean over to his ear and whisper, "I've waited so long for you, too."

That's all I get to say as he slides inside me in one go. It begins slow, but as soon as he's sheathed all in, we both let out a long exhale.

I wait for that sting people say happens the first time, but it's barely there. Or maybe I'm too lost in the moment and drunk on Xander to feel it.

There have been times where I've lain in bed and imagined how it would be, my first time, I mean. Whether it was fast, slow, passionate, or emotional, it didn't make a difference. Because in all those times, Xander's face was the only one that appeared.

No fantasy could've prepared me to the way he's taking it easy and being gentle. To the way his entire body is getting accustomed to mine. To the way he's holding my back with strength but also care.

But I don't need care right now.

I need him to take me, to make me feel how much he wants me and to prove that he has indeed thought about me before.

"Harder, Xan," I breathe out.

"I don't want to hurt you."

"I want you to hurt me."

He chuckles, the sound like music to my ears. "My bossy Green is back, isn't she?"

"Yes. Now do it."

"I'm big and you're too fucking tight," he rasps. "It might hurt for days."

"I want it to hurt for days."

"Fuck me." His blue eyes twinkle with mischievousness. "Why do you want it to hurt for days? So you can remember us?"

I nod.

His smirk coupled with those dimples might've secretly slaughtered me. "You won't have to, because I won't stop for days."

A flash of emotions covers his face as he kisses me while picking up his pace. He's right, I'm too tight, and because of that, each thrust hurts. But it's the pleasurable type of pain, the type that pulls me in deeper with every second.

My breathing picks up and my nails dig into his golden hair as his hips jerk with the force of his thrusts. My back pounds against the wall and a wave forms at the bottom of my stomach, strong and unyielding.

"Xan… Oh, God…"

"Oh, fuck, fuck!" he grunts against my lips. "Are you close?"

"I think so."

He reaches a hand between us and flicks my clit, adding a maddening pressure to my pussy. "I can't hold it in anymore."

"Neither can I."

The heels of my shoes dig into his arse as he rams into me with harshness so violent, it makes me delirious for a second, unable to remember where the hell I am or what I'm doing.

His hips jerk over and over, like he can't control the force thrumming in him.

"I've wanted you for so long, Green. For so fucking long."

"So have I," I admit through a moan.

"I wanted you even when I shouldn't have."

"I don't care."

"I wanted you to be mine so much it hurt."

"You did?"

"I wanted to kidnap you to somewhere no one knows

us and fuck you until we could no longer move," he confesses against my mouth. "I wanted to take you from the world and keep you for myself."

So why didn't you?

I don't say those words aloud since a harsh wave snaps inside me. It's sudden and wild and before I know it, I'm drowning in it.

His scent is the only thing I breathe, a little bit like an ocean, a lot like mint, and so much like belonging.

Xander has always been the one I can belong with, the only one I've never felt as if I should pretend in front of.

He's been my knight, my anchor. My one and only.

I'm slowly coming down from my wave when I feel something warm dripping down my thighs.

He stares at me with an apologetic expression, even though lust still lingers in there. "I'm surprised I lasted this long with how much I've been fantasising about you."

I bite my lower lip, then release it at the corner. "You've been fantasising about me?"

"All the damn time. It drove me fucking insane."

My fingers get lost in his hair as I peek at him through my lashes. "Even when you were with others?"

"What others?" He brushes his lips against mine. "You're my first, Green."

THIRTY

"You're a virgin?" My eyes widen as I ask for the hundredth time. "Really?"

"Lay off, would you?"

"No, I need details—*all* of them."

"Details? Really, Green? Besides, you're kind of distracting."

I glimpse down at myself and realise that after he carried me to bed, he stripped me as I continued to ask him about the bomb he dropped earlier.

I'm currently kneeling between his legs as he throws his shirt behind his back and kicks his trousers and boxer briefs away. We're both stark naked like when we used to take baths together as toddlers.

It's different now, though, and it has something to do with his semi-hard cock that I can't stop staring at.

The only reason I break eye contact is because of the dark look in his eyes. So many promises lurk in there, taunting, luring. My skull tingles in anticipation and my thighs unwillingly clench.

It's strange how I've stopped thinking about my body in front of him, or rather, how he sees me. It's because of the way he looks at me, I swear; it's so full of heat and want, there's no room for those nasty doubts.

A part of me wants to dive into his arms and never resurface, but my curiosity needs answers first.

Wrapping the sheet around me, I lean over so my entire front is glued to his. The thin cloth is the only barrier between us. "Better?"

The groan that leaves his throat is so manly and raw. "You're killing me, Green."

"I'll stop if you tell me."

"Maybe after round two."

"No." My fingers splay on his chest and I run the tips of them over his nipple. It's hard like the rest of him.

"For starters, stop doing that or I'm coming all over your sorry excuse of a sheet."

I still my hand but don't remove it. "So it is like the articles say, male nipples are also sensitive."

"What type of articles have you been reading?" His tone is amused.

"You know, stuff."

"What type of stuff?"

I blush. "Sex stuff."

"Sex stuff, huh?"

"That's how I keep myself knowledgeable. Happy now?"

He chuckles, and I can't stay mad or pouting when he does that. It's like a happy song. My own happy song that only I know its lyrics.

"I'm actually not surprised."

"You're not?" I ask suspiciously.

"You were always a curious little kitten." He taps my nose. "Why would you be different about sex?"

"You remember that?"

"I told you. I remember everything about you."

"No, you don't."

"Try me."

I narrow my eyes. "When did I have my first tooth removed?"

"First grade."

"When did I decide pistachio is my favourite flavour?"

"During pre-school's summer."

"What's my favourite animal?"

"Tigers, but you settle for cats because you can pet them and raise them."

"Then why don't I have one?"

"Because you were traumatised after Luna's death. You still miss her and don't want to have your heart broken again."

My chin trembles, but I continue asking. "What's my second favourite colour?"

"You don't have one, because all other colours aside from green suck."

God. He does remember. "When did I have my first kiss?"

"Sloppy smooches or real ones?"

"All."

"It was with me when we were ten and I kissed you on the mouth, not the cheek." He pauses, jaw tightening. "As for the real ones, I don't know."

"Ronan's party, with a certain drunk arsehole who kissed the daylights out of me, then told me I was disgusting."

"You know I didn't mean it. It was my defence mechanism, remember?"

"It still hurt."

"Green…"

I lift a shoulder. "I won't lie to you, Xan. I won't say it's all fine now. Bottling emotions is what led me to where I am today, so I'm trying not to let the pain settle on the inside."

"I'm cool with that." He clutches my hand that's resting on his chest. "I'll cooperate. Hit me with your pain."

"I just did. I'm not as cruel as you."

"Ouch. I deserve that."

"Let's agree you deserve more, but I'll never hurt you, Xan."

"You did." He sighs, the sound loud and deep. "You just

didn't know it. The hardest thing I've ever had to do in my life was to pretend I hated you when I never did."

"Never?"

"Not at all. Not even close," he repeats my words from earlier, but his tone is dead serious. "I'll do my best to make it up to you in any way I can."

"How about you tell me why you were a virgin."

He releases another breath, this one resigned. "You never give up, do you?"

"Nope." When he doesn't budge, I poke him. "The other time, Ronan was bragging about how he was the first to lose his virginity and Aiden was last. I thought you were somewhere in between." And I might've felt sick to my stomach at the time.

"You think I would tell Ronan I was a virgin? He'd shun me then drug me and bring me a hooker."

Yup. That's so Ronan. "If you had those risks, why didn't you just go with the flow?"

"I told you, I've always wanted you."

"But you could've still had sex." Even as I say the words, I can't help the bitter taste exploding at the back of my throat.

All the times I've seen him with other girls trickle in. Those pulses of pain and the tightening of my chest nearly return as well.

I hated it when he was with others.

And I hated myself for it, too.

He lifts a shoulder. "I never wanted anyone but you."

My lips part. "Then why did you parade Veronica and Summer and everyone else around? You went to rooms with them."

"But I did nothing with them except having them watch porn with me. If they were two girls, I watched them go down on each other. They didn't say a word about it, because they cared more about the fantasy and being with me. They cared about the image, not me."

"So you did it for the image, too?"

"No. I did it to push you so you'd never want me like I fucking wanted you." A faint smile breaks on his lips. "I was that sick."

"No, not sick, flawed."

"Flawed, huh?"

"Yeah, so flawed it's a bit sick."

"Just a bit?"

"Yeah, just a bit. Because the truth is, I'm the sick one."

He raises an eyebrow. "Go on. You can't leave me in suspense here."

I hide my face in his rock-hard chest and speak against it, "I always dreamt about you coming from my window to take my virginity."

No answer.

Did I ruin it? Damn it, I need to learn how to stop oversharing. We're just getting back together. He doesn't need a one-way ticket into my brain.

I peek up at him and pause at the expression on his face. He's watching me with eyes so intense, it's like he's about to devour me whole and leave nothing in his wake.

"I'll do that next time," he says in a hoarse voice.

"No, that's not—"

"I love your mind, Green. It's so similar to mine."

I bite the corner of my lip. "Really?"

"Oh, absolutely." He runs his fingers through my hair. "Does that mean you fantasised about being mine?"

"Maybe."

"Maybe isn't good enough. Try harder."

I reach up and run my fingertips over his lips. "Maybe I wanted to come here, too. Maybe I watched you relaxing half-naked by the pool."

"Someone is a stalker."

"Shut up. You're also a stalker. Both Ronan and Cole told me you watch me."

"Snitching bastards."

"Just admit it."

"I have a better idea."

My brow furrows. "What?"

"Did you know that the whole time you've been lying like this, you've been torturing me, Green?"

My cheeks redden, but I don't attempt to move, not that I can.

"Or are you doing it on purpose?"

"I'm not."

"Remove that sheet."

"W-why?"

"Remember what I told you the other time? When I order, you…" he trails off, waiting for me.

My breathing catches and I take a few seconds to regulate it before I slowly peel the sheet off me. It glides against my hard nipples, creating tormenting friction.

"Now, place both your hands on my shoulders and lift yourself."

The way he orders me gets me into a high alert mode. It's a want so deep, I can barely contain it inside my body.

I want to scream it from the top of the roofs and shout it at the stars.

Even though my body trembles, I do as told, clutching his shoulder and staying suspended atop of him.

He strokes his cock and when I'm momentarily transfixed by the movement, I ignore my shaking limbs.

"Now, come down."

"Xan…"

"Do. It." His non-negotiable tone springs me to action and I slowly, too slowly lower myself onto his hard dick.

We groan together as his cock stretches me. My thighs shake the more I take him in.

"You feel so fucking good."

I stop, breathing harshly and trying to fit him in.

"Go all the way, Green."

"But you're so big."

"You said you liked being hurt."

I nibble on my lower lip. "I do."

"But you like it better when I do it?"

My eyes widen. How can he read me so fast?

I don't have to say anything, though. He grabs me by the hips and brings me down in one merciless go. His balls slap against my arse with the force of it. I cry out, then squeal when he flips me so I'm lying underneath him.

Unlike earlier, I don't have to tell him to go harder. He thrusts into me with the urgency of a desperate man.

Of someone who has nothing before him or after him.

The harder he pounds into me, the tighter I hold on to him.

I'm sore and it hurts slightly, but that's the last thought on my mind right now.

Xander isn't the only one who's desperate. I am, too.

I've waited for him for so long, it almost feels unreal now, like maybe I'll wake up and all of this will be a dream.

If it is a dream, then I have no interest in waking up.

I can be trapped here for eternity, thank you very much.

"You're so beautiful, Green." His eyes hold mine captive as his cock owns me. "You've been driving me fucking insane."

I don't know if it's his words or his rhythm, but I come undone in a minute. The record time would be embarrassing if I had the clarity of mind to care about that.

Xander's name is the only thing on my lips as I reach that peak, that place of freedom. There's no fog here, no pain. Just a pure high.

"Say it again," he grunts.

"What?"

"My name."

"Xan." I brush my lips against his. "I missed you, Xan."

He groans as his back turns rigid and he joins me over the edge.

Xander brings my bandaged wrist to his mouth and kisses it so tenderly, it actually hurts.

Not physically, but emotionally. The fact that he sees it, that he saw it even when I refused to see it myself, makes me want to hide.

But I don't hide, not from him.

He's been the only one I could never hide from.

"I missed you, too, Green."

THIRTY-ONE

Xander

C ole wasn't wrong to call me a watcher.

I am. It's not something I can resist.

My gaze follows Kim as she disappears into her house, a huge grin on her face.

Her flushed, reddened face that I haven't gotten my fill of.

The face that will never leave my vicinity, even if she wants to.

Now that all those facts have come to light, I've passed the watcher state and gone into a different type of category.

Addiction.

There's a difference between being obsessed and watching from afar and the inability to stop thinking about something.

It's even worse than alcohol because that addiction only started to kill this addiction.

Needless to say, it's not working.

"Turn around," I whisper to myself as I stand by my front door.

If it were up to me, she wouldn't leave my bed for…years, that's about right.

We'll begin with the seven years I resisted her and me and everything that made sense, and I'll multiply them for recompensation.

And then I'll tie her to me because there's no way in fuck she's staying out of my sight now.

Kim stops at the threshold and glances over her shoulder, trapping the corner of her lip under her teeth.

Fuck me.

"You're killing me, Green," I mouth.

She smiles. It's a special one, her smile. There's still pain in that green gaze, so much bottled pain that I know won't be healed magically, but she still fights. She still wants to smile and be normal. She still gives her entire heart and secretly believes in magic, and that's probably why she has that much pain.

That pain will be mine now, just like the rest of her.

I remain there like a fucking idiot long after she disappears inside.

After I fucked her in the shower this morning, I had a perfect plan to spend the day between her legs. But as much as Kim enjoys pain, she was sore to the point of moving funny.

So I came up with plan B—kissing her entire body, worshipping her mouth, then moving on to her cunt.

However, that plan can wait until she gets something she needs after being discharged from the hospital—going out, being out there, and believing in the confidence she's slowly building without even realising.

That's why I suggested the date. I smile at how her eyes rounded the moment I said 'date', but then she said Kirian is feeling bad and she'll have to spend time with him. Now, it's a date for three. Not that I mind. Kirian can be bribed by games and brownies.

That's why she went back home—for a change of clothes and to get Kirian.

I go inside and pour myself a cup of coffee. I search under the cupboard for a bottle of liquor, anything will do. It doesn't have to be vodka.

Even whiskey is game about now.

I slam the cupboard shut after recalling that Daddy dearest banned them from the house. I run a hand over my brows. People feel headaches after hangovers; I feel them when I don't have my morning 'coffee'.

"No alcohol. Get used to it." Dad stands by the stairs. For the first time in ever, there's no actual malice behind his words.

He's wearing his pyjamas—that's another first. Even if it's the weekend, Dad always finds a dinner here, a charity there, a brunch somewhere.

Every occasion is a way in with people, and people are his speciality.

Just not this person right here.

"You know I actually keep a stash everywhere, right?" I lift an eyebrow. "Ahmed can't find all of them."

"I know that." He rubs his jaw. "That's why you're going to rehab."

"Sure thing, Dad," I say with sarcasm. "I'll finish whatever program then come back to do what I'm good at: ruining your career."

"Ruining my career?" he repeats with the same level of my sarcasm. "Can't you understand you're ruining your life, not my career?"

I'm not an idiot. I know that. "If it's a step closer to the great Lewis Knight's fall, I'm happy to make sacrifices."

For a second, he says nothing, just continues watching me as if I'm his worst enemy but also his closest ally. His life is lonely like that, despite all his party's members and what-the-fuck-ever, he trusts no one.

"How about her?"

His question makes me pause. "Her?"

"Kim." He rubs his jaw again before letting his arm fall to his side. "What do you have to offer her if you ruin your life? Her mental state is complicated enough. I won't allow you to make it worse. Calvin won't either."

His true colours are showing now. At the end of the day, his actual biological child is the one who matters.

Dad has always asked about her, made sure she's well

taken care of, and he told Ahmed she and Kirian have free access to our house.

When she was hospitalised, I heard Calvin talking to him a few times. Dad barely finds the time to eat, so it's a surprise he called someone outside of his work circle. And not just anyone—Calvin.

For years, he's been showing his care in a subtle way like a doting uncle. Because his career doesn't allow him to be obvious about an illegitimate child.

Well, since Dad doesn't like surprises, time to ruin his morning.

"She knows," I say.

"She knows what?"

"That you're her father, just like I know you're not mine."

He remains silent, but his face doesn't change.

"Wait. You already know?"

"Calvin told me."

"Right." I scoff. "Since when did you two keep your line of intel open?"

"That's not important right now."

"Of course, you're important. Your career. Your fucking elections. Your party. Is that why you didn't face her? Because you're scared to tell her that your political career comes before everyone else, her included?"

"I didn't tell her for the exact reason you need to stop drinking. Her mental state doesn't need any more pressure right now."

"Sure, I believe you."

"Xander," he says my name with that impatient tone like I'm the last thing he wants to deal with. "You think it was easy for me to give up my daughter? My own flesh and blood? It was the hardest decision I've made in my life, but at least I get to see her, talk to her, and make sure she's fine. Calvin said she's still fragile. I won't allow you to make it worse."

"Did your pen pal Calvin perhaps mention that I knew, too? For fucking seven years, if I may add."

"Language."

"Fuck that, Dad. Oh, wait, you never were. And the worst part is, I didn't need a DNA test to figure that out." I stride towards him and point a finger at his chest. "You stopped being my father the day Mum left because of you."

Then I storm out of the house. Dad calls after me, but I consider it as if he doesn't exist.

I take deep breaths before I go to pick up Kim and Kir. They don't need to see me on the verge of combusting.

The Mazda comes into view and then I see the fucking bastard who used to call himself my friend.

He's pinching Kim's cheek and grinning down at her like in some cliché film.

My first thought is to break his arm.

Forget it. That's not only my first thought, it's all the thoughts running rampant in my head.

No one touches her now, not him and not anyone else.

Although I've often had those thoughts before, this is the first time I get to act on them.

Except for kicking Ronan's arse the other time, or the one before that. If he keeps doing this, he'll get himself fucking killed by me.

I march towards them as they chat happily about something. What, I have no idea. All I know is that I hate whatever they're talking about.

Instead of punching him in the face like a part of me wants to, I just shove him away, grab Kim by the arm, and hug her to my side. My hand grabs the curve of her waist in a possessive hold.

A slight shiver goes through her and reaches me through our clothes. I avoid looking at her because that'll soften me up and I need all my harshness to deal with this fucker.

"*Bonjour*, Knight." He grins, then narrows his eyes. "Now let go of my Kimmy. I was inviting her to a date."

"She's not your *Kimmy*." I pull her even closer to me until there's no line that separates her tiny body from mine.

"Of course, she is. It's not like you—"

"She's mine." I cut him off.

A huge weight lifts off my chest as I say those words. I can't even recall how long I've bottled them inside. All I know is that it's been so long that the inability to say them became painful at some point.

I chance a look at Kim, but she's not watching Ronan or the scene. Her entire attention is zeroed on me, lips parted and that spark shining in her deep green eyes.

If they're an enchanted forest, I'm ready to get lost in there and never be found.

Ronan raises an eyebrow. "Oh?"

"That's right." It's with reluctance that I wrench my gaze from hers. "Now, shoo and keep your hands off her or I'm beating you the fuck up."

"You're forgetting something, Knight." His lips curve into a smirk. "She went out with me first. Didn't you, Kimmy?"

"You fucking—" I'm about to lunge at him, but she wraps both her slender hands around my arm. It's just a touch, but it's enough to quench all the fire inside.

"Stop it, Ro," she scolds.

"Fine." He rolls his eyes, then pins me with a glare. "One fuck-up and I'm taking her. Remember, prince charming is better than a knight in shining armour."

"Fuck you." I flip him off for good measure.

"No, thanks." He waves at us on his way to his car. "Heard Captain has first privilege for that."

"Fucker," I mutter under my breath as Kim's shoulders shake with laughter. "What are you laughing at?"

"The fact that Cole has first privileges. Elsa and Teal told me about how you and Cole were…you know."

If she knew it was only because of his eye colour, she'd probably think I'm a freak, so I keep that bit of info to myself. "And you're laughing because…?"

"I don't know. It's kind of weird but also strangely perverted to imagine you and Cole."

I raise an eyebrow. "You've been imagining me and Cole?"

"No!" She hits my shoulder. "Well, maybe. I mean everyone at school has been talking about it. That doesn't mean I want it to happen."

"Why not?"

She lifts a shoulder. "I don't like thinking about you with other people."

"Is that why you punched Veronica?"

She winces but plants a hand on her hip. "Maybe I punched her for the same reason you wrestled with Ro."

"His name is Ronan."

"What if I like Ro better?"

"Kimberly," I warn.

She wraps both arms around my waist and buries her head against my side so when she speaks, her voice is slightly muffled. "Say it again."

"Kimberly?"

"No, the part you told Ronan earlier."

"You're mine?"

She nods several times.

I lift her chin so she's staring at me when I say it this time, "You're mine, Green. Now and always."

"Always?"

"Fucking always."

I lower my head to claim her lips when the clearing of a throat stops me.

Calvin stands at the door, helping Kirian with his backpack.

As soon as the little man sees me, he abandons his father and storms towards me to hug my leg. "Xan!"

Kim blushes like a sack of tomatoes as she untangles herself from around me.

"Hey, Superman." I give him a fist and he blows it.

"Are we going in your car? Are we?"

"Of course." I throw him the key.

"Yes! I don't want Kimmy's car."

"Hey!" she scolds. "What's wrong with my car, Monkey?"

"It's not cool." He hides behind my leg and gives her a face.

"I'm going to tickle you to death. Here comes the gorilla for the monkey."

"Nooo!"

She starts chasing him around me while he shrieks and asks me for help.

While I would've under different circumstances, I just can't seem to look away from Calvin.

He's still there, carrying Kirian's bag and smiling with warmth at the scene in front of me.

That man is my father. My biological one, at least. Despite all my talk earlier, it's weird to imagine anyone but Lewis as my father.

Besides, Calvin has always been Kim's father, and the parent she needs in her life.

Despite his absentee status, he's always looked at his children as if they're the only ones who matter. Not like Dad, who only looked back when his family was causing some sort of problem for his career.

Calvin's gaze meets mine, and his smile doesn't falter or change. It's the same warmth, the same care.

I shake my head. I must be imagining things because I didn't get my usual dose of alcohol.

Calvin is the last thing on my mind, and while I didn't admit it to Dad, he's right about how fragile Kim is during this period. We should focus on her, not on any other clusterfuck.

I pick up Kirian and he squeals with delight as I place him over my shoulders.

Kim tries to jump, but she can't reach him. "Hey! That's cheating."

"Team Superman!" he shouts. "Xan, wrestle Kimmy like the other time."

"Shut up, Kir." She blushes, voice low.

"But you said it was special wrestling." He stares at Calvin. "What does special wrestling mean, Dad?"

"No idea, Kir." Calvin's smile doesn't change, hiding his reaction perfectly.

Fuck me. This little man will be the reason for the explosion in Kim's cheeks.

She snatches the keys from Kirian's hands and runs to the car. "I'll start the car up."

She leaves me alone with Calvin. Perfect. Not awkward at all.

He passes me Kirian's bag and I take it from him. In the last second, he keeps it between us and says in a cool tone, "Take care of them and of yourself."

I give a sharp nod. "Yes, sir."

His lips curve in a smile. "Calvin's fine."

I smile back. "Yes, Calvin."

THIRTY-TWO

Kimberly

Healing is a slow, painful process.

For the following week, I discover how weak I actually am. Even when Dad, Elsa, and Xander say otherwise.

I'm weak, because I still hide whenever Mum is in sight. I'm weak, because I'm scared of eating, and whenever I do, I vomit it right back up.

I'm weak, because I'm starting to think I'm a burden to everyone, even when my therapist has been trying to purge those thoughts.

Then in the midst of weakness, like now, he comes in.

Xander.

My knight, even if it's in a different way than when we were children. He used to carry me on his back, and now, he pulls me to his side as if I've always belonged there.

After I return to school, he's there every step on the way. Without saying any words, he announces to RES's student body that I'm now his and if anyone breathes in my direction, let alone says anything, they better start preparing their funerals.

He holds my hand and kisses me in the halls as if we've been doing it for eternity.

He whispers things into my ears, like how much he misses me, even though I'm right there.

I've become so used to his presence, as if we were never separated, as if we're picking up right where we left off seven years ago. Maybe that's why whenever he disappears, the fog begins to slowly creep in through the cracks.

Today, I met Silver in the library, and although we didn't speak, it brought back memories of the times where I hated myself and envied her body.

Through the years, I've always wondered why she grew up to be so beautiful while I became a potato. And sometimes, like now, those thoughts return with a vengeance. That's why I'm hiding in the back garden.

Elsa's been watching me eat my food and has been following me to the bathroom to make sure I don't stick my finger down my throat.

Since that infamous night, I haven't done it, but I can't help feeling the involuntary need to puke. The doctors say it's psychological.

Eating disorder.

Mental disorder.

Life disorder.

All I want is some solitude to collect myself and go back in there.

I'm not even three minutes in before Xan's silhouette appears from between the trees. His blond hair is styled back and his Elites' jacket forms to his bulging muscles. I wonder if there will ever be a day where I'll look at him and not think he's blindingly beautiful.

He slides beside me, and I can't help the smile that breaks out on my lips. I might have wanted solitude, but not from him—*never* from him.

I let my head drop on his strong bicep. "I thought you guys had a meeting with the team manager?"

"We're done. Or I'm done, anyway."

"Are you still suspended?"

"Doesn't matter."

"Of course it matters." I lift my head and sniff him, and the waft of alcohol hits me, even though mint comes from his breath. "You've been drinking."

"Define drinking." He grins, but even that doesn't charm him into my heart.

"You have a problem, Xan. You need to stop."

"It's all under control."

I reach into his jacket and retrieve the small bottle of *Absolut Vodka* he usually keeps there. "How are you keeping it under control? You're like an old alcoholic man."

He inhales, then tries to snatch it away. I throw it ahead letting it smash to pieces against the asphalt.

"Why the fuck did you do that?" he snaps.

"Because you need to stop."

"You're starting to sound like Dad."

"Well, maybe you should listen to him. Can't you see that you're poisoning yourself?"

"No, just like you're not seeing how you're starving yourself."

I pull away from him.

"Fuck." He runs a hand through his hair. "I shouldn't have said that."

"You're right, I didn't see how I was starving myself. I didn't see how I was slowly hitting rock bottom both emotionally and mentally, but I do now. And the reason I'm not eating is because I don't want to vomit. It pushes me back to those times and I hate those times. I told Calvin and Elsa about it, though. I also asked the doctor if there are any food supplements I can use. I'm trying, Xan. I just want you to try, too. Don't throw your life away because of some grudge against Lewis."

He strokes my cheek and I lean into his hand, briefly closing my eyes. "It's not only because of Dad."

I glance at him. "Then what?"

"You know that moment when you think your life has no

purpose, and it's kind of numb? Alcohol and fighting make me feel."

"Just like cutting made me feel. There was so much pain and sometimes, I couldn't breathe, and that's when the cutting and the pills began. They made me feel something other than that pain. They were a pain I could control, a pain that could purge it all out with the blood. The physical cut was more tolerable than the thousand emotional and mental scars I walked with every day. But you know what?"

His finger never leaves my face. "What?"

"When I almost died, I realised how temporary those feelings are. The guilt is way more permanent and long. Besides, I want real feelings, not forced ones through addictions. Don't you?"

He thins his lips into a line but says nothing.

"What's more important? Me or alcohol?"

He scoffs. "The alcohol started because of you, Green. I mean, it was my choice, but you're the reason."

"Then I'm ending it."

He smirks. "You're ending it?"

"Absolutely. Watch me."

"Meh, I don't think I can."

"Why not?"

"Climb on my lap so I can watch you clearly."

I hit his shoulder. "You're awful."

"Come here, Green." He taps his lap and he doesn't have to say it twice.

I crawl on top of him so my legs are on either side of his strong thighs and my arms are wrapped around his neck.

"You know, with this position, I can see your underwear." His lips tilt upward. "Green. Seriously?"

"I thought you'd appreciate it."

"Oh, I fucking do." He brushes his lips against mine, then quickly pulls back.

"Tease."

"You know why I tease you?"

"No."

"Because you still have an adorable-as-fuck pout."

"Hey, I'm not a kid anymore."

"Thank fuck for that." He thrusts his pelvis and his bulge nestles against my knickers.

He groans in his throat as my thighs shake. God, I think I'm broken. One touch from him and I'm already soaked. Shouldn't I have gotten more self-control by now?

He grabs my hip with a large hand and claims my mouth with his. My body melts into his hard one as he thrusts his tongue inside and kisses me deep and slow.

From the outside looking in, I must appear so tiny against his body, almost nothing.

"Wait." I pull away, my head slightly dizzy. "We're at school."

"So?" He rubs his cock against my underwear, and I whimper as he gets harder with the contact. "Remember the time I cornered you here at the first day of school this year? You were wearing that short as fuck skirt and Silver spilt coffee on you."

"How could I forget? You told me to not dress like that." And it was the first time he got so close in years.

"That's because I wanted to take you right then and there." He rotates against me. "You were killing me, Green."

My throat dries, but I managed to say, "Xan…we'll be suspended."

"Not if we're not caught."

"But…" I trail off when he dry-humps me.

Oh, God.

"Besides, it'd be worth it."

"Xan—" My words die out as he claims my lips again.

He rubs his cock against me over and over and I moan in his mouth, being found be damned.

A part of me wants someone to see us, to witness this moment in time, because I want to commemorate it.

I want to paint it on one of those blank canvases and keep it for life.

Xander releases my hip and snakes a hand under my skirt. I tighten, then tremble when he pushes my knickers aside and thrusts a finger inside me.

"Fuck, you're soaked," he groans against my lips.

"For you," I whisper back.

"You're killing me, Green."

"And you're owning me, Xan."

"Only me?"

"Only you," I breathe out.

His finger picks up speed and he adds another, filling me and triggering that hazy phase. It's a phase where everything disappears—no noises, no smells, no sights—at least, not from the outside world.

All I feel is his touch, all I see is his deep ocean eyes, all I hear are his breaths.

Just him. Xan. Once my best friend, then my tormentor, and now, my everything.

"Can you hear the sound of your arousal, Green?" He bites on my lower lip.

My cheeks heat as that sloppy sound heightens the more his fingers come in and go out of me.

"It's a symphony made only for me," he murmurs. "*You* are made only for me."

I clench around his digits and tremble as the orgasm sweeps over me, then submerges me in its clutches.

How could his words set me on fire without any matches or gasoline?

"You're so exotic when you come. I want to eat you up." He kisses my cheek, my forehead, and my nose and finishes with a brush of his lips to mine.

"I can't believe we did that at school." I wince, even though I'm still delirious from the orgasm.

He pulls out of me and it feels heartbreakingly empty. I don't focus on it, though, because Xan brings his fingers up and licks them one by one, without breaking eye contact.

The same fingers that were inside me.

Holy shit.

He's licking me off him. Why the hell am I so turned on by that?

He places his other thumb in front of my lips, and I don't hesitate as I lick it, matching his rhythm with mine. The taste of his skin explodes in my mouth, and it's the best food I've had in a long time.

Xander's lips pull in a smirk around his fingers, his dimples creasing his cheeks. "Mmm. I think I found an alternative to alcohol."

"Please share." The masculine voice coming from our right startles us both.

Cole appears out of freaking nowhere, carrying a book. *On the Genealogy of Morality* by Friedrich Nietzsche.

"What the fuck are you doing here, Captain?" Xander sounds impatient.

"I'm supposed to ask you that. I was reading in peace until you two decided to interrupt it."

Oh, no.

No, no, no.

Please tell me Cole didn't hear all that. I hide my face in Xander's shoulder. I won't be able to look at Cole in the eyes for a lifetime.

"Control your voyeurism tendencies, Nash." Xan seems completely unaffected, unlike my self-melting state.

"Technically, I saw nothing, so no voyeurism there." A pause. "I'm thinking you're developing some exhibitionism tendencies, though."

"Which is none of your business."

"You're right. I lost interest after the truth set you free."

I squeeze Xander's shoulder so he'll urge him to leave. I can't show my face if he's over there.

Xan chuckles, then says with utter sarcasm, "But that'll never be the case for you, Captain."

There's a long silence, and I wish I could see the expression on Cole's face, but I'd rather die than do that right now.

"Come to practice," he says in a cool tone before his voice disappears altogether.

"Is he gone?" I whisper without looking up.

Xander keeps a hand around my head. "You should stay like this a bit more, just to make sure."

I smile, my fingers digging into his jacket. When we were kids, he'd always invent games to make me hug him or him hug me. He said it tuned out the outside world chaos.

Seven years later, he still has that habit of manipulating his way into my arms.

"You still love hugs, Xan?"

"Only from you, Green."

THIRTY-THREE

Kimberly

Another week passes in a blur.

Time is strange. One moment, it's long and excruciating and the next, it's so fast you can't savour it.

When my therapist asks why I think I feel like it's moving fast now, I don't even hesitate to answer.

It's because I have the most important people with me, and it frightens me that I'm not savouring my time with them enough.

While Mum and I still don't address each other whenever we meet by accident in the house, everything else is different.

Dad never went back to Brussels and has taken a long leave; he's putting in his papers to ask for a transfer to London. When I told him I was fine, he said he wasn't, and I might have hugged him to death.

There's also Elsa, who's been listening to my jumbled thoughts and things I didn't like to admit out loud, like how I hid because I thought she'd leave me the same way all those I considered friends did.

She said I'm stuck with her for life.

I also have my little happy pill, Kirian. He's been writing poems for me. One of them says:

I don't say this a lot.
Because I'm a big man.

Love you.

Now.

Tomorrow.

Forever.

He also took my hand and made me eat with him—small bites instead of large ones so I don't end up in the toilet.

Lewis visited, too, and I crossed paths with him in the Knights' household. He didn't address our biological relationship, but he told me he's there for me if I need him.

But above anyone else, there's this person who's now hugging me from behind as I snuggle between his legs. The one who kisses my body from top to bottom and tells me I'm the most exquisite thing he's ever seen.

I'm beginning to believe him, too, because even if words can lie, the look in his eyes can't. The way his body reacts to me, the way he hugs me definitely can't either.

He's just *that* person, the one you know you can close your eyes with and when you wake up, he'll be there.

We've been going to the places where we played as kids. We've visited every park and every shop and goofed around with scarfs and pistachio gelato and M&M's. I might have eaten my weight in them by now.

Being with Xander is like finally finding a missing piece of myself and slowly sewing it back in place.

I'm still trying to have him quit drinking and fighting, though. The fights have become sparse since I keep him 'busy'—his words, not mine. But he still sneaks alcohol into his juice and coffee. He still wakes up in the middle of the night to drink on the balcony.

Every time he returns and hugs me from behind, I bite my tongue to not start a fight.

I can't lose him now that I've found him, and the alcohol is slowly but surely taking him away from me.

"Just so you know, I would rather have you underneath

me right now." His breath dances on the shell of my ear as he speaks. "Or above me. I'm not picky as long as I'm inside you."

My face heats and I discreetly elbow him. "Stop it."

"Or we can leave."

"No, we agreed to this."

"We can always change our minds."

I shake my head. Did I mention he always tries to get what he wants whichever way he sees fit?

We agreed to watch the game with everyone else in Aiden's house. We kind of interrupted this habit after he got together with Elsa for the same reason Xander now wants to leave. Aiden is so possessive about Elsa and her time, he doesn't like other people around when they're together.

Elsa said he only approved of this night because he's having her do something later as payment for it.

Even now, he has her on his lap and his hand wrapped around her waist. He's not watching the game. Instead, he keeps whispering things in her ear that sometimes make her blush something fierce. But most of the time, she's an expert at keeping an indifferent expression.

Unlike me.

Ronan, Knox, Teal, and Cole are here, too. And I still can't look the latter in the eyes without feeling flustered. I can't get over the fact that he heard me and Xander the other time at school.

Ronan and Knox are standing and fighting like die-hard fans—for different teams. Ronan—and everyone else here—cheers for Arsenal, and Knox prefers Chelsea.

Knox doesn't seem to be scared about being outnumbered as he threatens to end Ronan's life.

"You're going down, Astor." Knox makes a motion of slicing his throat.

"Stop acting like a certain goth and admit that we're stronger than you."

Teal, who the jab is directed to, doesn't even look up from her phone. Her T-shirt for the day reads, *Nope. Not Today.*

She's sitting beside Cole, who's leaning his head against his hand and watching the game with a neutral expression.

Now and then, he tells Teal something that she answers with a simple nod and no words.

Teal doesn't care for football or the school's hierarchy, so she can't be here because she's delighted by the horsemen's company. If anything, I think she secretly dislikes all of them—except for Cole, because she speaks to him sometimes and doesn't give him that 'why are you talking to me' look.

She must've tagged along because of Elsa and Knox. While she doesn't show it, she's a bit attached to them.

"Just admit it." Knox jabs Ronan's shoulder. "We're stronger than you."

"Someone should take away your delusional pills because last I checked, we're winning."

"We'll turn the game."

"And we'll score one more and win."

"It's definitely your weed speaking, Astor."

"*Mais non.* It's your delusional pills." Ronan's gaze meets mine. "Isn't that right, Kimmy?"

Xander motions at him with a dismissive finger. "Finish your game and don't address her until the end of your life."

I smile to myself. Someone is jealous. No idea why that makes me so giddy.

"Are you sure you won't change your mind and marry me?" Ronan counts on his fingers. "I have a title, I'm rich, beautiful and don't care about wars. I'm like the Switzerland of this world."

Teal scoffs and says in a mocking tone, "That must be why you're called Death."

Cole's lips lift in a smirk.

"What was that, *ma belle?*" Ronan grins with no humour.

"She's calling you Death." Cole is still leaning on his hand as he stares between Teal and Ronan. "Maybe you should prove it."

"Yes, prove it," Aiden speaks for the first time tonight, finally lifting his head from Elsa's ear.

"We can think of ways." Cole proposes.

"Or we can make them." Aiden raises an eyebrow.

"I might have a suggestion."

"Or two."

"We can start right now."

"Yes, let's make this night a bit more fun." The smirk on Aiden's face shines with pure sadism.

Cole, however, remains serene. Unaffected even.

The most boggling thing is that during that back and forth, Aiden and Cole never looked at each other or exchanged glances. They were plotting mayhem without any prior plan.

Talk about team play. Or maybe it's more than that between those two.

"I agree." Xan's voice comes from behind me with mischievousness.

"What are you doing?" I whisper.

"Making Ronan pay by throwing him in front of those two." He brushes a kiss against the lobe of my ear. "Watch and learn, Green."

Ronan flips off Xander, who returns it with a huge grin, as if he's been waiting for this his entire life.

"Being Death is cool." Knox wraps an arm around Ronan's shoulder, instantly forgetting about their team-level disagreement. "Everyone is afraid of you on the field."

"Thank you, Van Doren!" Ronan squeezes him in a bro clutch. "I'm promoting you to my closest friend and firing all these fuckers."

"I never agreed to being fired," Cole says.

"You mean you were my friend?" Aiden scratches his chin. "I don't remember that."

Cole snaps his fingers as if he recalls something crucial. "But we do remember what you did last week when—"

"Don't make me go Death all over you, Captain." Ronan is smiling, but his usual playfulness and warmth are gone.

"Fine." Cole sighs. "Then let's play a game."

"I love games," Aiden encourages.

"Me, too," Xander chimes in, but his finger continues caressing my skin underneath my top in a sensual rhythm.

"*Bah, merde.*" Ronan flops to the sofa opposite everyone else and diagonally from us. "What game?"

"Something simple like…" Cole's gaze strays to Teal, who remains focused on her phone. "Truth or Dare."

"Let's make it more interesting by only doing dares," Aiden suggests.

Elsa rolls her eyes. "Why am I not surprised you want that?"

"Because I'm going to win and make you do that dare, sweetheart."

"In your dreams, Aiden."

"We'll see about that." He stares at her for a beat too long. It's as if he forgets everyone else is here, just like I do when I focus on Xan's warmth behind my back and his finger wrenching tiny bursts of pleasure from within me.

"Now, where were we?" Aiden addresses everyone else. "Right, dares. Let's do that."

"Teal loves dares." Knox rubs his hands together.

"She does, huh?" Ronan smiles genuinely for the first time since they started ganging up on him.

"Oh." Cole's eyes ignite. "That's a surprise."

Lie. He knew it all along and is now pretending like he didn't plot it from the beginning with Aiden.

And Xan's knowing help.

"She does. They're her favourite." Knox falls down beside her. "Aren't they, T?"

"Shut up, Knox," she hisses at him without breaking eye contact with her device.

"Why not? The more the merrier, sis."

"Not interested." Teal chances a glance at Elsa, but Aiden has already gone back to whispering in her ear, so she might as well not be here.

"Come on. Surely you can give it a go?" Cole asks in a persuasive, gentle tone that I'm certain resembles the devil's when he's luring people to sin.

"Afraid of losing, *ma belle?*" Ronan winks.

"Never." She meets his gaze for a beat too long, then focuses on the phone again.

"Leave her alone," I say. I won't stay still as they corner her.

Teal peeks at me for a second, silently relaying her thanks and I nod at her.

"Stay out of it, Green," Xander whispers in my ear, eliciting goosebumps on my skin.

I glare at him. "No, I won't stay—"

My words die in my throat when his other hand snakes between my legs. Even though I'm wearing jeans, all he has to do is touch my nub and I'll moan.

Shit.

"Now," Xan murmurs. "How about that alone time?"

"You're not fair." I clamp my thighs together so no one sees me. That only increases the pressure and my breathing.

"You know what's not fair, Green?" he speaks against my ear, causing me to shiver. "Wanting you and not being able to do something about it. I'm done with that phase."

He pulls me further against him and the bulge of his cock rests hard and thick at the small of my back.

I bite the corner of my lip so I don't groan aloud. I don't think I can keep my reaction bottled any longer.

Everyone else is busy with Ronan and I'm not hearing

them, but anyone can look in our direction and notice Xan's hand between my legs.

Like Cole.

I'll die of embarrassment if he catches us again.

"Fine." I jerk up to a standing position, interrupting the conversation.

Knox and Ronan give me a quizzical reaction, but Aiden and Cole exchange a sly glance.

Please don't tell me it's written all over my face.

"We're leaving." Xander wraps an arm around the small of my back, a victorious smile on his face. "Kim wants to sleep early."

"Tuck her in safely," Cole says.

Aiden lips twitch in a smirk. "After all, you just won your case against the court of human rights law."

"Screw you, King." Xander flips him off.

"Wait." Elsa wiggles from Aiden's lap, even though he doesn't want to let her go.

She reaches me in a few steps. "I thought we'd spend time together tonight. I'll watch K-dramas with you?"

"That's the first time you haven't called them soap operas." I grin.

"You know what they say, it takes practice." She pauses. "So? Are we going to spend girls' night together?"

"I vote against that," Aiden says.

"Me, too." Xander pins me to his side. "Later."

Elsa and I exchange an apologetic glance before Xander practically drags me with him out of Aiden's house.

As soon as we're outside, he removes his jacket and drapes it around my shoulders, nodding with satisfaction as it swallows me. "Now, you won't be cold."

I hit his shoulder.

"Ouch. What was that for, Green?"

"What was all that about? This is supposed to be a night with friends."

"Friends are overrated."

"Now, you're being cynical."

He hugs me by my waist and connects his forehead against mine. "I just want to be with you, Green. Not them. I hate anything that distracts me from you."

Damn.

How can I stay mad after he says things like that? Besides, it was just an excuse. A huge part of me wants to spend alone time with him, too.

He grins. "You just forgave me, didn't you?"

"Don't be so full of yourself."

"Only if I get to fill you." He brushes his nose against mine. "Told you, I'm not hard to satisfy."

"You're just so persistent and annoying about it."

"Annoying, yes. Why is that news? You always called me annoying when we were kids. But" —he lifts a finger —"you always came back to my side."

"That I did."

"Because you can't resist me."

"Stop being so arrogant or I'll kick you."

"Come on, Green. Arrogance is kind of my image."

"Even with me?"

"Especially with you. What if you leave me after I shed the image?"

"Not going to happen. Besides, you were always an arrogant, proud arsehole." And it's probably why he's refusing Lewis's help about the addiction. He doesn't want to appear weak in front of someone he believes ruined his life years ago.

"Proud arsehole, you say?"

"The worst," I joke.

"Have you seen my friends? I'm sure I score low on the arsehole scale compared to them."

"Ro does."

"Ronan. His name is Ronan. And believe me, he's not what

he seems. He likes to think he's Switzerland when he's in fact an imperialist power."

"Really?"

"He's Death, after all."

"And you're War."

"Easy to start and hard to end." He grins. "Remember that, Green. Actually, make it impossible to end."

For some reason, my heart thumps so loudly, I actually stop breathing for a second to come to terms with what he's said.

Impossible to end.

He doesn't want it to end.

"You weren't easy to start, Xan."

"Yes, I was. You always fantasised about me, remember?"

"And you about me."

"Guilty as charged."

"Wait, what did Aiden mean by you winning the case in the human rights court of law?"

He thins his lips but remains silent.

"What is it?"

"Nothing."

"Tell me."

"No."

I poke his side. "Xander Edward Knight, since when do you hide things from me?"

His lips move in a sly smirk. "I love it when you call me by my third name. You sound hot."

"You're not changing the subject."

"Bossy, too. Hmm. Now, I want to fuck it out of you."

"Xan! Stop deflecting and tell me."

"Fine. It's Aiden being the usual fucker."

"For what reason?"

"He knew I was a virgin and never let me live it down."

I burst in laughter. "So he called the case a human rights one?"

"Stop laughing." He scowls, pulling me closer into him.

"Sorry, I can't. It's so funny." I try to hold it in but laugh anyway.

"Let's see if you'll be laughing when I fuck you until you can't move tonight."

My thighs tighten at the promise, but I say. "Back to being arrogant, aren't we?"

"You still like me."

"Maybe." I pretend to look elsewhere.

He grips my chin between his thumb and forefinger, forcing me to stare at those eyes that are so deep, I feel like I'll never find a way out of them sometimes.

"Say it, Green." There's a certain edge in his tone, as if he'll take things to a different level if I don't comply.

I wiggle free from his hold and sprint down the street to our houses, calling behind me, "Catch me and I might tell you."

I might not be an athlete, but I always did decent at running, I mean decent enough to run ahead from him and reach the house before he catches me.

I'm panting after only a few seconds. Thank God the distance is short. My hair sticks to my temples and my clothes are glued to my back.

But I'm already near my front door. I'll—

Strong arms wrap around me from behind and lift me off the ground. I squeal as his warmth and mint scent envelop me whole.

"Got you, Green." He nibbles at my ear. "You really thought you could outrun me?"

"Ugh," I try to squirm free.

"Don't be a sore loser. Pay up."

"Fine. Let me down."

He does, but he keeps an arm around me as if he doesn't trust me not to try to run again. While I pant, his chest barely rises and falls with the effort.

"Are you a robot?" I groan.

"We need to work on your stamina." He ruffles my hair. "But first, payment."

I grab him by the T-shirt, get on tiptoe and kiss him. Just a peck before I pull away.

"That was the appetiser, right?" He runs his forefinger over his lips and I'm transfixed by the sensual movement.

Definitely an appetiser, considering all I can think about right now is kissing his lips until the morning.

"Let's go to my house," he says. "Dad won't be home for a while."

I fold my arms. "First, give me back my thing."

"Your thing?"

"My bracelet." I extend my hand. "Give it back."

I thought I lost it somewhere that night I was transported to the hospital, but it wasn't in my personal belongings. There's only one option as to where it went.

Xander raises an eyebrow. "And here I thought you forgot about it."

"Never. It's been with me for seven years, after all."

He reaches into his jeans and pulls out the bracelet. It's clean, not soaked with blood like the last time I saw it.

I'm so glad it isn't. Blood isn't something I want to see for some time.

Xander takes my scarred wrist in his. Although I removed the stitches, it's still ugly with long marks. He lifts it to his face and brushes his lips against them. My heart flutters and it takes effort to breathe.

I'm a mess every time he does things like that.

Then he clasps the bracelet around my wrist. "Don't ever remove it."

I nod.

He reaches into his other pocket and pulls out a pack of M&M's, digs into it, and places a green one in front of my mouth. "Open up."

"I can eat on my own." I try to snatch the pack, but he keeps it high over my head. "Ugh. You're unfair."

"We can stand here all night or you can open that mouth."

I huff, but I let my lips fall open. The moment he places the M&M inside, I lick his fingers, causing his eyes to darken. Xander's eyes spark every time I brush my tongue against his skin.

"You're killing me, Green."

"Mmmm." I grab the pack from him, take out a blue M&M, and place it in his mouth. "Have one, too."

While I brush my lips against his fingers, Xander swallows mine into his hot mouth, lapping them with his tongue. A flash of desire grips me, and it takes everything in me to speak in a semi-normal tone. "You never told me your favourite flavour."

He speaks around my fingers, "You."

Holy…

If he keeps saying things like that, I'm going to climb him in public.

"Now." He flashes me his dimples. "About that redo."

I'm about to kiss him when a presence cuts into our peripheral vision. I stagger backwards but don't leave Xander's embrace.

My mouth gapes.

The blonde hair, the elegant posture. It's almost like seeing a ghost.

Xander's entire body tightens as she smiles. "Hello, Xan."

THIRTY-FOUR

Xander

"**M**um?"

My voice is incredulous, even to my own ears. The woman I thought I would never see in this lifetime stands in front of me.

Her hair is straight and blonde and falls to her shoulders, just as I remember. She's wearing one of the elegant dresses fit for the upper class, and she still has a brooch over her clothes.

If I didn't know we'd separated more than twelve years ago, I would've thought we saw each other yesterday.

Her face has that familiar permanent small smile and her blue almond-shaped eyes have no wrinkles surrounding them.

"How have you been, kids?" She stares between me and Kim as if this is an everyday occurrence, as if she went out for a stroll and just returned.

"You've grown up so much, Kim." She smiles. "Thankfully, you don't look like your snake of a mother."

What the fuck?

First, my mum is here.

Second, did I mention my mum is here?

"Can I talk to Xander?" she asks Kim, whose eyes remain wide, as if she's witnessing a ghost's appearance and probably thinking about ghostbuster options.

Same for me.

"Uh…" She shakes her head, then squeezes my hand. "I'll be…home if you need me."

I don't even have the right state of mind to nod or do anything. I'm still staring at my mum and trying to figure out if I had enough alcohol to end up with another 'dream'.

Soft lips seal against my cheek and it's enough to pull me out of my trance. I glance down at Kim and she smiles in the warmest, most considerate way any human would.

Her smile says words she doesn't have to utter out loud.

I'm here for you. I'll always be here for you.

I smile back, showing her the dimples she loves so much. "Go ahead, Green."

She nods, chances one last glance at Mum, then slowly heads to her house.

The only two who remain are me and the woman who brought me into this world.

The woman who left because Dad was too much.

"Should we go inside?" She motions at our house—mine and Dad's, not hers. Because she left it without a look back.

I don't say anything as I stride through the door, knowing she'll follow. The sound of her heels echoes in the empty hall.

Ahmed greets us at the entrance and stops upon seeing her.

"Hello, Ahmed. How have you been?" She smiles at him with a warmth that she used to give me.

A warmth that's a little bit sad, a little bit forced, a little bit fake.

And I used to gobble it all down because it came from her, my mother.

"Hello." He turns into his completely professional stance. "Can I get you anything, Xander?"

A bottle of vodka would be grand, thank you very much.

"Nothing," I breathe out.

"A glass of wine for me," Mum says.

"I'm afraid we have no wine." He nods and disappears around the corner. I have no doubt that he'll call Dad and inform him about our unexpected guest.

Before Dad comes home, Mum and I need to talk.

Shoving a hand in my pocket, I turn around and face her. She's sitting on the sofa, both legs tucked to her side like a refined lady.

Mum was never a refined lady. She was a waitress prior to knowing Dad—and Calvin.

Dad brought her to the upper-middle-class side of the tracks and after that, she cut all contact with her extended family and switched social classes.

Her gaze sweeps over me. "You've become a man."

"No thanks to you," I say without even thinking about the words. But I guess that's all I ever wanted to say since that day she abandoned me in the middle of the street and never looked back.

"Xander, listen to me."

I lean against the counter and fold my arms. "I'm all ears. Let's hear what brought you back after ghosting for twelve years. Spoiler alert, the address didn't change."

She thins her lips. "I see you've become fluent in sarcasm."

"What can I say? Growing up with no mother made me fluent in many things. Like lying, drinking, fighting. You name it."

"I won't have you stand there and blame your life choices on me. You have Lewis and his money."

Is she for real? Is there a way I can reach into my eyes and somehow blind them so I don't see her face?

For twelve whole years, I've wondered what it would be like to see her again. If maybe she'd return and fill the hole Dad was never able to.

Hope is a dangerous thing; it makes you believe in things that might never exist.

I believed in Samantha Knight, and that hope is now dimming to nothing at the first conversation.

She's not here to save me.

"Why are you here, Samantha?"

"I'm your mum and you'll address me as such."

"Nope. You kind of, *sort of*, stopped being my mum the moment you abandoned me in the streets while I was crying and calling your name."

She stands up and I expect her to come at me or something, to try to prove her biological status, but she heads straight to the drinking cabinet Lewis always keeps at the corner of the room. She curses when she finds nothing, her fingers shaking.

"Remember that drinking problem I have?" I tilt my head to the side. "Dad banned alcohol from the house because of it."

"He's such an expert at throwing away good liquor." She rubs her neck and her fingers tremble.

I reach into the side cupboard and retrieve a small bottle I keep there, then throw it her way. "I see where I got that problem from."

She clutches the bottle and opens it with over-eager fingers. "Vodka, seriously? Don't you have any wine?"

"Everyone picks his poison of choice, I guess."

"Whatever." The moment I see her gulping the liquid like she's been in a desert, a sense of disgust hits me.

It's so hard, I physically clutch the counter for balance.

I look like that. Just like her.

Now that I think about it, she always walked around with a cup of wine in her hand. She even mixed it with my redberry juice once, and that was my first sip of alcohol. I finished it all and was acting weird. That's how Dad found out about it and they had a huge fight.

Then he took me to the doctor and I might have had my stomach cleaned.

Maybe that's why Dad has been an extra dick about the drinking since the beginning of this year.

"Are you even sorry?" I ask.

She wipes the side of her mouth, but doesn't give back the small bottle. "Sorry? For what?"

The fact she's asking is enough to say she's not, but I speak anyway, "That you left your only son behind with a man who isn't even his biological father."

"You know," she murmurs.

"Yup, kind of figured about all the cross-breeding."

"Just so you know, I don't appreciate sarcasm."

"Just so you know, I don't fucking care."

She shakes her head. "I didn't leave you with a stranger. Lewis considered you his son from the very get-go. Besides, he and Calvin came to an understanding a long time ago to supervise on their biological children from afar. Why do you think Calvin picked you up sometimes and Lewis picked Kim up at others? Or when the four of you had fathers' days out in the park and all that rubbish? They had it all planned."

I figured Dad and Calvin were exchanging information behind the scenes, but I never thought they were this much in tune about how everything was playing out.

"Did the arrangement bother you?" I ask. "Is that it?"

"I didn't care."

"Of course you didn't. That's why you left."

She says nothing, and her silence is more painful than her words. I thought I was immune to pain about now. Turns out, I was fucking wrong.

"And why did you come back?"

She sits on the sofa again and takes another drink of my vodka, more gracefully this time since she doesn't have an itch to satiate.

"Whatever happens, you're my son, Xander."

"Bullshit."

"What did you just say?"

"You heard me."

"Listen here, Xan, as your mother, I demand respect."

"Bullshit," a stronger male voice says from behind me.

Dad.

That was faster than I thought. He probably was in Silver's father's house nearby.

He places his briefcase on the table and strides inside to stand beside me. "You heard him."

"Lewis." She smiles. "I've been waiting for you."

"I told you not to ever come here."

"Wait." I stare between them. "You meet? Are you like tea parties' mates? I thought she was in fucking Brazil or something."

"Can you leave us alone?" Samantha's hand trembles around the bottle's lid.

"Fuck no," I say.

"Just go." Lewis motions behind him.

"I can't believe this." I stare at her. "You're here for him, not me?"

She taps the lid of the bottle, keeps her posture, but says nothing.

I scoff as I exit the room, but not the scene. I hide behind the corner and do something I used to when I was a kid—eavesdrop on my parents' fights, hoping they'd end soon.

When they didn't, I went to Kim because she was the only one who weaned down the chaos. She still is.

"What the fuck are you doing here, Samantha?" Lewis yanks on his tie.

"You're not answering my calls."

"That's because I don't want to. Take a hint."

"You don't get to ignore me, Lewis."

"Watch me." He stands by the table, towering over her. "I told you last year that would be the last fucking time you're getting money from me."

"Mike's business went bankrupt again. We need help."

"You won't be getting it from me. Last I checked, I'm not your husband's sponsor."

Wait a fucking second. She remarried and Lewis has been giving her money all this time?

What in the actual fuck?

"You better well be." She stands up, clutching the bottle in a death grip. "Otherwise, the press will know about your illegitimate daughter. How do you think your campaign will go, huh? The mighty politician Lewis Knight has an illegitimate daughter and is raising another bastard child as his own. I can see it as the headlines. And remember, I have the DNA tests to prove it."

"You thought I was giving you the money because I'm scared of you? What a mess have you become to think that way? I only funded your loser husband's companies because you're the woman who gave birth to my son and I don't want to see you hit rock bottom, but if you threaten my children in any way, I'll bury you and Michael so deep, no one will be able to find you."

"We'll see who'll be able to bury the other one first." Her face reddens. "Either I find the money in my bank account or you can kiss your peaceful children's lives goodbye."

She heads to the door.

"Samantha," he calls after her.

When she turns around, a hopeful expression covers her features. "Changed your mind?"

"Don't you ever show your fucking face here again. Keep your alcoholic influence away from my son."

The door closes behind Samantha with a loud clink. Lewis breathes harshly and runs a hand through his hair as he sits down and retrieves his phone.

He places a call to Sebastian Queens to tell him he won't be making it to the rest of the meeting, then to his secretary to let her know there could be changes to the plan, and finally to Calvin to inform him about Samantha's visit.

As soon as he finishes that call, I come out of my hiding spot, placing both hands in my jeans' pocket. "Why didn't you tell me she'd remarried? Why did you tell me she was in Brazil?"

He lets the phone drop beside him and stares at me. "I should've known you'd eavesdrop. I'd prefer it if you'd never heard that."

"You mean the part about my mum being a gold digger?"

"That part, too."

"What else did you hide from me? Because hiding things seems to be your modus operandi around me."

"Doesn't matter."

"It matters to me." My voice rises. "This is my life; I have the right to know what's happening in it. I'm not a kid anymore and you don't get to make the decisions on my behalf."

"Fine." He sighs. "Samantha had an affair with her current husband for the last year of our marriage. I asked her to stay for your sake, but she didn't want to. She said this life wasn't as she expected it to be and it was suffocating her. She hated being a mom and this whole lifestyle. She also became neglectful of you and your safety. When she decided to leave, I didn't stop her."

My fist curls in my pocket. "Why haven't you told me any of that? Why did you let me hate you all these years?"

"For that exact same reason. You already blamed me, so I didn't want you to hate your other parent, too."

"Well, don't expect any applause, Dad." I turn to leave.

"Xander." His stern voice stops me in my tracks.

"What?"

"You said you're not a kid. So don't act like one."

I face him fully. "What do you mean?"

"The drinking needs to stop. Don't make me use force, because I'll do it."

I release a long breath. "How about you think about a solution to her threat? If this goes to the press, it'll fuck Kim up. People will start thinking of us as siblings and that's off the table."

"How about you?"

"What about me?"

"You said it'll screw Kim's life, but it'll also screw yours."

I lift a shoulder. "I can manage."

"It's okay if you can't. You have me for that."

"I don't need you," I mutter.

"I know. I'm just putting it out there in case you do." He rises to his feet and places a hand on my shoulder. "You are my son, no matter what DNA tests say."

I wiggle him away. "Sappy doesn't suit you."

"I figured as much." He chuckles, the sound rare and I know it shouldn't be taken for granted. Lewis Knight doesn't laugh, at least not genuinely. He doesn't stand there and offer his hand without expecting something in return.

For the first time in forever, I stare at him through a different lens.

He's my dad.

While I respect Calvin, Lewis is my dad.

All biological ties be damned.

With that thought, I ask him something I would never ask of other people.

Kim is right, I'm too proud to ask for things. Help, for instance, or a brake to put on my life that's spiralling out of control.

"Can you stop her?"

"I'll do everything in my might," he tells me.

"What if you can't?"

"Worst-case scenario, we all have to leave the country."

"Calvin, too?"

"Especially Calvin. He works for the diplomatic circuit

and that's even more scrutinised than politics. No scandals are allowed."

"Shit."

"I know, but we have to think about the worst-case scenario. I can always give her money, but she will never stop. Besides, I won't deal with someone who threatens you."

"Thanks…I guess."

"No sarcasm this time?" He smiles.

"Don't get used to it."

He squeezes my shoulder. "I need you to focus on you now. Think about that program."

"Fuck."

"Fuck indeed, young man. This situation will not go on."

And the dick Lewis is back. *Good to see you again, Dad.*

"Kim is worried about you," he says.

I lift a brow. "Since when are you and Kim pen pals?"

"I told her the other day to tell me if she needs anything. I found her pacing in front of her house earlier and once she saw me, she ran to me and said these exact words, 'You said to tell you if I need anything, and I do. Whatever you have to give me, give it to Xan. He needs help as much as I do; he's just too proud to admit it. So don't give up on him. One day he'll look back and thank you for it and I will, too.'"

THIRTY-FIVE

Kimberley

I can't stay still.

    Ever since Samantha showed up, I've been pacing the length of my room, back and forth like a trapped animal.

After I talked to Lewis, I spent time with Kirian and Dad. We played Scrabble, then we put my baby brother to bed. Now, I'm in my room, feeling out of sorts.

Dad just told me about what Samantha is threatening, and I might have died inside a little.

Yes, the threat of the press and being known as Xan's sister is crippling, and the thought of media attention makes me shake, but that's not the reason I've been on the verge of crying.

It's Xander.

It's the boy who was running after that red car when he was so small. It's the image of his crying face and the sound of his screams as he begged Samantha to stay, right before he tripped and fell.

That image has never left my mind. It was pain in its truest form, raw and deep.

The fact that the same woman has returned to inflict a different type of pain on him makes me want to punch her in the face.

She disappeared for twelve years just so she could come back and ruin his life.

Our lives.

I retrieve my phone and check my messages. Nothing from him, so I type.

Kimberly: Are you there?

No answer.

Kimberly: You know I'm here for you. I'll never leave, just like I promised.

Still nothing.

The thought that he's out drinking or fighting freaks me out.

I tuck the phone into the pocket of my pyjamas and head to the kitchen for some Lady Grey tea—Dad may have made me a fan lately.

On my way downstairs, I text Ronan.

Kimberly: Did Xander come by?

Ronan: Who's that? Oh, the traitor. If he shows up, he'll be slaughtered.

Ronan: Want to come to my party of one?

Ronan: Or two if you count the weed.

I shake my head, then text Elsa.

Kimberly: Did Xander get in touch with Aiden?

Elsa: No. Is everything okay?

Kimberly: It's fine. I'll tell you tomorrow.

Elsa: This is Aiden, make it after tomorrow. Or better yet, next week.

I consider texting Cole, but I don't dare to after what he witnessed the other week.

"It's final, Jeanine. I've made my decision."

Dad's voice stops me in my tracks at the entrance to the kitchen. He's at the table, talking to Mum with his usual cool tone.

Her head snaps in my direction as if she senses me. I freeze in place, and even my phone remains in my hand. I'm acting like a criminal who's been caught stealing.

"It's because of her, isn't it?" Mum snarls, pointing an accusatory finger in my direction.

"No, it's because of you. You're not fit to be the mother of my children. This is long overdue."

"I can't believe you're divorcing me because the brat cut her wrist." She glares at me.

There's that need to melt into the wall or to dig a hole in the ground and bury myself in it.

Since I was a kid, the moment Mum has looked at me like that, I've been reduced to nothing.

"Shut your mouth," Dad scolds her. "I won't allow you to speak to her in that manner."

"I'll speak to her however I please. I'm the one who gave birth to her, yet she hasn't done anything to reward me for that sacrifice." She shakes her head, staring me down. "I should've got rid of you when I could."

"Jeanine, if you don't shut up right now—"

"Maybe you should've," I speak over Dad with a calm tone. "That way, I would've never had the misfortune of being your daughter."

"What did you just say to me?"

"You were never a mother." Now that I've started talking, I can't stop. The words tumble from my mouth like a prayer. "You made me feel so insignificant and small that the thought of finishing my life became the first thing I'd wake up to and the last thing I'd sleep on. You made me believe I was a mistake, a disgrace, a disappointment, but I'm not. *You* are. You love yourself too much to care about any other human being. Your narcissistic type shouldn't have been allowed to give birth to children. DNA doesn't make you a mother, it makes you a vessel."

She barges towards me, raising her hand. I stand my ground, glaring back at her.

Now that I've told her what's on my mind, there's no way

she'll be able to bring me down. Once upon a time, I used to slave for crumbs of her attention and approval, but now, I realise I was emotionally abused by this woman.

Physical abuse is nothing compared to the scars she's left in my soul, scars it will take me a long time to heal.

But I'll get there. I'll build back my life, and she won't be a part of it.

"Touch her and I'll burn your studio down," Dad speaks in a non-negotiable tone.

She stops right in front of my face. Of course, the threat to her precious art, the translation of her ego, would stop Mum. No, it's Jeanine. She was never a mother to me.

Her nostrils flare as she glares down at me. For the first time in my life, I don't bow my head down and leave. There's no need to cry or to hide. My bloodstream is filled with adrenaline as I meet her stare with mine.

Dad comes to my side and holds me by the shoulder. "I expect you to leave the house immediately."

"What? You can't do that, my paintings and supplies—"

"Everything will be packed and sent to you tomorrow. You're not allowed to spend another minute under the same roof as my daughter."

"You don't understand," she hisses. "I have an exhibition. My family is expected to be there."

"Your exhibition is none of our business." He motions at the door. "Now, get out of my house."

I should feel bad, a tinge of something, but she killed that part of me a long time ago.

Now, there's a new me, and it's no thanks to her.

THIRTY-SIX

Kimberley

I spend the next hour tossing and turning in bed and checking my phone like an obsessed freak.

Xander never responds to my texts.

I call, but there's no answer.

Once, I read an article about the brain's reaction when someone is scared. The first instinct is to run.

That's what's happening to me right now. I want to run to Xander's house and find him. I want to run in the streets and search for him. If he's fighting, I'll pull him out of it and punch him in the chest for hurting his beautiful face.

If he's drinking, I'll confiscate the alcohol and punch him again for ruining his liver.

Okay, so maybe punching isn't the right solution, but I'm nearly going out of my mind with worry here.

The showdown with Jeanine earlier didn't put me out of my element as much as not knowing Xander's fate.

Dark thoughts keep creeping into my mind. What if he's hurt? What if he's passed out somewhere and no one finds him? Worse, what if the wrong people find him?

I should call Lewis and—

A sound from my balcony jolts me. It's like a bird or an insect. It happens again, and this time, I jump up from the bed.

I contemplate calling Dad, but it's probably nothing that warrants waking him up.

Slowly, I slide the balcony's door open. A gust of wind blows my hair back and seeps under my thin clothes, causing me to shiver. I'm about to peek outside when a strong hand wraps around my mouth and shoves me inside.

I shriek, but it's muffled.

My limbs flail around and I try to fight, but then the rest of my senses kick in. Mint and ocean scent, the dimples, and his warmth.

Xander.

"Shh." He throws me on the bed and kicks his shoes away before he follows.

And by follows, I mean he traps me underneath him, pinning my wrists above my head with one hand as his palm continues to cover my mouth.

The hardness of his body against mine sends shivers of pleasure between my thighs. The position is so intimate and close—so close.

"Is this how your fantasy starts, Green?" The glint in his eyes coupled with his dimples are a sight to behold.

I remember there's something I want to ask, something I want to make sure of, but now that he's imprisoning me like this, I've lost all thoughts.

I'm just glad he's here, he's safe, and he's with me.

He's the only thing that remains. His intense edge and his solid form. His body against mine, our breath mingling.

It should be forbidden to want someone this much.

To yearn for him this hard, even when he's all over me.

I miss him already, and he just got here.

"Do you know what I'll do to you now?" He hovers over me, his lips inches away from my throat.

I shake my head once.

He grins, the motion sly, and even his dimples appear

sinister. "That's the point. The fantasy is yours, but the direction will be all mine."

He releases my mouth and I exhale harshly into the air. It takes effort to suck breaths into my starved lungs.

Xander yanks my top to above my breasts and I moan as he grabs one roughly.

"These perfect tits are mine." His mouth latches on my nipple, teasing it against his teeth.

My back arches off the bed due to the strength of the stimuli. Is it crazy that I'm about to orgasm here and now?

No idea if it's because of the position, the torturing sensation in my hardened nipples, or the fact that he's dominating my being right now.

His other hand reaches between us and he shoves down my pyjamas and underwear in one go.

The tips of his fingers sample my tender folds before he cups me. "This cunt is fucking mine."

"And if I say no?" I challenge, and it's just that, a challenge. A way to rile him up because I might be going out of my mind with pleasure and I want him to give me his all.

To show me his true self—uncut, imperfect, but so utterly whole.

"No, as in it's not mine?" His tone is calm, but his grip tightens around my core, creating delicious friction.

"Yes."

"Oh, you fucked up, Green."

He releases me for a beat to fumble with his jeans. "You know what will happen now?"

"No?" I don't know why it came out as a question, but I'm too aroused to think about that at the moment.

"I'll fuck you so hard, you'll only want to be mine. Now, tomorrow, and fucking always."

Xander lifts both my legs so they're resting on his shoulders. "Keep them there."

I do, even though I'm shaking, my body whirling with that need for something, *anything*.

The build-up will kill me any second now.

He slams inside me so deep, I can feel him all the way inside. Oh, God.

My mouth opens in a wordless cry.

With my hands above my head, I'm too helpless to move or try to wiggle free—not that I want to.

It takes one thrust, one single thrust, and I'm screaming my orgasm.

He shoves a palm against my mouth, muting the sound as he powers into me. With every thrust, he hits a magical spot that drives me insane.

I don't even come down from the first orgasm, and another one bleeds into it. My continuous shriek is interrupted by his rhythm. The way he's muffling my mouth and pinning my hands over my head while owning my body is more than a fantasy, it's undoing me.

It's finding pieces of me I never thought were there.

It's belonging in its truest, rawest form.

His pace escalates with a strength that leaves me breathless. "You." *Thrust.* "Are." *Thrust.* "Mine."

He releases inside me with a groan. I feel so full of him, it's making me delirious.

I'm panting. My hair sticks to my nape and temples with sweat. Perspiration covers my entire body and shines on his hard muscles.

I'm still shaking so bad, I don't think I'll ever come down off this high.

So this is what it means to be thoroughly fucked.

Xan doesn't pull out of me, but he lays my feet on the mattress. His hot lips make their way up my belly, my breasts, and my neck before he removes his hand and claims my mouth in a rough kiss.

And then he's moving inside me again, slow and measured, almost as if he's savouring my body for the very first time.

Another type of pleasure grips me, one that's filled with years of longing, of missed chances, and toxic habits.

Xander and I started with a tragedy, but we found company in it. We fought our pain with hugs and kisses and small touches.

Now, we're fighting it in a different way. Now, we'll taste it on each other's tongue and see it in the scars left behind, whether physical or emotional.

And with pain comes release.

With pain comes freedom.

I've never felt freer than when I'm held down by him.

He's slowly but surely taking away my pain, and I'll also take his.

He might have been my knight, but I'll be his now. I'll bring back his armour and his sword.

So he can stop the war.

His hips jerk with the power of his thrusts. The moment he flicks my clit, I'm a goner again.

Completely. Thoroughly. With no way back.

"I'm going to miss this, Green," he grunts. "I'm going to miss you when I'm gone."

THIRTY-SEVEN

Xander

There are a few expressions I never want to witness again on Kim's face.

The first is that pale, hollow one with her wrists slit.

The second is seeing her cry, because she does it with so much pain, it rips me open.

The third is the fake look and the smiles she's forced in the past in order to appear normal.

Now, I find another one.

Fear.

As she lies in my arms while we're facing each other, she stares at me with widened eyes and her chin trembles, although she's clearly trying to control it.

It's not working.

She's about to break down and there's no way around it.

As I watch her, I wish there was an option where I could stop it. If it means I have to rip my heart out and lay it before her on a plate, then so fucking be it.

"W-what is that supposed to mean?"

I say nothing. I don't know what to say.

She grips my bicep with her tiny hand. I can't help staring at those scars—long, disfigured, and a witness of the time she had no other way to go. Even though the bracelet hides some of them, they're still visible and angry against the world.

A world I'm leaving her alone in.

"Xander, you said you'll miss me. Where are you going?" she insists.

I take her hand in mine and brush my lips against her scars, and like every fucking time, she shivers, as if I'm not kissing her skin but her soul.

"To heal," I say against her most beautiful part. The proof she's a survivor.

"T-to heal?"

"Rehab. Dad and I agreed on the thirty-day program, but it could go to the sixty-day one."

"Oh," the word leaves her lips in a breath. She's happy about it, but like me, she has that imminent doom lurking in her expression.

The fact of our separation.

I stroke her green strands back. Another beautiful part—her quirky old self shining through. It's proof that the little girl is still there, broken but able to pull her pieces together.

"Then there's the whole shitstorm with my mother. If she carries on with her threats, we'll be under a lot of scrutiny for being siblings and I don't want you in the middle of that."

She places a hand in front of my mouth, cutting off my sentence. "I don't care what the world says. You were never and will never be my brother. I have one sibling and it's not you."

I kiss her fingers before removing them. "Thank fuck for that."

She bites on the corner of her lip. "Dad says we might have to leave the country altogether."

"Mine did, too."

"I don't care, you know."

"No?"

She threads her fingers through mine. "It's not places that keep me rooted, it's people. This place is my home because you're all in it. If we go together, we'll just be relocating home."

I'm glad she's thinking like that, even though she's forgetting important things—like our friends and everyone we know.

But I keep that to myself and change the subject. "If this shitstorm had never happened, where were you planning to go next year?"

"Imperial College, and I was going to take Kirian with me. There's no way in hell I was leaving him with Jeanine. Now that Dad is around, my plans have slightly changed."

"To what?"

"I don't know. The sky is my limit." She strokes the back of my hand. "What about you? Do you still want to go to Harvard?"

"How do you know about that?"

She blushes. "I heard you talk to Lewis once."

I smirk. "Stalker."

"Shut up. So? Are you?"

"No."

"Why not?"

"I only wanted to go there because it was the farthest place I could go to be away from you. I chose it to escape you. Now, that won't be happening, even if you beg for it."

Her smile is contagious and I can't help pulling her cheek to me and kissing it.

"Then what's your plan now?" she asks.

"You."

"M-me?"

"Yes, you. Wherever you go, I go."

"Come on. You must have some dream in mind. Do you still like reading the economic part of the news?"

"Yes, I do."

"So you're following business?"

"Probably, but only if it doesn't keep me away from you."

"Of course it wouldn't. Besides, sacrifices need to be made for success."

"The only sacrifice I'm making is the rehab. I mean, healing, not sacrifice."

Her expression falls and her deep green eyes fill with wretchedness.

"When are you going?" she asks in a small voice.

"Tomorrow."

"That soon?" Her words break at the end.

"Yeah, Lewis Knight's friends work fast."

"They do."

"I'm sorry."

I also don't want to leave this soon, but I have to do it anyway, so I might as well rip it as a Band-Aid.

"Don't be." She leans over and brushes her lips against mine. "I'm proud of you."

"I'm proud of you, too, Green."

A tear falls down her cheek and she wipes it away quickly.

I cup her chin. "Hey, what is it?"

"It's just, I waited so long to hear you say something like that to me."

I kiss her tear away. "From now on, you'll be hearing it the entire fucking time. You're mine, Green, and I'll protect you with my life."

"I'll protect you, too."

"Is that so? From who?"

"From yourself. From the world. From anyone who tries to harm you."

"So you're like my knight now?"

"Uh-huh. Get used to it."

"Let me see about that." I pull her to me and lift her leg so I can slide my dick into her cunt.

She's already so wet. Both of us moan as I'm sheathed deep inside her.

I fuck her as slow as the time that passed while I waited for her those seven years.

I fuck her while staring at her, letting her know that she's it for me. I don't have to be thirty-something to know that. I've known it since the moment the woman who gave birth to me abandoned me and Kim hugged me, promising never to leave me.

I knew it when she held my hand and cried with me, even when I told her I didn't like seeing her cry.

I didn't understand the levitation in my chest back then, but now, I do.

What I feel for Kim isn't only about our bodies' connection or our history, it's also about our pain. It's about the fact that her presence dulls the emptiness like no alcohol ever will.

The orgasm that hits her shakes both of us to the core. She wraps her arms around me and hides her face in my neck as she whispers, "I love you, Xan. I've been in love with you for so long, I don't know when it started or if it'll ever end."

And just like that, I'm a goner.

THIRTY-EIGHT

Xander

After tangling herself around me, kissing me, and whispering things in my ear, Kim finally loses the long biological battle with sleep and drifts off.

My chest still aches at remembering the words she said. Like how much she loves me, how much loving me has saved her.

At that moment, I couldn't speak. I still can't, because I have no right to say those words when I'm leaving.

I stand by the bed, fully dressed, and stroke the stray green hair off her cheek. She moans softly, leaning into my touch.

Everything in me shouts at me to stay.

To hold her.

Kiss her.

Never leave her side again.

But Dad is right; I don't deserve her. Not yet.

With one last glance at her, I step out of her room. Before leaving, I have to go to a place and get her a gift, but first, I bring out my phone and type.

Xander: Remember that day you named me your knight? We were in the park and you were wearing that green princess dress with ribbons and lace and shit. Your hair wasn't brushed, and you had this green crown on top that you made Calvin buy you for Halloween. Then you said, 'Hey, Xan. Every princess needs a knight and you're honoured cuz I'm making you mine.' The moment I knelt in front of you while you blessed me with a bamboo sword, mimicking the queen, was my happiest childhood memory. It was the first time you dressed up and smiled after your grandmother's death and I felt so damn proud to bring joy to your life. That's why I hugged you straight after and nearly squeezed you to death. When you looked at me with those huge eyes, I wasn't only a knight, I was a fucking God. I still feel the same whenever you look at me, and that's why I had to hate you after I overheard Dad and Jeanine.

I knew. I just knew, even at eleven, that I didn't want to be your brother. I fucking hated it and I wanted to shout it out loud. I wanted to grab Dad and ask him why, but I bottled it all inside. For years, I looked at you and knew I couldn't touch you. For years, I ached to talk to you, to tell you it hurt without you, and that I missed you. I missed being your knight, your armour against the world, but most of all, I missed being your closest friend. The more I wanted to do that, the harder I hated myself and I directed that hatred at you. I hurt you because it hurt me. I hated you because the opposite was fucking impossible. I became War because wars are mass destruction to everyone—me included.

I couldn't be your knight anymore and it slowly killed me. Finding out I'm part of the reason you decided to end your life was the last chip in my armour before it was destroyed to pieces. But then it started building again because of someone. You. Since that night you barged into my room, hugged me, and told me we share no DNA, I've been slowly shedding War and building back my armour.

You were right. I was honoured to be your knight. Now, I have to be a worthy of that title and you again.

I'll heal, like I'm sure you will. I won't fix you and you won't fix me. We'll just hug each other like we used to do in the past. If Samantha stirs any shit up, I'll kiss you in front of the world and shout that you're mine, their judgement be damned. The universe doesn't matter, Green, you do.

Then. Now. Always.

THIRTY-NINE

Kimberley

Loneliness is a morbid thing. It starts with that small feeling of emptiness and morphs into something completely unavoidable.

That's how it's felt since Xan left weeks ago.

Lonely. Empty. Miserable, even.

It's true that we were practically separated for seven years, but even back then, I saw him every day. In his garden, with Kir, at school. He was always a constant in my life.

Now that he's gone, I feel like my air supply is slowly diminishing and will one day dim to nothing.

That morning, I cried for so long after reading Xan's text that Dad thought something was wrong with me.

But Xander didn't stop there. No. He left me a gift in a green box in front of my room. When I opened it, a small silver kitty came out and climbed into my hand.

With the kitty was a note.

I never told you how sorry I am that Luna died. It's a few years too late, but it's time to move on and embrace a new life.

P.S. You're mine.

Xander

I fell to the ground, hugged the kitty, and cried again. I

cried so hard that I thought I wouldn't stop crying or missing him.

I didn't. Stop missing him, I mean.

Considering the nature of his rehab, he's not allowed any contact with the outside world except for a weekly call with a family member, as in Lewis.

I always go to his house on that day, lingering outside as a creep until Ahmed opens the door.

While Lewis talks to him on the loudspeaker, I remain completely shut in the background, just listening to the tenor of his voice and boxing it for later when I'm alone and all I think about is him.

Lewis offered me to talk to him, but I shook my head, because if I did, I'd just cry. I don't want to cry and disrupt his rehabilitation in any way.

And I'm always on the verge of crying when Xander's first question is, 'How is Kim?' It's as if he awaits the weekly calls to ask about me, my therapy, if I'm eating, if I'm doing better at school.

Lewis answers all his questions with a smile while I battle with the need to drive to wherever he is and maybe kidnap him or something.

He doesn't need to worry about me. I've been healing, slowly but surely.

I think my actual healing process started the moment Jeanine left the house, and it only thrived after she and Dad signed the divorce papers. None of us went to her exhibition. Even Kir preferred a mac and cheese night with Dad and me than to celebrate Mum's success.

And she did succeed. The articles praised her and the critics fell at her feet. She sold out with millions of pounds for a single painting.

That's what Jeanine does best and what she should've been doing since the beginning.

In all the interviews she took, she said that she and Dad agreed for an amicable divorce. I scoffed and moved along.

She didn't even try for Kir's custody. It's like she was somehow looking for this chance at freedom, a chance where she gets to disappear into her studio and forget she gave birth to children.

Samantha, on the other hand, didn't leave peacefully. She tried to keep her promise to Lewis and ruin him, Dad, and all of us. Even Jeanine's career.

There were nights where I wanted to hide beneath the blanket, shaking with the fear that she'd cause a ruckus and soon enough, everyone at school and in the country would judge me and Xan.

I lied to him the other day and said I don't care. But I actually do. I don't want to be labelled as his sister in any way.

And I don't want to have to leave all our friends behind.

Instead of surrendering to that fog, I joined Dad and hugged him, then I talked to him about those thoughts. That's my weapon against them. The moment I talk about them, they lose their lethal edge and disperse into nothingness.

Then, one morning, I woke up to find Lewis at the steps of our house, smiling with triumph.

He got Sebastian Queens, Silver's father and Cole's stepfather, and Jonathan King, Aiden's father, involved.

Sebastian is the future leader of Lewis's conservative party and expected to become the prime minister, so his power kind of overrules everyone else. Jonathan King kind of owns the country and everyone in it, so his power is even stronger than that of politicians.

According to Lewis, Samantha and her husband were sent outside the country and they'll never return.

I asked if she could do anything from wherever she is, but he shook his head with complete confidence and told me, "She won't be able to do anything from there."

Those words sent a shiver down my spine and I kept wondering if it wasn't a simple relocation. But then I thought about how she planned to destroy our lives, and I stopped feeling anything about her situation.

She won't get to disrupt our lives again.

Or whatever life I'm trying to maintain now that Xan is gone.

In the spiritual trip I took to Switzerland last year, a Buddhist monk told me that souls are attracted to each other.

Now, I know why.

Xander's soul completes mine.

Life without him has no meaning.

On day twenty-three of Xander's rehab, I'm walking down the hall at school with Elsa as she tells me about the latest prank Knox pulled on her and Teal yesterday.

Even though I'm listening to her, I'm not registering anything. The halls and the students have all turned into grey, that shade that you see in old films.

Colours have been slowly diminishing from my life.

Elsa rubs my arm, bringing me out of my stupor. "He'll come back, Kim."

"I know." I sigh.

Doesn't mean this ache in my chest lessens. It's like being caught in a net and not having the ability to move.

We stop in front of the class and I face her. "How would you have dealt with this if it was Aiden?"

"I can't even think about it." Her expression is apologetic. "So I guess that means I wouldn't be able to make it."

I nod. That's what I love about Elsa the most—her honesty.

"We can have a game night?" Elsa suggests with a hopeful smile.

"Sure."

"Did someone mention a game night?" Ronan grabs Elsa and me by the shoulders.

"You're coming?" she asks.

"Depends on where I should come." He waggles his brows. "Threesome, anyone?"

Both of us laugh.

"I'm not joking, *mesdemoiselles*. In fact, I haven't been this serious about anything in my whole life," he whispers so only we can hear. "I'm sure you've heard the legend around here about my package. Here's a secret, it's true."

"Here's a secret, you'll die." Aiden yanks Ronan's hand from over Elsa's shoulder, tucking her to his side, and glares at him.

"Fine, I'll just have my Kimmy."

"Nope." Cole brushes Ronan's other hand from my shoulder and subtly but firmly pushes him away from me.

"What's in it for you, Captain?" Ronan demands.

"Knight asked me to, and I quote, 'keep your octopus hands off Kimberly'. I'm just being a good sport here."

Somehow, I don't believe that Cole is being a good sport for no reason. Even Elsa said there must be something in it for him.

"I agree." Aiden strokes his finger on Elsa's waist. "Reed is the reason Knight won the case against the human rights court."

My cheeks heat at the meaning behind his words and Elsa elbows him; so that means he must've told her about it. I wouldn't be surprised; Aiden doesn't keep anything from her.

"Human rights court?" Ronan stares between us.

"Knight's virginity." Cole hits his shoulder. "Keep up, Astor."

"Wait a fucking minute." The expression on Ronan's face is

to die for. It's like he just realised the world is ending and he's the last to know. "Knight is a virgin?"

"Was." Aiden smirks at me and it takes everything in me not to hide.

"What the fuck?" Ronan shouts. "What's with all the girls he took to those rooms and—"

"It was just a ploy," Cole says, and I can't help smiling.

"The sneaky fucker. Who else didn't know?" Ronan stares at us and when no one answers, he snaps, "Only me?"

"If you want to blame someone, start with your big mouth," Cole says.

"That's it. Friendship is over."

"You won't see me complaining about that," Aiden says.

Ronan flips him off and turns around.

"Are you coming to the Meet Up later?" Cole shouts behind his back.

"Fuck you and the Meet Up, Captain."

"How about the game night?" Elsa asks.

"Only for you, Ellie." He glances back and winks at me. "And Kimmy."

We both smile at him and he winks again.

While staring behind him, he bumps into Teal, who loses her balance and falls on her butt.

Some of the students snicker at the impact of the fall.

She glares up at Ronan, who instead of offering her his hand, shoves them both in his pockets, sidesteps her, and pretends she doesn't exist.

What the hell?

That's not the Ronan we know. He might act bitter, but he's not a dick.

Elsa and I rush to help Teal, but she's already on her feet.

"Are you okay?" Elsa retrieves Teal's bag and gathers the books that have fallen on the floor.

"I'm fine."

"What was that all about?" I ask no one in particular.

"It's nothing." As Ronan disappears down the hall, Teal stares at his back with so much malice, I can feel it under my skin.

Nothing? More like something.

Xan and I began with nothing, too, and now, I'm begging for air until he returns.

One more week.

Just another week and I'll be able to breathe again.

FORTY

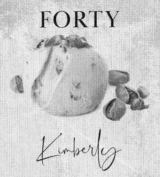

Kimberly

"Come on, Kimmy!"

Kir is about to start his excited dance in front of my door.

Elsa and I promised to take him to Elites' game and he's been stoked since the morning.

I don't share his enthusiasm. Going to Elites' games and knowing Xan won't be there is like inflicting torture upon myself.

But this has been a long time coming for Kir, and he'll definitely throw a fit if I don't take him today.

The other week Dad and I took him out for ice cream to celebrate Dad's new job approval. He'll now work in London and in the mornings alone, so he'll have plenty of time for Kir.

Still, the little shit was only asking about when we'd be taking him to a game and told us that he can totally buy tickets online now.

My baby brother is getting bigger way too soon and I don't even like to think about it.

While I'm hurrying to get ready, London jumps on the bed, demanding to be petted. I scratch under her chin and she purrs, then gets distracted by my keys and begins playing with them.

The door to my room opens as I'm rushing to gather my phone, one arm in my denim jacket. "Coming, coming."

"On my face or around my dick?"

I stop in my tracks, jacket hanging off my arm and my bag open as the voice registers. That deep voice with a hint of playfulness.

His voice.

Please don't tell me I'm imagining things, because that would be much too cruel.

I briefly close my eyes before slowly opening them.

There he is, standing at the entrance of my room, wearing a simple grey T-shirt and black jeans that outline his athletic frame.

He's gained some muscles over this month, making him appear a tad more lethal, a tad more attractive.

His lips are curved in a small smile, creasing his cheeks with those hot as hell dimples.

The blue of his eyes swallows me whole until he's all I can see and all I can breathe.

It's him.

Xander.

The sensation that hits me is so violent, the bag falls from my hand, its contents spilling on the floor.

"This isn't a dream, right?" I whisper.

He strides in my direction and reaches me in a fraction of a second. By the time I stare up at him, smell him, I'm already done for.

He lifts me up in his arms and I gasp as his lips crush to mine, his tongue invading me and feasting on me.

I don't even have time to focus or to think. Xander kisses me with the desperation of a man on the verge of breakdown.

Like me, he hasn't been breathing, and now, we're sucking in each other's air for the first time in forever.

I wrap my arms around his neck and my legs around his trim waist as I kiss him with everything in me.

He's here.

He came back for me.

"Does this answer your question?" he murmurs near my mouth.

"Not really." I brush my lips against his. "I need a bit more to make sure."

He chuckles, the sound easy and heartfelt as he claims my mouth again. This kiss is slower, more passionate. He's tasting me as much as I'm tasting him.

There isn't that constant aftertaste of alcohol. Now, he's only like mint and ocean and…Xan.

My Xan.

He's breathing me in as much as I'm breathing him.

He's feeling me as much as I'm feeling him.

He came back.

Oh, God. He came back.

"Wait." I shake my head, needing to get out of my haze. "You still have a few more days, no?"

His dimples make an appearance as he grins. "I came out early for exemplary behaviour."

"Really?"

"Really. I had to come back for you, Green."

"I missed you so much." My voice breaks with my confession.

He groans, "You're killing me, Green."

"You have no idea how much I missed you."

"And you have no idea how much I love you."

I pause, blinking. "Say that again. I didn't catch it the first time."

"I love you, Green. I'm in love with you. It probably began that day you hugged me and told me you'd never let me go. It's only heightened since then, and I might have hated you for it over the years, but I never once stopped loving you."

If there were a moment I could freeze in time, this would be it. I want to grab it, snap a shot of it, box it, and look at it in the future, preferably every day.

My heart nearly bursts as I let my fingers roam to his nape and I whisper, "I probably started loving you before. It became a torture over the years, but it was so worth it."

He leans over and bites my lower lip into his mouth. "So worth it, huh?"

"Absolutely."

"As in you wouldn't change anything about it?"

I pause before I say with conviction, "No. It's because of that I became who I am."

"And you became mine."

I can't contain my grin as he narrows his eyes.

"You have to say it."

"Say what?" I play nonchalance.

"Mine?"

"Yours."

EPILOGUE ONE

Kimberly

Three years later

I wake up submerged in pleasure.

Literally.

My legs are wide open as Xander feasts on my pussy. His wicked tongue runs up, then thrusts inside me.

I back off the bed and grab his blond strands with a force that must hurt. That doesn't stop him, though.

He eats me like a hungry predator and I'm his poor, willing prey.

His thumb finds my clit and he does that masterful thing, flicking and circling. It's insane how much better he knows my body than I do. How he drives me crazy with the simplest touches.

The moment he teases it between his fingers, I'm a goner.

Complete and utter goner.

I scream his name as I come undone around his tongue. My breathing is harsh and fast as he licks my sensitive folds one more time.

When his face reappears from between my legs, he's grinning so wide that his dimples form deep creases in his cheeks.

He darts his tongue out and licks me off his lips, and I can't help the whimper that escapes me.

Oh, God.

That will never get old.

Since we started living together in college three years ago, Xander always wakes me up this way or with his dick deep inside me. Bottom line, he always wakes me up with an orgasm and those mischievous dimples.

I try to wake him with my lips around his cock, but that doesn't happen too often. One, he's always up first, and two, he usually doesn't like it when I take away his 'morning fun' as he calls it.

"Morning, beautiful." He climbs my body with slow, sloppy kisses up my belly.

I stopped my life-draining diet two years ago. It took too much to make that decision, so as soon as I began to keep my food in, I decided to adopt a healthy lifestyle but without starving myself.

Xander became my personal trainer for runs, and I might have wanted to kill him at the beginning for all the long jogs we did, but then I started to look forward to them. And, okay, the way he looked in his running clothes might have helped a bit. Fine, a *lot*.

He's just delicious, and all the girls who jog in our park agree.

When I glared at them, he teased me and told me while fucking me that I'm the only woman he sees and ever will.

True, I still have those self-confidence issues sometimes, but now, I have my mechanisms and I've learnt how to easily move away from them by digging into my self-empowerment.

Now, I can look at myself in the mirror and finally smile. I can be myself and not want to be someone else.

And the person who played the most important role in all of that is this man who's now kissing his way up my body—my non-perfect, full of stretch marks and scars body—and still has that wild, lustful look in his eyes.

He flicks my nipple with the pad of his thumb and I moan deep in my throat and run my fingertips over the place where his heart lies. He had a tattoo inked on his skin as soon as he returned from rehab and stayed away from Absolut Vodka. We do drink, but he never loses himself to it now.

Green.

That's what's on the tattoo. Just one word next to his heart.

He got me inked on him for life, and I still feel close to tears whenever I see it.

Xander is mine as much as I'm his.

His chest sticks to mine as he grins at me with that sloppy, sleepy, lustful smile.

"Morning, Xan." I ruffle his blond hair. I can't keep my hands off it and I might be too in love with the colour. It's shining under the morning light coming from the balcony of our bedroom.

He leans on his elbows so they're on either side of me. "Happy graduation."

"Ugh, don't remind me of all the things I have to do today. Kir was demanding to come here."

Dad, Lewis, and Kirian will join us for lunch after the graduation ceremony, and then I've already made plans with Elsa, Aiden, and the others.

That is, if Aiden doesn't decide to kidnap Elsa somewhere.

We always have family lunches and dinners now. Lewis and Dad are our fathers, and although I don't call Lewis 'Dad' and Xan doesn't do the same to my dad, we have that unspoken mutual understanding, sort of like the one Dad and Lewis had for years.

It's easier this way and doesn't give us grief from any prying eyes.

Mum moved to Paris two years ago. She sends us invitations to her exhibitions, but we don't go. There isn't even pain as we talk about her now. She's like that distant relative no one actually cares about.

Even Kirian, who's supposed to be attached to his mother, doesn't want to spend time with her and is now striving to be a 'proper' man like Dad and his Uncle Lewis—his words, not mine.

"I'll bribe Kirian with brownies so he doesn't spend the night," Xander says.

"Why can't he?"

"Because we're celebrating."

"We'll be doing a lot of celebrations for one night."

"We'll have to add one more then. The most important one." He reaches under the pillow and retrieves a ring with a blinding green jewel on top.

My eyes widen as I stare between him and the ring. This can't be what I think it is…?

"I've wanted to do this since RES, but Dad and Calvin said all that adult shit about college graduation and whatnot. Besides, I didn't want to distract you more than I should. Needless to say, I've waited so fucking long to make you officially mine, to call you my wife, my life, and my future."

I'm crying like a little girl by the time he finishes. "Yes! Absolutely yes!"

"I wasn't asking. That means you have the chance to say no and I'm not having that, Green." He slips the ring on my finger. Perfect fit—of course it is.

Sometimes, I think Xander knows me even better than I know myself.

He stops and looks at me more than I'll ever stop to look at myself.

And for that reason, he's not only perfect for me, but he was made for me.

Just like I was made for him.

"I love you so much, Xan."

"And I love you, Green." He claims my mouth in a slow kiss that robs my breath.

I'm melting and I have no interest in stopping it. London mewls, then jumps on the bed, demanding to join the celebration. She hates being left out.

Xander pulls away, "Now, for the wedding date."

"What about it?"

"How about tomorrow?"

We both laugh as our lips meet again.

EPILOGUE TWO

Xander

Five years later

You know that feeling where you love someone so much that you'd kill for them, but sometimes, you want to kill them?

Those tiny moments where you want to strangle them while you fuck them.

This is one of those times.

Those thoughts have never stopped swirling in my head since the company dinner we had at Ronan's house.

And now, Kim is walking by my side, interlacing her fingers with mine as if nothing happened.

We'll see about that.

I enter the code to the apartment, and she goes inside first.

"I'm craving something to eat. What do you think we—"

Her words catch in her throat as I pull her by the arm and slam her against the apartment's door. I grab both her wrists and shove them above her head.

She gasps and her green eyes fill with excitement so tangible, I can feel it over the black rage swirling in my brain.

"What were you doing back there, Green?"

"I don't know what you're talking about."

She's provoking me on purpose and fuck if it isn't working. I yank her dress up, then my trousers and boxers down.

She bites her lower lip, her tits rising and falling heavily against my chest.

"You don't know, huh? Because it seemed to me you were allowing that fucker from accounting to flirt with you before I kicked him out."

"I was?" Her eyes widen with mock disbelief.

I lift her up by a hand under her thigh and she doesn't need an invitation as her legs wrap around my waist.

"You'll pay for it, Green."

"I will?" she whispers in my ear.

I slam inside her so hard, my balls slap against her arse. Fucking fuck. She feels so right—so damn right.

She moans aloud as I fuck her hard and fast against the door. The bangs and the slaps of flesh against flesh echo in the silence.

Thankfully, for the neighbours' sake, the apartment is soundproof.

Kim's groans fill the air and her mouth opens in that wordless O.

"You like provoking me, Green? You like how I pulled you out in front all of them, claiming you as mine?"

"Yes," she whimpers as I hit her sensitive spot over and over again until she's screaming my name.

I follow her soon after, the force of my release knocking us both cold. Her head falls against my shoulder and she stares up at me with that dreamy, utterly pleasured smile.

"I love it when you don't hold back, Xan."

The haziness of the orgasm slowly withers away as I recall the reason why this particular release felt good. It's because I haven't fucked her this hard in weeks.

"Oh, fuck." I carry her to the bedroom and lay her on the

bed. Our cat, London, jumps away but remains at the door. I swear she's the biggest voyeur on this planet.

Kim bites the corner of her lip and still has those 'fuck me' eyes that keep luring me close.

I place a hand on the bump of her womb. "Is she okay?"

"She's fine." She pulls me over by the neck and removes my tie, then undoes my buttons. "You're awfully overdressed."

She doesn't stop until she removes my shirt and nuzzles her nose against her name tattoo on my heart. My wife loves that a bit too much.

My fingers lay in her hair that still has her signature green strands, although they're not as loud now. "The baby, Kim. What if I hurt her?"

"You didn't." She gives me a dirty look. "If you hadn't started holding back, I wouldn't have provoked you today. Blame yourself."

"But I don't want to hurt our baby." It freaks me the fuck out that I could damage her if I keep my usual rough pace.

The doctor said it's fine, but it still makes me nervous as hell.

It doesn't help that my beautiful wife has become so hormonal since the pregnancy that she even interrupts me during work, lying on my desk and demanding pregnant woman care.

Since we both have crappy mothers that are thankfully out of our lives now, Kim has been nervous about the mum's role, but I know she'll be the best one alive.

She's been a mother figure to Kirian his entire life without even realising it. That's why he never asked about Jeanine when she left.

Now, he's excited about becoming an uncle and has begun threatening me to take care of his sister or he'll 'kick me'. Dad and Calvin have been calling daily and sending all sorts of shit since they learnt we're expecting.

For the past eight years, I've spent with Kim, I've been the luckiest and happiest bastard alive.

There hasn't been a day where she doesn't make me laugh

with her goofiness, or where she doesn't root for me to be the best version of myself. Just like I do to her.

That's what we've been doing all this time, being the best we could.

Kim has never stopped healing, but now, she looks back on that last year in RES with nostalgia. She doesn't hide her scars anymore. She could've had plastic surgery for her wrist, but she's chosen not to. Whenever someone asks her about it, she says it was a time when she was lost, and then she found me and I found her.

And after that, we were never lost again.

Kim kneels on the bed and runs her fingertips over my semi-hard cock. "If her mum is happy, she'll be happy."

"Is that so?"

"Totally." She grips me harder.

I groan. "You're killing me, Green."

"Admit it, you love it."

"Oh, I do." I take her scarred wrist with the bracelet dangling from it. She's never removed it since that day I put it back on her.

Just like the wedding ring. And no, I didn't marry her the following day of the proposal. I had to wait an entire month.

Small price to pay for finally having her by my side in all possible ways.

People marry their soulmates or those who complete them. I married the woman who gave meaning to my life.

She's not only my soulmate, my life wouldn't have existed without her.

"Make me yours, Xan."

"You already are, Green."

"Will you remind me again?"

"Oh, I will."

I flip her over and she squeals, then gasps as my lips claim hers.

BONUS SCENE

Xander

Age eleven

Cole is an idiot.

He's been saying these things to me lately that I can't get out of my head.

He said Kim will hate me, that she'll eventually choose some other tosser over me. He said girls always change for the worst and I'm only her friend.

Friendzone.

I asked Dad what that means, and I don't usually like asking him for things.

Dad said a friendzone is when a girl only likes you as a friend and that's all.

That's not *all*.

Kim is my best friend, but she's more than that. She's... everything.

Ever since Mum left, Kim has been the shoulder I lie my head on. Her lap is the best place to sleep on. Watching her eat the green M&M's I picked for her is the best scene I've ever laid my eyes on.

I love lying on the grass with her as she reads from her fantasy books. It's not because of the way she narrates, she's bad at that considering how she skips over words when she's too excited to know what happens next.

What I love is the way her green eyes turn round and huge whenever a plot twist happens.

More than anything, I love how she only comes to me when she's feeling low about how Jeanine treats her, but also when she's thrilled about the smallest things.

Kim is more than a friend, she's family. No, not only family, she's more.

She's my Green.

I don't want to be stuck in the friendzone or whatever that tosser Cole said.

He told me I need to keep my distance, but I don't want to. So instead, I'm going to do something friends don't do.

I'm going to do something that will keep me as her knight forever.

We had a pact. I'll always be her night. Today, tomorrow and in the whole future.

Kim is standing over her little brother's bed. She's singing to him in a soft tone. It's a song she invented about how he's so pretty and that she loves him.

Kirian's eyes are fluttered closed, but she keeps singing some more until he sighs in his baby voice.

As she stands there, I inhale a deep breath and tap her shoulder. She turns around and a smile breaks on her round face when she sees me.

I lean over and press my lips to hers.

I don't know what I'm doing, but Cole said he did it, so that means I can do it too.

Kim freezes, but she doesn't pull away. She just remains there and I do too. She tastes a bit of pistachio. I love pistachio just because she loves it. I brush my mouth against her one last time and step back, rubbing my nape.

"Xan?" she asks, her cheeks turning an adorable shade of pink.

"What?" I shove a hand in my trousers' in my pocket, not wanting to blush too.

"What was that?"

"We're not only friends," I say. "We're more."

She grins and takes my hand in hers. "Of course we are."

I tuck her to my side and hug her so close, she protests then giggles as she wraps her arms around my back.

Green and I are more.

So much more.

We're everything.

THE END

WHAT'S NEXT?

Thank you so much for reading *Black Knight*! If you liked it, please leave a review!
Your support means the world to me.

If you're thirsty for more discussions with other readers of the series, you can join Rina's Spoilers Room on Facebook.

Next up is Ronan's book, *Vicious Prince*.

Vicious Prince's Blurb

He's prince charming. Just not hers.

I have a secret.

I stole a heart, or rather a marriage contract.

It wasn't mine to own, to look at or to even consider.

But it was there for the taking so I took it.

Huge mistake.

Ronan Astor is a nobility in this world.

Arrogant player.

Heartless bastard.

Vicious prince.

Now, he's out to destroy me.

What he doesn't know is that I'm out to destroy him too.

My name is Teal Van Doren, and I'm where princes go to die.

ALSO BY RINA KENT

For more titles by the author and an
explicit reading order, please visit:
www.rinakent.com/books

ABOUT THE AUTHOR

Rina Kent is a *USA Today*, international, and #1 Amazon bestselling author of everything enemies to lovers romance.

She's known to write unapologetic anti-heroes and villains because she often fell in love with men no one roots for. Her books are sprinkled with a touch of darkness, a pinch of angst, and an unhealthy dose of intensity.

She spends her private days in London laughing like an evil mastermind about adding mayhem to her expanding universe. When she's not writing, Rina travels, hikes, and spoils cats in a pure Cat Lady fashion.

Find Rina Below:

Website: www.rinakent.com

Neswsletter: www.subscribepage.com/rinakent

BookBub: www.bookbub.com/profile/rina-kent

Amazon: www.amazon.com/Rina-Kent/e/B07MM54G22

Goodreads: www.goodreads.com/author/show/18697906.
Rina_Kent

Instagram: www.instagram.com/author_rina

Facebook: www.facebook.com/rinaakent

Reader Group: www.facebook.com/groups/rinakent.club

Pinterest: www.pinterest.co.uk/AuthorRina/boards

Tiktok: www.tiktok.com/@rina.kent

Twitter: twitter.com/AuthorRina

41903682R00189